Gods Among Us:
Alienthology

A Novel by
Rafael Madureira

Published by Skinny Brown Dog Media
Atlanta, GA USA and Punta del Este, Uruguay
www.skinnybrowndogmedia.com

Distributed by Skinny Brown Dog Media
Developmental Editing and Design by Eric G. Reid
Cover Design by Skinny Brown Dog Media
Content Editing by Timothy Swiney
Publisher's Cataloging-in-Publication Data

Paperback ISBN: 978-1-957506-14-2
Hardback ISBN: 978-1-957506-15-9
E-book ISBN: 978-1-957506-26-5

ABOUT THE AUTHOR

Rafael Madureira is the author behind the *Gods Among Us* series. He is an IT technician, aviation operations specialist for the United states army reserve, and a proud veteran of Operation Enduring Freedom 2010. He grew up being fascinated with aliens and mythologies and has always had story ideas for fiction writing. This book is the first of his works in fiction writing, which he hopes to publish many more. In his other life he is also a software development major at Western Governor's University.

Contents

PROLOGUE   1

CHAPTER 1   An Unlikely Meeting   11

CHAPTER 2   The Hunt   37

CHAPTER 3   Voyage Through the Stars   71

CHAPTER 4   To Asgard   97

CHAPTER 5   Extinct by Kindness   141

CHAPTER 6   Are We Back on Earth?   155

CHAPTER 7   Much to Explain   185

CHAPTER 8   Raytech   229

CHAPTER 9   To New Worlds   245

CHAPTER 10   Round Two   275

CHAPTER 11   The Statute of Secrecy   305

PROLOGUE

Imagine if the legends were real. The gods of all races were at one point in time watching us. Though that is our depiction of them anyway. These beings, called Celestials, all agreed that being referred to as gods was just too vainglorious; like taking credit for being the actual Creator responsible for intelligent design. All the Celestials had assisted in the creation, but being considered gods was a misrepresentation of what an advanced race with far superior technology could do.

Welcome to the story of some of the first gods of mythology, as the revelation of their true identities comes to light to the modern man through concepts ancient man simply could not grasp.

***

The Celestial had watched the skies from the world of Asgard for quite some time, now learning as much as she could about planet earth. From her palace, she had a clear view of the open universe. A magnificent light shot into the sky from a perfect crystal sphere at the tip of its white marble-like towers, reflecting upon the thin atmosphere and illuminating the entire palace even in the darkest night. The sphere doubled in its function, also giving Asgard a perfect view of the stars like a Hubble Telescope while illuminating the palace for its inhabitants. This Asgardian telescopic technology was superb in regard to observing everything in the universe.

Perfect weather was always present as the realm traveled passively through the galaxy, floating islands suspended by artificial gravity in the air around the palace. They were immaculate small meditation gardens.

Kili sat cross-legged on a large boulder on one of the realm's many floating islands as it floated passively around the palace. She was in deep meditation. Her sparkling hair floating through the soft breeze, transparent and golden, creating a crystalline shine in perfect harmony with her light blue skin. Like all Celestials, she appeared to be made out of gorgeous glass crystals. Still, Kili was attractive even by Celestial standards.

Baldr landed on Kili's island, his feet gently touching the soft grass as he began walking in her direction.

"Is it time?" asked Kili, opening her eyes as he approached from behind. All Celestials moved gracefully, but Baldr was the most pleasant to spot due to his jolly aura; everything in his presence seemed to flourish just a little more, from the soft blades of grass to the birds as they flew by him.

"Yes, Kili, the time has finally come. It won't be much longer before the Maku threatens the existence of another developing race."

"I have been observing their species. They can be rather brutish, not at all graceful, and have some rather self-destructive tendencies," said Kili as she looked upon the stars. The sky showed all constellations clearly from their realm, allowing them to observe all forms of life with their abilities.

"We once were as they are now. They are the new race, but they contain the basics of our very own way of being. They are merely basic blocks to something much greater, and we must guide them in the right direction. We've come a long way ourselves," Baldr smiled warmly.

"Well, it should be interesting to arrive in this period for them; if memory serves right, you and your brethren were gods in their eyes. I came to be way after we left their existence, and let's not forget, if they knew who my father was, I'm not sure how welcoming their species would be."

"You may have some…. circumstantial origins, but you are one of us and the one most appropriate for the job. Besides, you know the rules; it must be their own doing to rise. We have learned from the results of our interventions," said Baldr as they walked to the edge of the island.

As they stepped off the edge, an aurora borealis swept under their feet, allowing Kili and Baldr to gently glide down to the ground, walking their way towards the Bifrost room on a path seemingly made of light.

They gently landed on the soft grass and made their way to the stone road that led just outside the Celestial palace. The harmony of nature with the mixture of crystal and stone of the court was unrivaled. Of all the planets in the universe, Asgard was by far the most prosperous.

"Well, I suppose this will be an experience. I have only known our planet and a few others since I came to be. It should be fun to travel someplace anew."

"Many of their lore, their constructs, and their ways are similar to ours. I think you will find it strange at first, but you'll like it there," said Baldr as they entered the bridge to the Bifrost.

This was different from the rest of the realm. Unlike the palace, which appeared crafted of light-emitting stone, the Bifrost seemed to be a dome with an open-top made from gold and other metals encrusted with jewels and expert craftsmanship. It gave it a much older appearance than the palace, water flowing into pipes turning to steam and waterfalls drifting off the sides.

Handcrafted by the Celestials, the bridge served both aesthetic and functional purposes. Part of it was a majestic masterpiece of art, wide enough for a dozen horses to run side by side from end to end, and long enough for a small army to set up camp.

It led to the very edge of the realm as if the end simply hung from the stars. It was a majestic machine to behold, allowing the Celestials to travel to all realms with almost no effort.

"Welcome! To what do I owe the pleasure?" Asked Heimdallr as Kili and Baldr approached the machine room at the end of the bridge.

"It is time, old friend," said Baldr. "The Maku have set their eyes on a new world, and for the peace of the universe we must avert the events that will come should they succeed."

"Name your champion, your destination, and your cause," said Heimdallr in a booming voice as he opened the massive doors, revealing a giant room full of intricately designed machines.

The room was crafted to perfection in design. The ceiling was a dome shape with a perfectly round aperture at the center through which was revealed the night sky and all other realms within reach. At the center of the room, an enormous globe appeared to show all destinations, beside it was a flowing light that formed the shape of a tree with branches flowing in varying directions. Next to the globe and tree, there was a round, glowing platform pulsating with different colors of light.

The Celestials were firm traditionalists, setting all their technology to react lavishly to poetic words and actions, making their movements and phrases even more graceful. Many were from across the known universe and beyond, and they all followed golden rules for their traditions.

"I am Kili, daughter of the trickster and entities unknown. I travel to Midgard to ensure the protection of the realm and the known universe."

Kili looked at the object on her left wrist. This device was a nanotechnological marvel designed by herself. The device appeared to stare back at her through a crystal screen, a glowing blue eyeball staring at her awaiting command.

"Well, this won't do to mingle among them," said Kili, looking down at herself. "Brief me and prepare proper attire," she said to the small device. The eyeball nodded in agreement.

Her crystal white clothes matched the shine of her hair and somewhat the hue of her skin, as did all Celestials. If there was such a thing as perfect harmony, every aspect of their bodies attempted to achieve it. The crystal wristband came to life as it displayed a hologram with several pages, some with information and some with images of human females in modern clothing.

Kili touched parts of the hologram-like computer screen and engraved letters in a glowing blue hue in the air out of pure light. She read quickly through the information in front of her, which scrolled like a list on a piece of paper floating in front of her as she walked.

"May the guidance of the Celestials grant you true and accurate direction," said Heimdallr.

"So, I am to find one of them and bring them here? Are the clans still active? How will I find a suitable individual?" asked Kili, in confusion.

"They evolved from clans, but the head clans still share the bloodlines. It must be a lineage that has had contact with us before. They have almost no awareness of such, so it is at your best discretion," said Baldr as they approached a large machine which sat before the holographic globe and started placing the coordinates himself.

"Very well, I suppose it's time to assimilate myself physically," said Kili as she looked at the small screen on her wrist. The device had shown her the look of a young woman in her mid-twenties dressed in a tasteful combination of black and blue, not far from the attire of the Celestials, but relatively familiar to modern humans.

"That will do. Well done, Nano; execute." The device suddenly turned to a metallic liquid form, spreading like water and reshaping her clothes as well as her body somewhat.

The blue hue began fading from her skin, slowly turning to a lighter human complexion. Her clothes switched colors from their flowing crystalline white to a more normal dark blue as the metallic liquid seemed to pass through, her hair going from golden translucent to a slightly dirty blonde. Even her height was changed to a more human height, although still somewhat tall for a human female. The metallic substance receded to her wrist and took the form of a digital smartwatch once more.

"How do I look?" She asked Baldr as she spun herself in front of him.

"Like a mighty shield maiden!" Baldr chuckled slightly. "Now go forth and find us one of the chosen. We put a lot of effort into that race, and it must continue to prosper."

Heimdallr drew a sign in the air with the tip of his spear, the end of the blade cutting through the air as he made different signs. Before Kili and Baldr, a mandala appeared on the crystal platform next to the globe, glowing in red light in the giant globe. The same mandala burned on a particular spot, a little blue marble floating in the mass of the globe. On the flowing tree-shaped light, a route was traced brightly from Asgard to Kili's destination.

"The portal is now open, as it once was over two thousand years ago," said Heimdallr as he took a step back. Planting his spear firmly on the ground, the mandala on the floor pulsated a faint green glow with the echo of his spear.

Kili stepped onto the crystal platform and the mandala expanded and glowed brightly. Baldr raised his hands with his palms facing Kili.

"Seriously?" Kili looked somewhat impatient.

"Tradition is imperative," said Baldr as he began the blessing. "May the All-father Odin grant you the wisdom to guide you in your journey, may the mighty Thor provide you strength and safe passage in your travels, and may… " Baldr paused for a moment as Kili raised an eyebrow, "… may your father grant you laughter every step of the way."

The room suddenly became flooded with light, a bright white light encasing Kili completely, making the shape of a perfect silver sphere around her as the Bifrost powered up and began launching the Celestial to her destination.

And in a flash of light, the portal to Earth opened for the first time since the era of the gods.

CHAPTER 1

An Unlikely Meeting

"**C**ome on, Josh, just two more cups! We're almost the champions!" said Pete as Josh tossed the ping pong ball, barely hitting the cup successfully.

"It's all you, Pete! One shot, buddy." Josh crossed his arms. Pete took the shot, and his ball hit the rim of the cup, bouncing off and landing on the cup Josh aimed at.

Unfortunately, the other team took the last shot, finishing the game.

"Well, to a man of my stature, this is particularly difficult," said Pete, half-drunk as he drank the last beer cup.

"Yes, yes, you're very talented except for beer pong. The boards of scholarships sure appreciate your talents," said Josh, chuckling slightly.

"It's gotten me this far! Besides, I'm the correct height to be a great surgeon! I can reach all that matters!"

"Yeah, that means your head's at tit height,

you pint-sized perv," Josh laughed. "You're going to create some real butterfaces when you graduate med school."

Pete and Josh had been friends for a long time; they met in their early years of college at their dormitory in their first semester and kicked it off since. Pete detested dwarfism jokes, as he was a dwarf. Otherwise, he had a great sense of humor and learned to cope and use as much sarcasm as possible in response.

Academically speaking, Peter, or Pete as he preferred to be called, was nothing short of a genius. Josh, on the other hand, had always been the "ok" student with a great sense of wit. Pete was from a wealthy family in New Jersey and simply wanted to get away from his parents, but felt that the typical colleges for rich kids simply weren't his scene, so Colorado it was.

Despite being a dwarf, he wasn't bad-looking with his blonde curly hair and medium build. Josh was also a regular medium build short brown-haired guy. Josh wasn't a rich kid, but came from a relatively average household in Florida.

Together, they started their fourth college semester as Pete wanted to be a plastic surgeon, and Josh wanted to be a mechanical engineer since he got a chance to play with some of the more advanced gadgets during the time he served in the army.

"Didn't your momma ever teach you it's the inside that counts… and also below the neck where I can see and reach best," said Pete as they took a break from the beer pong match they just lost and sat down at their tables.

Josh was the designated driver, so water was his only choice of drink. Pete, on the other hand, consumed astounding amounts of alcohol for a man his size.

"You see…" said Pete, stumbling and very drunk, "The trick is to think grand as you do things. Every day I am a dwarf, but in my head, as I drink more, I am an epic dwarf of tales!"

"You lack the beard, Pete. Besides, no one wants to get cut up by a dwarf from Lord of the Rings," Josh jested.

"They would if they ended up pretty and with pointy ears! That's how hot elf girls are made!" Pete got up again. This time they made their way towards a game of darts with some more local college students.

Despite his stature, and no matter how many drinks, one thing Pete had learned was the coordination to win at almost any bar game. He had an unmatched perverted lust with humor and a skill no man of any stature could match at darts, pool, horseshoes, or any games played at a bar or party, except beer pong due to his short size.

Josh, on the other hand, was a reasonably decent player at any game, nothing too impressive, really highlighting Pete's skill at all games they played together, and as best friends and roommates, they took on anyone who would step up to the challenge.

"Another one bites the dust! Thank you, gentlemen!" exclaimed Pete in one breath as he downed another beer and took the last shot at the dartboard, hitting the target flawlessly.

"Thank you for playing. Please leave your tips at the bar; the nice lady who has been feeding me alcohol all night will know what to do as always, don't you darling?" Pete playfully looked at the bartender, a young brunette in her early twenties.

The bartender smiled at him as she took another empty glass, filling up the next one. It was getting late and closing time was coming fast, but who cares? It's the weekend, and Pete was up to drinking; Josh was the driver. That was their agreement tonight.

And so, Pete drank and found creative ways to get other people to fund his drinking spree for the rest of the night.

"Finally, time to head on home!" thought Josh as they made their way towards the door. It was late, or early, depending on the point of view. It was two in the morning as the bar was beginning to close. There were barely any people left in the bar as Josh helped Pete stumble out the door towards Josh's car.

Josh's car was nothing special, an economic model Honda Civic with an engine that almost stalled whenever the air conditioner turned on and made a funny noise whenever Josh made steep right turns.

The overall lack of horsepower meant Josh had to drive politely. Good luck outrunning anyone or cutting anyone off with the super slow economic model acceleration. The car was reliable. It did get him and Pete through almost four years of college without breaking and made over 40 miles to the gallon.

Josh loved his car and took great care of it. Pete lent him a helping hand here and there. Unfortunately he had a few questionable ideas for it, but Josh kept him on his toes about it. He tried to put tacky dice in the rear-view mirror, attempted to decorate the back with stickers, and even wanted to modify the exhaust to make it louder; pretty much all imaginable cliché things you can do to a college kid's car, but Josh usually shot down any idea that didn't have to do with general maintenance. And so Pete, accepting defeat, simply helped with gas and provided financially with some of the maintenance costs.

Josh and Pete went through college renting a small in-town apartment after their first semester. It was just outside the campus's city and an hour's drive to a fun little town for outdoor activities. Rent was significantly lower than the dormitories as there was no nightlife after 7 PM. Winter would shut off the rafting, hiking trails, zip line, and pretty much any fun activity, and there weren't any real restaurants besides small diners. But the peaceful environment away from the campus gave them just the right time to study and the choice of whether to be social or not.

Pete and Josh chose to be social most nights, but occasionally it was time to relax in a quiet place where you didn't have to work too many hours to afford a home while in college. The perfect balance.

It was a moonlit night that cast a bright shine over the road, so bright you didn't need headlights. It was the beginning of February, so the air was still chilly. Random snows would hit the area, followed by days of sunlight despite low temperatures. Josh and Pete drove through the night as they made their way home.

"Canyon City! Ah yeah, it's funny to have a whole city named Canyon when it's firstly a town. Secondly, the thing near it is a gorge, not a canyon. Seems like two ironies," said a fairly drunk Pete analytically.

"And just how many people at the time of the settling and naming of the town knew the difference?"

"Well, that's a fair and valid point, but at the same time, in our time, I'm sure they could change it legally," Pete replied.

"At least it isn't named springs; Idaho Springs, Colorado Springs, El Dorado Springs, Manitou Springs. It feels uninspired. Besides, there aren't that many springs in any of those. Think of all the hassle; even Google Maps would have to change it. Too many places to change the name just to be accurate,"

"Fair point, but did it not occur to anyone before it became so popular?"

"Well, probably not considering the whole state's background in…" Josh was interrupted by a bright light shining beside the road just ahead of them.

The light shone in a mixture of white with an array of colors. Josh slowed his car as they approached closer to it. A shape was taking place inside the circle of light; it stood several feet off the ground on four legs, seemed to have a reptilian body and a long thick tail, its head also looked reptilian, like a crocodile that had grown too tall but also had a torso and arms on top of its four legs.

The reptile creature looked directly at Josh and Pete as it let out a loud, ear-piercing shriek. Josh took no time in speeding right past it as the beast gave chase, now running after the car as they attempted to speed away from it.

"Holy shit! Faster, Josh! It's catching up!" screamed Pete, as he looked back in desperation. The creature was almost touching the rear bumper of the speeding vehicle as Josh floored the gas pedal, trying to get away from the hideous creature.

Another light shone in front of the car as the creature suddenly stopped; Josh swerved out of the road to avoid it as they were approaching it fast, coming to a dead halt as his car veered off the road abruptly. He watched the bright light carefully as this time a female figure emerged from the same type of light the nightmarish creature came from.

It was a tall female, slightly taller than Josh. She was well dressed in dark blue and black clothes, black leather long coat with blue, and two small daggers seemingly made of light in each hand.

"Well then, it appears you arrived at the party early. Come and get it, big boy!" exclaimed the female warrior as the creature shrieked and charged forward. The woman didn't hesitate and charged forward as well. In one movement, she sliced off the creature's left arm as it slammed into her, sending her flying back into the trunk of Josh's car.

The creature was shrieking in pain and immediately was met with a hail of bullets as Josh and Pete exited the vehicle, and Josh unloaded his 9 mm pistol at the beast, the bullets having little more effect than a slap in the face.

The beast growled at the trio as it rapidly made

a run for it, disappearing towards the mountains as it dived into the trees and boulders near the road.

"Valiant attempt of you, mortal, but I recommend abstaining from this bout; its hide is too thick for your projectile weapons," said the mysterious woman as the creature fled into the darkness of the night.

"Ok, what in the hell was that? Who the hell are you? And what in the world is going on?" asked Josh.

"First, let us seek shelter. We are too exposed, and that creature is far from dead!" She touched what looked like a smart watch on her wrist; the bracelet came to life in a blue hue.

"Repair them," she uttered to it as she pointed to Josh's car. The watch suddenly turned into the shape of some sort of power tool, a kind of strange looking small cannon, as it encased the female warrior's hand. She fired a small marble made of a strange silver liquid that landed on Josh's damaged car like a splash of rain. The dent where the female had landed began to unbend.

In a matter of a few minutes, Josh's entire car was back to normal. The liquid rose from the now-repaired car and sprung onto the woman's watch again, glowing in a dark blue hue as it sank back into her wrist.

"I was able to repair the physical damage with the nanodevice, but unfortunately, nothing could be done about the primitive design or lack of adaptive technology. Now, escort me to shelter and I shall disclose all that is necessary for you to know, mortal. Well, after I deal with this," said the female warrior.

She turned towards the creature's severed arm that was still twitching on the ground. The warrior raised her left hand towards it and her wristwatch again suddenly morphed, transforming into a circular form over her hand into what seemed to be a small cannon of some kind again. The cannon had lights in a blue hue this time, pulsing until it reached a solid dark blue all around.

"Incinerate," she said to the device as its blue light suddenly turned red and the strange hand cannon fired a fierce flame, burning everything in front of it for several yards.

"Whoa, whoa, whoa! You can't simply burn everything in front of you with that... that thing!" exclaimed Pete.

"The statute of secrecy must be maintained per treaty agreement. That was the simplest way to sanitize all trace evidence of the battle," stated the warrior.

"Don't you think people will question the massive burnt land several yards from a state road?" asked Pete.

"That is not my concern. A giant scar on the scenery shows no evidence. A severed reptilian appendage warrants investigation. Now, if you gentlemen are done squabbling here, shall we seek refuge on this rock of a planet?"

"First off, apartment; second, yeah, that might be a good idea; it's almost sunup," said Josh as he motioned for the female warrior to enter the car.

Josh and Pete started the car and drove without hesitation. After all, she had saved their lives and they both wanted to get out of there fast.

The patrol units arrived shortly; SUVs with their new overhead LED lights, two of them, they were impressive new vehicles, but it was all that the small Sheriff's department could afford as it in fact belonged to a small town after all.

The Sheriff was already out there looking at the giant charred scar as Deputy John made his way towards him.

"So whatcha thinking, John? Them college kids playing with flamethrowers or something?" asked Sheriff Dan.

"Maybe, I don't really see how it would make such a mark though. This is like a giant fireball just shot right through the side of the road. And look at the barbed wire fence; it got liquefied when whatever it was shot right through it."

John touched the edge of the fence; it was still hot. He looked over at the fence post and saw something shiny. John picked it up; it was a small crystal blue scale, a little larger than his thumb. Not very sharp but strong, it wouldn't bend or break no matter how much pressure he applied to it with his fingers. John put the small scale in his pocket as he stood and walked towards the Sheriff.

"Find anything?" asked Dan.

"Nothing that matters." He thought of mentioning the strange object to Sheriff Dan, but decided against it for some reason.

"Hell, I reckon if anybody's gonna figure that out, it'll be you," said Sheriff Dan.

Sheriff Daniel Pownell was in charge of the department, since he had been in the force for so long they just had to put him in charge. Out of all his new deputies, guys who only had 2 or 3 years in the department, he favored Deputy John Brady the most since he seemed to be the smartest of the lot according to the Sheriff, and since he had known his dad since they were kids.

John, or Deputy Brady, insisted on calling him by his title multiple times, but Sheriff Daniel Pownell simply refused to accept it from any of his guys. In public, he was Sheriff Pownell to John, and just Dan when hanging with the department, as the deputy consistently reminded him. He was like a dad to every young deputy in his department, and he was an old-fashioned cop. Law and order were easy to maintain in town.

"Why don't I check on our resident trouble-makers and see if either of them has some insight into this, Dan? Pretty sure they're going to have something to say about it, especially since this road leads to and from Canyon City, and the call was for a disturbance and possible explosion on the road,"

"Say hi to them for me, John; they're good kids, even if they screw up sometimes," said Dan, laughing. John took off in his patrol car heading for Canyon city. He knew just where to go to get answers. "And don't stay out too late." John nodded as Dan chuckled while he got in his patrol car.

The car ride home went a lot quieter than before. No longer the festive mood Josh and Pete were in prior to witnessing a fight between a horrid monster and a strange, but very strong lady. Josh was sure this woman was not from this planet, especially after watching the miracle of his car being wholly repaired.

"Ok, lady with the crazy alien technology, this is a long ride; please begin explaining to us what the hell is going on so we don't have to sit here quietly," said a still somewhat drunk Pete as they made their way to their apartment in the long empty road.

"Ok, that was a dragoon, a Draconian's subordinate. Low intelligence, predatory, very tough to kill. And if that has journeyed here, it means its master can't be anywhere farther than 100 miles," said the woman.

"Ok, so it is not of this planet. Got it. Who are

you, and why did you come here?" asked Josh.

"My name is Kili, Daughter of Loki. I am of Asgard. My assignment is to make my way here, as your planet is in grave peril; my kingdom is one of many that watches and governs planets, including this one. And if sources from my planet are correct, your world is to end unless I succeed in my mission," said Kili.

"Daughter of Loki? Asgard? That makes no sense. Are Norse gods aliens?" asked Josh.

"We prefer the term Celestials. That is the term bestowed upon a small group of individuals in any race that has reached biological immortality and a certain technological advancement such as carbon mastery. We have visited your planet before and have encountered your species. At the time, you were primitive and lacked any technological understanding. Naturally, to you Simians, we were portrayed as gods back then," said Kili somewhat arrogantly.

Josh and Pete had caught on to the way she referred to them. Pete, despite being drunk, was not fond of it.

"Whoa, whoa! Simians? I like to think we are a tad more evolved from mere monkeys!" said Pete in protest.

"Your attempt to blast a Draconian underling with a primitive projectile weapon proves otherwise. Anyway, at the time my forefathers had landed on this planet, your ancestors perceived us as gods. A long time has passed since we left for our planet, but we have maintained careful watch on you from afar, anticipating the day this threat would emerge. Your advancements in space and nuclear technology have made a footprint in the universe. We don't know exactly what it is that triggered this specifically, but a certain malicious organization has taken a high interest in your civilization. And that organization has had an unusual number of visitors to this realm lately, so naturally, they sent me here in response,"

"So, one of you to deal with an entire alien invasion? That seems like great odds!" exclaimed Pete, as he was beginning to sober up.

"I am more than a match for the Maku," Kili raised her head high as she proudly proclaimed her superiority. "Celestials are the stoutest, most advanced form of life in the known universe! We are the elite of our very own Asgardian race. Besides, there truly aren't that many of us, and per hierarchy, only very few of our kind are even sanctioned to meddle in the affairs of mortals like your species to maintain a certain order in the universe. And there is the statute of secrecy established by the Universal Council stating a planet not sanctioned to be in knowledge of all matters within the universe is to remain ignorant of universal affairs, and all agents and visitors must make the utmost efforts to maintain said secrecy."

"So, in other words, you're not exactly an army or numerous, so much as a few very capable advanced beings, like the special forces of the universe, and you are to leave no trace of being here or of anything you do. So only a few of us are allowed to know you exist. Why us?" asked Josh as they reached the street their apartment was on.

"We no longer need armies, and we are biologically immortal. If we were to breed excessively like you bipedal apes do, the entire world would simply end due to a shortage of resources. That's why Celestials are a small elite. And well, our encounter was by chance. I can make one or two individuals aware, as that is inevitable. Still, we are not to alert the masses of the existence of extraterrestrial beings into the universe until sanctioned by the Council," said Kili as they exited the car and entered the apartment. Pete still frowned at how she referred to them in general.

"Well, this is rather primitive, but will suffice for shelter, I suppose. Dwarf, you live here with this regular simian absent any accommodations from your home world? How did you obtain permission to be on this planet, anyway?" asked Kili as she turned to Pete.

"First off, it's Pete. Secondly, I am not from an alien race occupying this planet by invasion; it's a genetic condition called dwarfism. Third, can you please drop the superior alien attitude? We get it-you're from an alien race years ahead of us as we have just seen you repair our car with your wristwatch!" exclaimed Pete. "Furthermore, we are not simians; we are not apes, we are not monkeys, we are humans! Homo sapiens! The dominant species on this friggin' planet!"

"Apologies Pete; I meant no offense. Our race is used to studying and cataloging species, and yours originated from a similar strain as those large black fur apes. What do you call those here, by the way?" asked Kili, completely oblivious to any offensive words.

"Chimpanzees. Ok, so what is it you need? Where do you begin looking for this organization? And what is it they're after? Is it a weapon? A place? Why are you here?" asked Josh.

"Well, the first step is to find a mortal whose clan lineage intermingled with us in the past. Back a few epochs, your species had clans and small nations that sometimes dabbled in the affairs of our species. Naturally, your world has evolved from that system as it became more populous, but there should still be some indicator of your ancestors. As I stated, this human should be the most appropriate person to train first, as his clan had access to our technology on special occasions. We will need the assistance of this human I mentioned. Your technology has gained the interest of an organization that seeks to seize the planet for its resources. Unfortunately, I don't have that many details on what they're specifically after."

"Now, the dragoon I mutilated will likely seek a dark place to heal and rest, such as a cave or tunnel. I suggest you both do the same as we hunt for it at sundown. I need to finish it off before it regenerates its entire arm back. You, human, what do you call yourself?" asked Kili as she removed her coat.

Her arms were slender but muscular and covered in marine blue tattooed symbols, similar to Norse runes. Josh handed her a blanket and a pillow as she made herself comfortable on the couch.

"My name is Josh. Good to meet you, I guess. And well, we have to tailor the way you talk about our planet. You can't simply call people apes and say you're from the planet Asgard if you intend to keep secrecy."

"Likewise. Well, we will need to research and seek this human after we eliminate the dragoon; as I stated before, we rely on a few elite individuals instead of large armies. So, this human will be crucial to us. And yes, I do need to become better acquainted with your customs."

"Well, that sounds very exciting, except I am still fairly drunk so, we shall hunt for this dragon thing tomorrow when the world isn't spinning for me. Goodnight, heavily tattooed alien lady," Pete made his way to his bedroom.

As soon as Pete's door closed, Josh heard a loud knock on the door. Josh looked through the side windows to find Deputy John Brady standing on his doorstep.

"It's John. He is a local deputy, Kili. Do not mention anything about aliens or your planet to him," said Josh in a low voice.

"Well, that's a given; I will be as casual as I can," replied Kili in the same tone.

"What's going on, Officer?" Josh opened the door to Deputy John Brady.

He was uniformed, which indicated he was still on duty; his patrol car, one of the newer SUVs his department had just bought, was parked in the driveway with no lights. The deputy had been a buddy of Josh and Pete, but he came by less and less often to hang out since he joined the department when he graduated from college.

"Well, look at this fancy new cop car!" said Josh. "You get promoted or what?"

"The old man likes me best and we need to test these before we roll them to the other guys, so it's just mine for now," John chuckled. "Mind if I come in? I got a few questions to ask about some weird shit that happened tonight."

"Sure, man, come on in. You want a beer?" Josh was too late; Pete had already gone out of his room and placed a six-pack on the kitchen table.

"Y'all gonna get me in trouble again. Lemme at

least take the damn uniform top off, so I don't look so on duty. Hello lady, good to meet ya."

"Pleasure to meet you as well. I am Kili, and you are?"

"Normally, Deputy Brady. But tonight, thanks to these two troublemakers, it's just John, I guess."

"Come on, it's not like you can even get into trouble; you got everything working for you," said Pete.

"Yeah, we both know I got lucky; my dad and old man Dan go back a while since they both grew up in Texas. Lucky my dad is a Texas Ranger now, and the old man is who he is; otherwise, I'm just a smart cookie out of college who got in the department." John sat down and opened a beer.

Kili got up from the couch and joined them.

"So that gives you predilection? What is this Ranger from Texas you speak of? Sounds mighty. Our rangers can eliminate a target without ever being seen from the shadows."

"Wow! I mean, the Texas Rangers are the best of the police down in Texas, but damn! You in the military or something, lady?" asked John, confused.

"She's a foreigner!" blurted Josh, making eye contact with Kili and trying his best to tell her to go along without sounding suspicious. "An old contact from a foreign government I had back in the army days came to visit now that we are both out."

"Uh, yes! I'm not a denizen of this nation; our military is similar to yours in some ways," said Kili.

"Well damn! Looks like we ain't the only ones who got Rangers for the elite. I like that," said John.

"Yeah, well, the Army Rangers aren't too shabby either, you know," said Josh.

"Army Rangers, Texas Rangers, Rangers from… your country, Park Rangers, seems a little widely used of a term," said Pete.

"It's a good title for the elite. Anyway, originally I came here 'cause we had some weird stuff going on at the road, and I wanted to see if you guys saw anything or knew anything about it?"

"Nope, we got back from the bar near the college a while ago. What happened?" asked Josh, trying not to sound suspicious.

"It was some sort of giant burn mark on the side of the road, like someone blew something up with a giant fireball torch or something. You guys know anything about that?"

"Fireball torch, now that's a new name for a weapon," said Pete. "No, we definitely don't, but have you ever noticed how most weapons that deal massive damage like that seem to be thought up by a five-year-old?"

"It does not; come on, man!" said Josh, chuckling. "Not this again."

"Now hold on, hear me out now," said Pete as he raised a finger. "From what you told me back when you were in the army, a machine gun grenade launcher, a remote-controlled airplane that shoots missiles, and you did mention a robot with a gun that you push a button to kill people? I rest my case, thank you!"

"You know, when you put it like that, it sure does sound like a 5-year-old came up with it," said John.

"You have strange weaponized concepts, loads of offense, but where's your defensive capabilities?" asked Kili.

"A wise man once said the best defense is a great offense," said Josh.

"I suppose so, still, sending an automaton to get destroyed just to save yourself instead of designing a superior defense and training. A waste of technology, we simply lack the numbers to throw away both technology and personnel where I'm from," said Kili.

"Well, you also have fewer people where you're from," said Pete, giving Kili a sideways look. Kili acknowledged the look and said nothing in return.

"Well, here in America, we got the people, and remember, our army fought plenty of wars. We have the combat experience," said John.

"Well, let us hope it doesn't come to another war," said Kili.

"What?" asked John, confused.

"Let us hope no wars come soon is what she

meant," blurted Josh, also giving Kili a sideways look. She almost blew her cover for the second time. "You have seen the craziness going on around the world. The little chubby dictator and all."

"Oh, that guy! Nah, I reckon he'll calm down, eventually. You know how these crazies are; every time they need stuff, they threaten with war. I did want to show you guys something, though; I picked it up from the site."

John pulled out a metallic object from his pocket; it looked like a fish scale but was much larger, almost the size of his thumb. The strange scale had a particular silver-blue shine to it.

"At first, I thought it was just a piece of metal, but look at how it shines. Also, this thing is hard, harder than my steel multi-tool. I can't even get a scratch on it,"

Kili's eyes widened as she tried to hide her expression.

"You guys got any idea what this might be from?" asked John.

"Nope, definitely not. Maybe some new tech or something. Weren't the robotics students doing some sort of project out there?" Pete also tried to hide his expression at the sight of the scale.

"They're looking into drones for surveillance, but I don't think they're inventing new armor for them. I dunno, man. It's the only thing I could find, but hey, keep your eyes open. Let me know if you guys see or hear anything. Maybe it's aliens."

Josh stepped on Kili's foot as hard as he could to keep her from saying anything. Kili immediately looked at Josh with a somewhat angry look.

"Still actively engaging in your crazy theories, I see," said Pete. "Remember that paper in sociology you presented on how aliens could differ from us in social structures?"

"Hey, that paper got me an A, didn't it? Besides, who knows? Maybe I'm right and they are out there."

"Maybe, I guess we'll find out at some point if your shiny scale turns out to be something from them," said Josh as he grinned and looked at Pete, who replied with a reasonably fake grin himself. "And if they come back for their shiny scale. Oooohhhh."

"Yeah, yeah, listen, man, I've taken enough of your time. I gotta get out there and get one last patrol around town before I turn in the car. But you guys let me know if you hear anything about any of this craziness going on, ok? I'll see you guys out there," John got up and put his uniform back on. "It was nice to meet you, Kili. I hope I get to see you again before you take off."

"Likewise, John, I'm fairly certain you will. I have a lot to do before that happens."

John again looked confused by her words but brushed it off as talk from a foreigner. "Well, see you guys later," he said as he made his way through the door.

"Later, man," replied Josh as he closed the door behind him.

"Kili, you need to be more cautious," said Pete. "You almost gave away the whole 'I'm an alien thing' a bunch of times and would have raised a ton of questions."

"Apologies Pete, I thought I was doing fairly well. Besides, is he not your friend?"

"Aside from being an old college friend of ours, he is still a Police officer; he is with the local authorities. There's no telling if he would contact more people from the government or not," said Josh.

"Well, we shall work on my ability to speak with commoners in your town. What was it you told him again regarding where I'm from?"

"You're a foreigner, a foreign contact from when I was in the army. Or maybe an international student; let's try simple covers like that. You're from somewhere in Europe," Josh was too tired to think of any better covers for Kili at the moment.

"Very well then, we'll make it more elaborate tomorrow in the morning. Meanwhile, this is finally goodnight," Pete made a second attempt at going to his bedroom for some sleep.

"Goodnight, Pete, and you, Josh," Kili laid back down on the couch.

"Goodnight," Josh headed for his room, the recent events still running through his mind.

CHAPTER 2

The Hunt

"Wake up, mortals," said Kili as she knocked on Josh's door with so much force the hinges shook. "We have to hunt the dragoon, dusk falls upon us, and he will hunt soon!"

Pete came out of his room, half hungover, half grouchy. "Whoa! Easy superwoman; the door may fall off! Why are you so concerned with hunting that creature anyway? We are in Colorado; he has plenty of game to go after and isn't going anywhere far according to you," said Pete as he made his way to the restroom.

"Dwarf, as a genetic mutant, you should be mindful that he is highly mutagenic. His blood can cause several mutations in many biological species on this planet. Let us hope whoever set the creature here did not intend for that to happen to begin with," stated Kili. "And I am not exactly thrilled one of your government agents or police... cops got their hands on a scale from the dragoon either."

"What? Genetic… what did you just call me?" asked Pete as he left the restroom.

"We really need to work on your social skills," said Josh, "You expect to pass for a normal human, but you can't speak arrogantly to every person you meet or use this alien technology anywhere. Also, the term is Police Officer. But John is a deputy in the Sheriff's department. 'Cop' is just a slang term for that."

"I will be more mindful of your customs, but right now, we lack time to discuss this topic further. We must eliminate the threat and make our way back to Asgard. Also, what's slang?"

"It's a commonly used term, and wait, what do you mean we?" asked Josh.

"Well, you must assist me in hunting it. As locals, you know the area, leave the killing to me,"

"Whoa! Wait a minute! Are we coming with you?" asked Josh, bewildered.

"Yes, you primitive fool!" said Kili, "Now, the dragoon should be in an area with proper water and food sources as well as natural formations that will provide him cover. Where can we find such a location nearby?" asked Kili.

"Well, Tunnel Drive Trail would be ideal for that. Water nearby, plenty of caves and tunnels. Might be just the place," said Pete.

"Very well, that's where we shall initiate our

hunt. Gather your weapons; although they will be useless to damage it, but will provide a good distraction to prevent it from leaving again," said Kili as they made their way to the car.

"That's the intent. Hence we are bringing guns. Besides, it gives us some comfort and thoughts of safety," said Pete as he carried a relatively small pistol gripped shotgun. He had bought the thing at a gun show for home defense and had only fired it once for practice... The shotgun kicked like a mule; it was enough to push anyone out of the door of the house or through it, quickly if need be.

Josh had holstered his handgun on his hip and brought an AR-15. He wasn't sure how great a decision to have bought that firearm shortly after he left active-duty military. Now, he had just found an actual purpose for the rifle.

The three began their drive through the town. It was already late evening and local businesses were starting to close, city lights coming down to only the streetlights as the open signs were powered off. The city had the charm of a small town, and like many small towns, it had a bedtime.

None of this applied to Josh, Pete, and Kili as they made their way just outside of town and to a dark parking area near the tunnels. They parked the car at the spot hikers used for parking. The evening was darker as the full moon, which gave them high illumination, was gone. The trio was in complete darkness in the cold air of the end of winter.

"The police and emergency services typically stay in a skeleton crew for the night; we shouldn't encounter any hindrances from here," said Pete.

"Good; I would not want to fight skeletons as well as a dragoon, although I am unsure how a skeleton poses a threat," said Kili as they exited the car.

"I think he meant a small crew, not actual skeletons. It's a term we use for… You know what? Nevermind," said Josh, chuckling as he shook his head.

"Either way, let us get moving. Stand in a circle before me," said Kili as both turned to face her.

She turned the watch upwards towards them and uttered, "Nano, Night vision." A faint orange light shot out of the watch and immediately shot at both Josh and Pete's eyes, making them wince at the bright light that just rushed into their faces.

It was a strange feeling; Josh's eyes grew warm for a moment as he shut his eyes tightly, when he opened them again, he could see in a hue of sepia colors.

Josh looked over at Pete and saw his eyes were glowing an orange color. Every living creature he saw in the mountains and trails had a faint orange glow, making it easy to see everything from bunny rabbits to bats. It was a pitch-black night, but Josh and Pete could now see almost as clear as day.

"It will not last forever; you should be able to see and hunt the beast for a while," Kili's eyes also glowed orange. "When the glow fades in a few hours, your vision will return to normal. This ability is natural to us, but we found a way to artificially replicate it for mortals."

Josh and Pete loaded their guns and began their walk on the trail, paying attention to each crevice and rock formation around them.

"We won't have much luck merely following the road; let us look into these caves. They are not deep, but they are near water sources," said Kili.

"Are you insane? What should we do if we find what we're looking for and we get split up?" asked Pete.

"That is just it, is it not? We are not splitting up; we are merely looking more in-depth," noted Kili.

Pete had no further protests except for the ones regarding heights and reach. Being a dwarf was undoubtedly a handicap in a situation with any sort of climbing. Pete occasionally uttered a swear-word as he attempted to catch up to Josh, and all found themselves slipping slightly on loose rocks and dirt as they made their way towards more intricate rock formations.

Their eyes could still see very clearly into it as they began making their descent to explore the small caves. Most of them were relatively shallow with a small decline. They veered off the original trail and began taking beaten goat paths.

"Shouldn't we have more gear for this sort of expedition? At the moment, I feel a rope and some climbing gear would be in order," observed Pete as they crossed a rock formation that stood in their way and made it to the other side, the trail going somewhat high at that point on the hillside.

"Would you like us to go back to town and grab the equipment? I'm sure the local shop would be happy to oblige at this hour given the current circumstances," said Josh sarcastically.

Suddenly before Pete could reply, something pounced on his back as they walked a small trail, knocking the breath out of him. It clawed and bit at his neck and back while he tried to shake it off on the ground.

Kili swiftly kicked the creature off Pete before it fully grasped him, the force of her kick sending it into a large boulder as Pete cried out in pain while standing up. He was a little scrapped up from the short melee, and one of the claws had dug into his shoulder rather profoundly.

The creature fell to the bottom of a crevasse from the trail, stood upon four legs, and hissed loudly at them before slinking into a rock formation.

"What the hell?" Pete still felt the sting of the wound on his shoulder. He staggered as he stood for a moment, regaining his balance.

"Mountain lion must have made its nest here. You ok Pete?" asked Josh.

"I will survive, but that's going to leave a mark. Thanks for the quick rescue."

Kili acknowledged his gratitude with a nod.

"Do we have any medical supplies?" Pete asked as he examined his wound. It wasn't deep enough to require stitches thanks to his jacket, but there was blood where the claws gripped him. The cold air didn't help either.

"I have brought a few, just in case, Let's stop at the next flat area we find and patch you up," said Josh.

"We were fortunate. Had that beast been the one we seek, it would not have been so easy to ward off. We should be reaching the bottom of this descent soon," said Kili.

The trio descended down a goat path into a small area; it was closer to the river and ran near the trails. Josh applied proper medical care to Pete, disinfecting the wound and patching him with gauze before they continued their hunt.

"You know, I'm surprised with all this technology you don't have medical supplies," said Pete.

"We Celestials are highly resilient. Our bodies are robust and seldom sustain injury that requires healing aids, so carrying those supplies would be a waste for our missions. That and our defensive capabilities are highly efficient when it comes to avoiding harm. Besides our healers are normally the primary source for that sort of thing anyway. But they are only dispatched to combat missions, this was categorized as a reconnaissance mission so healers were not deemed necessary."

"Do you hear that?" asked Josh as he heard a strange noise. It was a mixture of a low growl and a few peculiar roars, followed by what sounded like a skirmish.

"It's the dragoon; it must have discovered your mountain lion," said Kili. "This provides us a better location on it. Fortune favors us in this hunt!"

"On the other hand, it is a bad night to be a cat," said Pete wryly.

"Consider yourself lucky it only managed to graze you, though," said Josh.

The trio approached the spot where the roar originated. It was a clearing of land from the rocky terrain with a small stream that led back into the river. A set of stacked boulders made a little cave den for the creature. The dragoon stood before the stream, facing off against the mountain lion. The lion clawed at the dragoon as it attempted unsuccessfully to grab at it. Both keeping just barely out of each other's reach.

"I would prefer not to engage both a lion and the dragoon simultaneously. But, considering the dragoon and the feline are near a water source, this can end bloody and dangerous. We cannot let them contaminate the water; blood contamination from a dragoon is rather unpredictable," Kili had a concerned tone as she made this observation.

They approached the area near the stream. Kili's wristwatch transformed into an odd-looking hand cannon.

"Freeze," she uttered to the cannon as it fired a blue flame, which froze the stream the moment it came in contact with the water near the brawl. Unfortunately, this also got the dragoon's attention, who turned his head from the mountain lion to the trio.

The lion took the opportunity to leap at the creature's head, only to be impaled by the dragoon's claws, right in the center of its chest. The mountain lion hissed loudly in pain as one of its claws dug into the dragoon's face, blinding it in one eye.

Unfortunately, the blow came too late as the dragoon sliced the lion open with its claws. Blood pooling from the mountain lion as it attempted unsuccessfully to retreat, the mountain lion slumped over, and it was no more.

The dragoon was snarling in anger as it charged the trio. Josh and Pete dodged the charging beast; the arm that Kili had previously severed had almost completely grown back but it still only had a nub for a hand.

Lucky for Josh and Pete, that was the arm that hit them, slamming them both into the ground, their backs stopped by large rocks with enough force to crack ribs.

The other arm raised its sharp claws to Kili, who stood her ground and made a ritualistic motion, touching her wrists together to form a pair of hard-edged blades made of pure light. These blades looked brighter and sharper, and were almost the length of short swords extending from her arms.

Kili stabbed the creature's hand and slashed its body several times before rolling out of the way to avoid the sheer mass of the charging behemoth, each of her slashes tearing scales and pieces of flesh off the creature.

Josh and Pete rolled into prone position and opened fire on the dragoon, but their weapons only irritated the beast. Pete's shotgun was like a mere punch while Josh's AR-15 pierced its skin, making small holes but not big enough to do vital damage. Droplets of blood streaked from the bullet holes.

"Well, at least the AR penetrates the hide," said Pete

"That's better than the last encounter, but it doesn't seem to do much," said Josh as they got up from the ground.

Pete reloaded his shotgun and paused for a moment as he aimed, trying to find a vital spot to hit. "Let's see if I can get a better hit this time as well."

The dragoon chuckled as Pete charged forward, pumping round after round at the creature's face. The dragoon reached forward at Pete and seized him by the arm, lifting him off the ground.

"Pete! No! Fall back!" screamed Josh as he emptied another magazine on the dragoon's body.

It was too late, the monster had Pete by the arm in the air; Kili charged forward and sliced the beast's leg. As the dragoon staggered to regain his balance, Pete took a shot right into the dragoon's good eye with his last round, this time blinding it completely.

Kili took the opportunity and Sliced at the dragoon's neck, taking the creature's head clean off as it shrieked in pain. Both the headless body and Pete, still hanging from its claws, fell to the floor.

"Way to go, alien lady! We did it!" Pete suddenly stopped mid-sentence as black blood still pumping from the headless body of the monster suddenly drenched him as he got to his feet. "Well done..." said Pete, less excited, spitting out some of the blood and wiping his face.

"Good idea dwarf! Your combat abilities far exceed expectations."

"It's Pete, not dwarf. And thank you, but that was a complete fluke!" said Pete as he suddenly winced, a small amount of steam coming from scrapes where the mountain lion had grabbed him previously.

"The dragoon blood, it has come into contact with yours!" exclaimed Kili as she looked at the device on her wrist.

"Injector, stabilizer," she uttered to it as it immediately morphed into an odd glue gun looking device. She pressed the tip against Pete's neck and said, "neurostabilize," as it injected Pete with a strange liquid.

Pete shouted in pain.

"Ouch! What was that all about? Will you give me a heads up before vaccinating me with your alien meds?"

"That was to stabilize your brain and central nervous system as the mutagenic compound invades your bloodstream. I can not stop those effects; there is no way to predict what it will do or how to reverse it until it finishes, but at least you will retain your sanity as your body mutates."

"As I... I'm sorry, did you just say mutate?" A bewildered Pete questioned.

"I warned you both the dragoon's blood was a mutagenic agent. You should feel some of the effects, but by the looks of it, your genetic condition seems to play a big part in keeping the mutations from being too drastic."

Analyzing Pete carefully, he didn't seem to be changing physically, nor did he act abnormal. Kili kept a close eye on him as she transformed the device into a flamethrower before leaving the area.

She incinerated the entire site of the battle with the beast, the water from the stream vaporizing into steam as everything else not made of rock turned to ash.

"I have to admit, I am becoming quite fond of that thing," said Josh as the device morphed into a smartwatch.

"Serves its purposes; I designed and programmed the nanodevice myself. Each Celestial has created a device here and there for their intents and purposes. Mine is simply more than just a weapon; a tool with multiple functions."

"Did you give it a name?" asked Pete as they began their way back to the main trail.

"I simply called it 'nanodevice.' It is comprised of nanotechnology in the form of many micro-electronic cells forming an artificial conscience. It caters to most of my needs but has limited communications as it typically just uses the communication signals in the existing planet."

"Definitely decades ahead of anything we can come up with on this planet so far," exclaimed Josh.

"Try centuries. Like you humans, our technology evolves in time; design improvements are made vastly over originals, and well, we already had extraordinary abilities by your standards back in the olden days. Just imagine what a few human centuries have done to our technology without annihilation."

"You take that into account too?" asked Pete.

"Of course, many civilizations went extinct due to their technology evolving simply towards war. You are not the first sentient species we watched over, nor will you be the last, but the Maku have a way of influencing a species towards their own self destruction. They seek to control and enslave the mortal races and shape the world strictly to their desire. If they win, you will all be enslaved and exploited for their intents and purposes, and they will eliminate all resistance. That is why we Celestials are duty-bound to assist in the prosperity of any young race that has demonstrated the gifts of intellect."

The way back to the trail seemed much easier for Pete, who appeared now more limber. He ran and climbed more effortlessly since the melee with the dragoon. Josh and Kili took notice of this as Pete went on ahead, but merely watched silently as their friend reached the end of the beaten path with ease.

"Well, now we must wait until the transitional planet is aligned with this one again. The Bifrost allows me to travel from Asgard to here in one shot, but travel back is tricky; I cannot store enough dark matter to power a portal all the way."

"You mean you're bouncing off another populated planet like earth to get to your planet?" asked

Josh.

"Yes, that is essentially the idea. Your scientists may have observed a few planets come in view beyond your solar system; those are mere small planets that allow us to travel through the cosmos. They are nothing like earth; they somewhat have species diversity, but they have only one or two major cities and serve more of a specific purpose. The next one should align itself in a few days, and I will be able to reach Asgard in a fairly decent time. Meanwhile, we must find one of the humans belonging to the original clans we have interacted with many centuries ago."

"Well, what's a way to do that? Last name search?" asked Josh as they headed back to the car.

"What's a last name?" asked Kili as they sat down and prepared for the ride home.

"It is a name given to the family in which you belong. I am Peter Lage; my given name is Pete, of the Lage family, like my father."

"Interesting. Perhaps that would be a way to determine the human I seek. What about you, Josh?" Kili produced a hologram of a screen with a list of names. The hologram showed a page in light blue with letters in a darker shade. "What do you call your family?"

"I'm Josh Gunnar." Said Josh as suddenly one of the names on the screen shined in golden letters; the trio looked at the name as it did. The words "Gunnar" read across the screen.

"This thing can hear us?" asked Pete.

"Of course it can, and it can see us. It has an artificial consciousness with full sensory input. And it has detected the name of one of the clans! Josh, it looks like you are one of the humans I'm looking for!"

"Talk about luck! So, what now?" asked Josh.

"Well, the answer is obvious: you must come with me to Asgard! As soon as Zion aligns with Earth."

"You're abducting him to a different planet?" asked Pete.

"More like inviting him to come along to visit the world of the old gods, as his ancestors would say," said Kili.

"Do I have a choice in this matter?"

"Of course, you can stay here and risk the annihilation of all your armed forces, the enslavement of your species, and total domination of your planet by a malevolent intergalactic organization or come with me to gain access to the means to keep them at bay until we can rid the world of them altogether."

"In other words, come with you, or we're screwed," said Josh.

"Well... there is nothing the Maku particularly state about breeding, but I suppose we can find you a nice maiden once in Asgard," said Kili, smiling.

"That's not what he meant…" said Pete. "Never mind. Josh, you have no choice, buddy."

"No kidding. But hey, while we wait, maybe we can show you around, teach you a bit about us and how not to be so literal all the time," said Josh, laughing.

"Perhaps. Cultural studies can be very beneficial to our cause," said Kili, "and I would like to study this strange language pattern of combining two words into one. It is… it's… an efficient means of speaking."

The trio made their way back and spent several days contemplating their next move. Kili shared information with Josh and Pete about the overall influence of her race and many others over their history, over the mysteries of many civilizations that had come to power with the aid of alien technology, of how traveling between planets had been made possible not by a ship but by the Bifrost, which vastly accelerated the ability to travel through the known universe.

Josh and Pete shared many customs and courtesies with Kili, to enable her to blend into everyday society as that was her goal.

Peter continued to display signs of improved mobility beyond his usual self but no drastic signs of mutation, which was a relief as Kili had explained she expected him to grow horns by now. Neither Pete nor Josh questioned her about this as neither of them wanted to know if this was a joke or not. Still, Pete's increasingly better physical abilities had become very noticeable for a dwarf.

Josh and Pete went as far as taking Kili to enjoy some of the attractions of Colorado, taking her rock climbing and shooting what she referred to as "primitive weapons."

"So everyone here does this sort of thing all the time?" asked Kili as they climbed the rock wall at a gym.

"Well, when we aren't at work. People spend most of their days at work. Five out of seven days of the week," said Josh.

"Why would you spend most of your days at work?"

"Because they need the money to sustain their lives. We can't all be rich, you know," said Pete.

"Why in Hel's name not? Are your basic necessities not met? In Asgard, even the lowest peasant has a hut. Now to have a more luxurious home, ale at his table every night, and a good life, he must work. But at least the basics everyone has without dying."

"Yes, well, things are a bit different here," said Josh.

"Yes, see, some of us make a ton of money, and the rest of us work for that someone for 40 or more hours of the week," said Pete. "That's capitalism in a nutshell."

"But what if there is nothing to do that week?" asked Kili.

"Well… you still have to show up," said Josh.

"That makes no sense! In Asgard, you train, feast and take care of yourself if you aren't on an assignment or performing your duties. But your time is your time if there's nothing to do."

"Well, we have people on salary for that sometimes, but it's kind of complicated," said Pete. "They normally work harder."

"So, one human works harder for the same quantity of resources as another who gains whilst he is at work, whether doing work or not?"

"Well, if by that you mean money, yes," said Josh.

"That makes no sense. Why would they work harder then?"

"Well, as I said, it's complicated," said Pete "That person is of more importance, so they have to be at work."

"And this money you speak of, is that currency? I saw you hand your credits in paper. Do you not have gold? Or digital credits?"

"We don't use gold anymore; too expensive." said Josh.

"But credits are made of gold. How can they be too expensive?"

"We generated currency because gold was too limited," said Josh. "Yes, we have digital, but it has to come to the same amount of money."

"The same amount of that green paper with letters and numbers and the face of your long-deceased leaders?"

"Yes. In a nutshell," said Pete.

"And does that 'money' not equal gold?"

"Well, it used to; now it's essentially a promise our government will pay and has covered what you owe," said Josh.

"Your society is very confusing, your weapons shoot solid projectiles that rely on kinetic force alone absent any energy. Your currency is made of a strange paper and most of your people have to dedicate one third of their lifetime to acquiring such green paper for such weapons as well as sustenance. Seems rather illogical."

Josh and Pete continued to do their best to educate Kili about their planet as the days passed. Josh and Pete still finished the school semester and had work, which left Kili at home with not much to do but research more online about their planet when the two could not take her with them.

February gave way into March, which became spring break. Then the time had finally come; it was a full moon, and all the stars were in the sky that night.

"Where are we going for this said portal?" asked Josh.

"Well, we need somewhere absent from prying

human eyes, somewhere with a clear shot to Zion. Somewhere the Dwa…" Pete shot a dirty look at Kili as she spoke, "Where Peter can make his way back without any questions," finished Kili carefully.

"Well, there is the Royal Gorge area; should be empty after hours, and I should be able to drive back. Josh, I've driven the Honda before; it is suitable for my height, especially now. I feel a bit leaner and can reach more lately. Besides, it's not like you'll be using it while doing whatever it is you intend to at Asgard."

"You nearly ran us down a ditch last time you drove, so please be careful this time. I want to come back and still have a car. Besides, the gorge is too far and has security and park rangers, so we need somewhere easier just to make a break for it once Kili does what she came here to do."

"Well, Sky Drive is just a mile from here, clear view of the sky, and not as many people. As for the car thing, well it was snowing."

"You could have slowed down and looked over to see where the road cut off."

"I am just over 4 feet tall; what is it you expect me to look over?"

"Well, if you two are done, shall we prepare for our journey?" asked Kili, "Pete will have assistance this time from the nano device. I don't intend to leave a mutating dwarf without some sort of monitoring while I travel to Asgard, even if you are stabilized!"

"Well, that's certainly unexpected; you're giving me your smartwatch?"

"It is not a… never mind; yes, I am lending you the device."

"It needs a better name; you're quite uncreative in naming things."

"How dare you, mortal!" said Kili.

"Ok! We will address these minor details later. Let's grab a bite before everything in town closes and head out!" exclaimed Josh. "Kili, what should I bring to this trip? A change of clothes?"

"What you are wearing will do; there is nothing you can do in this backward planet that will make you neither more presentable nor elegant before the council," stated Kili.

Josh was simply wearing a regular open hoodie with a t-shirt and jeans, nothing exceptional. Yet the fact that neither he nor Pete had any idea how Kili's people dressed made them simply take her word for it on this matter. After all the entire time she had been here, she had been wearing the same clothes as the night they met her with some small variations in color and design. The device on her wrist seemed to provide her with fresh clothes daily, so she never needed to shop for anything.

"Again with the insults; I thought we went over this," said Josh.

"To be fair, I am with her on this one, Josh.

Every gadgetry she has shown us and bit of knowledge so far implies they are centuries ahead of us. It's not an insult in this case, but Kili, do try to blend in when we go out to eat. This will be good practice for you."

"Well, that's exciting! Where are we going? A restaurant? One of those so-called taverns or pubes my predecessors spoke of?" Kili showed uncharacteristic enthusiasm.

"First, the word is pub, not pube; that is something else entirely. Second, we're going to our favorite burger joint for some dinner," said Josh.

"A burger… joint? What is that?" asked Kili, confused.

"It's like a restaurant but simpler, you don't have to dress very fancily and food is made fast on the spot, within eyesight even sometimes," explained Pete.

"Well, I look forward to seeing this 'joint' you speak of."

"Burger joint… what you said implies something different… Never mind; let's get going before we end up in another long conversation about this in which case the night might pass," said Josh, chuckling.

The trio left home, Josh looking back at it one last time, almost as if saying goodbye to it. He entered the car without another word and headed for what would be his last meal on earth for some time.

"Watsup, Gabe!" said Josh as they entered the diner.

"Not much, man; what can I get you?" replied Gabe from behind the cash register.

"The usual cheeseburger with fried mushrooms."

"Same for myself but with fries, please."

Both he, Josh and Gabe now stared at Kili, who was looking around the diner, taking in her surroundings. It was a small eatery indeed, no more than ten tables, some with two chairs, some with four. She could see the grilling area past Gabe's counter with ease.

Gabe wore a red shirt with the logo "Bunk House Burgers" on it in bold black letters over the print of a burger. Kili took in all the sights, silently looking around until Gabe addressed her almost awkwardly.

"Uh… and you Miss?" asked Gabe.

"Oh! Ummm… I'll have what these two gentlemen are having, please."

"Fries or mushrooms with it?" asked Gabe.

"Ummm… what should I pick?" Kili turned to Josh and Pete.

"Well, you know fries are typical but fried mushrooms..."

"Are a fungus so there's nothing wrong with typical fries," interrupted Pete.

"There's nothing wrong with mushrooms man,

let it go," said Josh, chuckling.

"There's plenty wrong with fungus; you wouldn't eat mold, would you?"

"There's a difference."

"I see no difference."

"May I suggest half and half?" asked Gabe. "These two will debate for hours if you let them."

"I concur! I've been inhabiting their home for a few days now. Half and half it is!" exclaimed Kili.

Gabe shouted the order to the cook in the back as he worked the cash register. "That'll be $32.71," said Gabe to Josh and Pete, who were still arguing over fries versus mushrooms as Josh inserted his credit card into the machine next to the register.

"So, you've been staying with those two, you from out of town?" asked Gabe.

"Yes, quite a ways away actually, another country."

"Wow! Cool! Where are you from?" asked Gabe excitedly.

"Asgard," said Kili.

"Asgard? Where is that? I never heard of it," said Gabe, confused.

"Uh, Norway!" said Pete as he caught the conversation mid-sentence. "She's a friend from Norway, foreign exchange program; she's trying to take a short vacation and learn our culture before giving it a go at the studies. Asgard is just the name of her town."

"Yes! That's it! Thank you, Pete!" said Kili as Josh quickly shoved her down the line away from the conversation.

"You cannot tell them you're from Asgard!" whispered Josh. "People will start asking where on Earth is that!"

"Well, I told him it was a different nation. Besides, clearly, how we speak is different."

"Yes, but most people on this planet know where most countries are. Try to be more discreet if you intend to keep secrecy!"

"Hey guys, your order is ready," said Gabe, still somewhat confused by Kili's quick getaway from their conversation.

"Thank you, Gabe; don't worry about her. Foreigners can be strange sometimes. I have a hard time understanding her myself, and her native language; man, can't understand a word of it," said Pete, awkwardly smiling.

"Hey, it's nice to show strangers around town, especially gorgeous ladies," said Gabe, smiling at Kili.

Kili smiled back awkwardly at him as they took their orders, filled up their fountain drinks, and sat down. Josh and Pete filled up their glasses with regular Coca-Cola; Kili merely mimicked their actions to appear more normal, eating her first burger and drinking her first Coca-Cola since her arrival on the planet as the past few days it had been Josh and

Pete's cooking that was the usual meal.

"I must say… this is much more preferable," said Kili between bites.

"Well, some things are simply not our gifts in life. Cooking being among them," said Pete.

"We cook well enough to stay alive, but this is actually legit earth American cuisine," said Josh as he took another gulp of his drink.

"You will find the feasts at the realm more elaborate than this, but this is quite tasty," said Kili.

"Yes, well, this is a small town, and we didn't exactly have time to prepare and go to a bigger restaurant," said Josh. "Maybe whenever we come back, we'll have time and be able to do so."

"Well, well, look who's taking a break from their college and home routine!" said Deputy John as he came from the restroom. "What you guys up to this spring?"

"Mostly just hanging out but we do plan on going on a short trip," said Josh, "Sit down, man; come join us. Did you order anything?"

"I did, but I already ate; I guess I'll just have a drink and hang for a minute," Gabe handed John a fountain drink cup. "On the house," said Gabe as John got himself a soda and sat down with the trio.

"I gotta tell ya, that piece of whatever it was I found, man that thing is tough! Took a round from my AR-15 to even dent it. I still don't know what it is, but if I can find more of it, we should all just start making body armor like that!"

"That's rather obsolete compared to some other armors, though. Reactive energy armor still wins the market." Josh kicked her leg. "Once it hits the open market, anyway. For the time being, they are testing it," finished Kili awkwardly. She was starting to understand why Josh and Pete consistently kicked her under the table during conversations quite well.

"Reactive what?" asked John.

"It's a project!" said Josh. "We had some people working on it when I left the army. It was mostly a concept back in those days, but now it's getting released to Special Forces. Details are classified."

"Classified, I haven't heard that from you in a while!" John chuckled. "I remember when you first came to the university, you used that a lot!"

"Well, seems Kili here is a bit better than me about those things."

"Anyone is compared to you. We could barely ask you how you slept when we first met you." said Pete jokingly.

"Well, how about that trip? You guys going anywhere special?" asked John.

"Time for me to see her country," said Josh. "Since she got a nice visit to ours."

"Well, color me impressed. Where did you say you were from again, lady?" asked John.

"Uh, Norway! It's rather secluded, difficult to

get in," Josh answered.

"So difficult I didn't have time to plan for this trip," said Pete. "I guess I'll just enjoy spring break alone."

"Well, it's just me and you for now, little buddy," said John.

Pete shot him a dirty look. Ever since they met, John quickly caught on that Pete wasn't fond of dwarf jokes, but John still pushed the limit from time to time. "I'm just joking, man," John chuckled.

"Picking on little people and minorities again, typical cop man!" Josh laughed.

"Hey, short lives matter, ok?" said Pete.

"Alright, alright, geesh, and then there's the damn college kids tag-teaming an honest officer just trying to make a living."

"So honest he cheated at poker that one night at Barry's," said Josh.

"Hey man, the guy is better than even Pete at cards, ok? Someone had to keep him from taking all the hands," said John.

"I told you I had him." said Pete.

"I could see your hand; you weren't gonna win," said John.

"I was warming up."

"Well, maybe we'll get a shot again; he's in the same year you guys are, right? Hit me up whenever ya'll go for another night after your trip, anyway,

I gotta head out. Nice seeing you guys; stay safe." John got up and left after finishing his drink.

"Is it just me, or are we seeing him much more often now that Kili's here?" asked Pete.

"He's coming around more; perhaps this trip is right on time," said Josh.

"Well, we do have ways to keep others from breaking secrecy," Kili said.

"You can't kill someone just to maintain your secrecy, Kili! Especially not a friend or a cop!" said Josh.

"I meant erase his memory, you barbarian! Life is unique and precious, which is why we Celestials also do our best to preserve it. Especially those of benefit to others. But there are plenty of other ways to keep someone ignorant of our existence. What do you think happens when you get déjà vu or forget why you entered a certain place suddenly?"

"You mean to tell me aliens erase our memories and escape when that happens?" asked Pete.

"Well, yes. Déjà vu is just the brain's glimpse of a previous encounter you forgot on the subconscious part of your brain because it erased your recollection of the event. Your brain gives you a familiar sensation since you have been there before, or around that someone before, but can't recall any details because certain key elements are missing. And the forgetfulness is when you catch a glimpse of something you were not supposed to see, but we caught it on time to wipe you."

"Well, that explains a lot. I thought we just had early dementia," said Josh chuckling.

"Your species is prone to that condition very early; it takes an average Asgardian at least six hundred years."

"Well, let's hope it doesn't come to that with John. He's a good guy. Being part of the police presents a problem for us, but he is our friend no less," said Pete.

The three stayed at the diner until closing time, eating and conversing about many things. To avoid raising suspicion, the conversation landed on typical American customs, which further emphasized to any bystanders that Kili was but a foreigner who was not very familiar with local customs.

Once they said their goodbyes to Bunkhouse Burgers and stepped outside, the topic of the conversation changed drastically.

"So, we need a space where you can get out easily Pete, yet it is up high and in clear view of the sky. This skyline drive, what is it?" Kili asked.

"Skyline Drive is a road that passes through a plateau. There are a few areas that are wide enough for… well, whatever it is you plan to do, and the way down leads straight into our neighborhood," replied Pete.

"That does sound perfect," Kili replied. "Let's

take a look at it. We only have eight more earth days."

"Well then, I believe we are ready," said Josh. "Let's head out."

The three went around the city to the entrance to the road they called Skyline Drive. It was a scenic route known for its altitude, its fossils of dinosaurs found along the mountains, and its fantastic view. Since it was early spring and the weather wasn't yet favorable for enjoying the outdoor views, the road was absent of any tourists.

Josh, Pete, and Kili drove up quickly along the road to a spot where there was a pull-off and a rel-atively wide area without anyone else there, making their deed for the night something no one would ask questions about.

Kili exited the car first, inspecting the sur-rounding area. It was a full moon and high illumi-nation night, so even when the car's headlights shut off, the three of them could still see reasonably well without the assistance of Kili's night vision abilities.

Kili drew two elaborate mandalas on the ground. Circles with detailed patterns, intricate intertwining squares forming a complex design. They were simple and identical, yet if you looked into them for long enough, you would get lost de-ciphering the pattern.

"Josh, stand in the center of one of those,"

said Kili, Josh did exactly as she told him to. "Pete, you have been invaluable both as a friend assisting me in the learning of your modern culture as you have been in hunting the dragoon; I lend you my nanodevice to keep you safe while we are gone."

Kili extended her arm, grasping Pete's in a tight lock. The nanodevice came to life and moved, half crawling, half turning to liquid form, traversing from Kili's arm to Pete's. The screen came to life and projected a pulsing white light over the mandalas.

"I guess I'll see you in a few, man" said Josh, not knowing what to say. He and Pete had been friends since freshman year of college and had been inseparable since then. This was the first time, absent from a family vacation, that Josh would leave his best friend behind.

"See you when you come back bud, I'll be here," said Pete with a slight smile. "And Kili, thank you. It's been… well… interesting. Josh, I guess I'll tell whoever asks when the classes start again that you had a family emergency or, in John's case, went to Norway. Seems legit, right?" asked Pete, Josh shrugged his shoulders and nodded in agreement.

"Well, we have said our goodbyes. Nano, Open the Bifrost," said Kili.

And with Kili's command, the device took a form similar to a projector, firing a blue light at the spot where the mandalas sat illuminated in white under their feet. Kili and Josh were encased in two globes that appeared made of silver, they were perfect spheres. The spheres shot upwards at an incredible speed—their light aiming directly at a faraway planet in the stars.

CHAPTER 3

Voyage Through the Stars

Josh saw his feet leaving the ground quickly from the mandala symbol on which he stood. Yet, he felt no wind, no force of gravity pulling him in any direction. His eyes saw the planet simply going away as he traveled. He saw planets passing by in harmony but no change in temperature as he moved further from Earth.

It was as if he were in an air bubble traveling through the stars. Josh could see flashes of light from the Bifrost as his body moved; they were flashes of varied colors, specks of light that followed his route like bright beams of light, gently moving minor asteroids out of his trajectory. It was as if he was riding on a rainbow through the galaxy. The only question in his mind was, "Where's Kili?"

Kili had taken off right by his side, but when they left earth, her trajectory deviated from his, and he could no longer see the silver sphere that had encased her. This slightly concerned Josh as he had never traveled between planets before and had no idea what to do or where this interplanetary bridge would lead.

But Josh did not have very long to dwell on his thoughts. As soon as he passed Saturn and the asteroid belt, he quickly saw a planet approach. The planet grew increasingly more prominent as he passed Pluto and was still growing; he was headed straight for it, thinking he was going to crash but felt no inkling of gravity or wind.

Josh braced himself for impact as he thought he would come in contact with the ground hard, but to his surprise, he landed with no more force than he had taken off, blowing only a tiny amount of dust around him as he landed off balance on his hands and knees.

Josh felt slightly sick as his landing made a soft patch of dirt on the grass; his vessel simply dissipated into thin air and the mandala symbol drawn from Earth was under him, marked the same way Kili had on the soil when they had taken off. Josh stood up and looked around; this planet was beautiful, an Aurora Borealis on a purplish horizon, hues of green and blue dancing on the sky overhead.

The sun was just coming up in the planet over the mountains, the patch of dirt Josh landed on was surrounded by lush green grass, the field of grass led to structures not far away; golden stone structures that light almost entirely reflected off.

And from the structures, a vehicle appeared to

be coming in Josh's direction. It was disk-shaped, small for a plane, seemed to have a globe in the center, similar to the flying saucers of typical alien movies. The aircraft hovered several feet above Josh and began opening at the bottom; a bright light shined as a figure slowly descended from the craft.

The figure floated down gently until its feet touched the ground. The light from the aircraft faded, and it quickly sped away from the area, heading back to the strange structures on the horizon.

Josh could now see the creature the unknown aircraft lowered several feet from him; it was a few inches shorter than Josh, a hairless skinny and lean but muscular and grey body, an enormous head with large black eyes. You could see the iris and pupils inside the dark eyes; they were oval-shaped, as was its head. The creature stared directly at Josh as it extended its index finger and pointed at Josh.

"Human, do not be alarmed; I come in peace. I will now be commencing the probing procedure," said the alien in an almost robotic monotone voice.

"Commencing what?" Josh gasped as he took a step back, apprehensive as to the alien's intentions. The alien began robotically walking towards Josh as he began making an odd snorting sound. It sounded like an oddly familiar snicker as if he was holding back laughter.

Josh continued to take steps back slowly until

suddenly the alien burst out laughing.

"I'm just messing with you, bro!" said the alien, still laughing. "We don't do that nonsense, that's just cheesy movie stuff on your planet. Hi! I'm Jura, and your friend from Ass-Gard is waiting for you over at the capital."

Jura waved hello before indicating for Josh to come with him. Josh was taken aback by the fact that the alien, Jura, not only seemed typical of the movies he had seen as a kid with his identical appearance to every alien drawing, movie, or cartoon but was also very surprised at his humor, and that oddly enough he spoke English perfectly. But Jura seemed trustworthy enough, so Josh introduced himself and followed the grey alien.

Jura joked with most things and had a great sense of humor as they talked while walking towards the golden capital. It felt less like speaking to an advanced species of an alien race and more like hanging out with a fellow college student on a nice summer day. Jura was about as normal of a guy as it came for the second alien Josh had ever spoken to, humorous even.

"… so yeah, bro, this lighter gravity affects some species. My kind is used to it thanks to all the interstellar space travel we do all the time. But without any enhancements, their bodies are super fragile. Luckily, I live on this planet. Anyway, get ready, cause here comes one of the manta whales and we're just gonna hop on its back. I don't feel like walking all the way the hell over there. Don't worry, with the low Gs, you're gonna fly and land on top of it. You ready?"

"Manta what?"

A moment of panic came into Josh's mind as a giant animal glided through the air towards them. It looked like a huge whale, yet it was flying, gliding gracefully through colorfully visible wind currents. Its skin was different shades of blue, light on the bottom and darker on top. However, its fins were different; the animal had a round skin-like membrane running the length of its body in a slightly reddish color like a stingray, more like giant wings so it could steer itself as it glided.

Josh took a moment to be both amazed and a little concerned as the animal passed gently by them, barely taking notice of them. Its giant eyes saw them, but it appeared uninterested as it continued its route.

"Ready? Jump!" shouted Jura as they both leaped. Josh found the height of which they jumped surprisingly high, but Jura had warned him the gravity of this planet was much lower. Both landed on the manta whale's back.

Josh landed on his knees, but Jura displayed the grace of an acrobat as he came down feet first.

"You'll get the hang of it, newbie! This one should land us close to the palace. You're gonna like the station; it's a pretty dope place. You should come on back and check it out sometime when you guys aren't on a mission saving the planets or anything like that."

"Right, um, Jura? What exactly is this place?" Asked Josh as they glided through the air on the behemoth's back.

"It's the grand interplanetary travel station, bro! The city of Zion! The bastion of multiracial interstellar travel and one of the first cities to allow all species to travel between planets. Basically, it's a pit stop in the universe for interstellar travel that allows trade, business, and even interstellar diplomatic affairs. Man, this city is da bomb! Now get ready cause we have to hop off. This big baby doesn't exactly stop and wait for us."

The giant manta flew just above a station, pausing briefly to bite at a large vase with some blue plants that looked like berries. The whale munched on the berries for a moment before gliding again gently into the air.

"Now!" said Jura as they jumped off the manta whale, landing softly on the ground.

"They feed on those berries, so we planted them all over the city. It makes the mantas easy to travel on as they just pass where they please. They don't mind picking up a straggler or two."

"How does something that big even fly?"

"Bro, they got giant air sacs of some gas that's

way lighter than air in their body. Low gravity, lighter than air gas, and wings, man. Their bodies just produce that gas when they digest food and store it to make them light as a feather. Awesome animal!"

All around Josh, the city was full of life. Josh saw strange yet familiar-looking vehicles arriving and departing what looked like a train station with no rails. The trains seemed to run on the same path of light that had guided Josh to this planet.

The train-looking ships ran on the Bifrost. Aliens of all breeds and sizes would board and leave trains, glowing skinned upright tall beings that looked like royalty, hulking armored looking aliens, creatures of more petite stature that carried themselves with a look of far superior intellect, alien-machine hybrids with clearly robotic moving parts.

Literally, every race imaginable was arriving or going somewhere; some went into the city itself, some appeared traveling with their entire families, conversing in languages whose very sounds were foreign to Josh.

Jura led Josh around the crowd towards what looked like the entrance to a large building. The aliens stared clearly at him as Jura politely made way for the two through the crowd.

Some would utter the word "human" audibly in surprise or the sound as close to it as they could; they were astonished, and many appeared delighted to see one of Josh's kind walking among them.

"Eh, don't worry about it, bro! They just never seen one of you around here. They'll get over it soon enough. The races here are mostly upper-class travelers at this station. Trust me; you don't wanna land on a lower-class planet for travel," said Jura casually as they arrived at an elevator inside the building they entered made of gold and silver with jewels with carvings of strange symbols on each button.

Jura pushed one of the buttons, and the elevator came to life and glided gracefully up. Gracefully but fast, yet for the speed the elevator ascended, Josh did not feel the gravity force a standard elevator on earth would exert upon its passengers.

"You like that? This baby has its own gravity control technology nullifying the magnetic force you feel on your earth elevators. Top-notch stuff, eh?"

"Jura, everything looks made of gold and jewels and crystals, why is that?" asked Josh, still amazed as he looked around while they ascended.

"That's because it is gold, jewels and crystals. It's a slightly modified version of your earth's rare-metal, harder but still conductive, with an inner lining of your earth gold, the jewels and crystals simply make a natural insulator combined with a more resilient type of glass plus it all adds to aesthetic design, bro. In case you haven't noticed, we

aliens are all about the shiny and artistic, also min-
ing asteroids gives you unlimited amounts of it, so
this planet is richer than all the countries on your
planet combined in terms of precious material
quantity. And the technology behind it is insane!"

Josh and Jura reached the top floor of the
building, and the elevator doors opened with a
swift hum. They were entering an open room, no
furniture, a design on the floor that appeared to
be a compass rose, everything still had the same
embellished look as it did on the first floor, and at
the corner looking out the clear glass window was
a being that appeared made entirely of light.

Josh could make out the human-like features
as he faced him; he looked strangely familiar for
an alien being Josh had never seen in his life before. The being had a glow that defined his body; it
was a young man, short-haired, glowing in a golden
hue, his upper body showed clearly down to his
waist, where he became formless and appeared
float. From his chest glowed a tiny particle of light
which gave him his physical shape.

He was about Josh's height; the figure began
to glide smoothly towards Josh and Jura as they
walked forward to meet him in the center of the
room.

"Greetings Josh, I am Che-Ben," said the being
of light.

"Hello… uh.. sir?" Josh was unsure how to address him or even greet such a being.

"Please, just call me Che. I'm sure you have questions; I will answer all on time, yet time is not what we have aplenty. Your world is one step closer to the edge."

"What do you mean by that?" asked Josh.

"Every world has developed itself, and many are to evolve still. Some evolved and received wonder, others met with disaster, and some simply evolved. Your world is taking its next step in that evolution, but as of now, there are threats to it and entities that seek to deprive it of its evolution. That is the premise that has brought you here. Your companion should be joining us shortly."

Suddenly the elevator doors opened again, and through it walked Kili and another gray alien. This one was shorter, about half as tall as the previous one, same gray skin, body, and head shape, but his large eyes were blue, and he appeared to have the same attitude as Jura had.

"Hey! Did you do it?" asked the shorter alien.

"Yeah bro, he nearly shit himself!" answered Jura chuckling.

"Ah! I knew it! You're such a dick!" answered the shorter gray as he laughed. "Watsup, bro? I'm Todd, the other dude maintaining this whole place."

"Um… hi! Good to meet ya. I'm Josh. So, why are we all here?"

"Cause this is the place to be, bro!" said Todd. "This place takes you anywhere in the galaxy, man, sometimes the universe! Also, you need some modifications done to your communication device, according to Kili here."

"What do you mean?" asked Josh.

"Well, I figured since we are to travel across the universe and your cell phone device only works on your planet, we should make some modifications to adapt it to the entire universe," said Kili. "So, since we have to stop by here anyway, we may as well do that at once."

"So, I can use my cell phone anywhere in the universe? How will that work with my phone carrier?"

"Bro, cancel the friggin plan!" Jura laughed, "once we upgrade the hardware, the cell phone as you call it will simply connect with any signal it finds. Now you're gonna take a minute to get the software upgrade, and I mean a long minute! But once you got it, it's a full-on alien tech deal. You're never gonna need another device for communication in your little blue planet again, bro!"

"Sounds good. Well, here you go, I guess," Josh pulled his cell phone out of his pocket and tried to hand it to Jura.

"Nah, I don't like being handed things man; stand by for a minute."

Jura snapped his fingers, and the door behind

him slid open, revealing a room full of strange instruments. Some seemed to be used to manufac-
ture parts and gadgets; others looked like surgical
instruments. Todd made the same motion Kili had
done on earth, clapped his wrists together, he had
the same strange diamond-shaped tattoos on his
wrists Kili had.

A faint glow came from both wrists as he
moved his hands in the direction of the room.
Suddenly objects began to move inside the gadget
room, drawers opening, parts coming out of the
space simply floating towards the center of the
room Josh and the others were.

"Ok, hold out your phone on the palm of your
hand," said Jura to Josh as Jura likewise clapped his
wrists together.

Josh's cell phone began to float between Jura
and Todd, suddenly the screws, screen, and circuits
began to come apart from the casing, strange parts
attached themselves to the phone, some replacing
a few of the phone's original components. A peculiar metallic fluid in what looked like a test tube in
the gadget room floated from the tube and into the
circuitry and screen. The phone began to reassem-
ble itself in midair as both Todd and Jura moved
their hands in several strange motions, the touch-
screen moving rather quickly and out of rhythm
into other components.

"Easy, guy!" said Todd to Jura. "You always go

in too rough every time you do touchscreens for the biometrics."

"Oh, suck my schloong! I never snapped it since that time, did I? Besides, the organotronic barrier will keep it all in and regenerate damage, anyway."

Josh's phone was reassembled entirely, switched on as it floated gently to him. Josh held out his hand as it landed on his palm. The screen displayed the words "Updating Firmware" in green letters with a black background, a bar showing the status of the update under it.

"Figures," Josh Chuckled, "I get the latest cell phone, and it's updating."

"Hey, don't hate!" said Todd, "Whenever it's done, you'll be able to call anyone in the galaxy, possibly in the universe, depending on your location. On this planet, for instance, your signal is unlimited. You can call anywhere from here. Besides, that liquid from the lab is the latest nano-technology and makes that phone impossible to break unless you happen to let it fall into the sun or something. Also, I replaced your battery." Todd scoffed as he held Josh's old battery in his hand. "Lithium-ion my ass! You got a regenerative micro reactor battery now, plenty of charge for the next century bro!"

"Is that safe?" asked Josh, concerned. He didn't fully understand precisely what a regenerative micro-reactor was, but he was fairly certain Todd had just added a small nuclear reactor to his phone. He looked at his phone up and down; the case was more or less the same, but the charging port seemed to be gone, replaced by what looked like a small cover that fit completely flush with the phone's casing.

"Yeah, don't worry about it bro, we mastered that tech long ago. It's sealed so tight not even the most advanced radiation detection technology could measure a particle leak! But the update may take a few weeks; it's a lot of data, and it's all over the air, five petabytes worth. Your planet hasn't even reached that yet," said Jura.

"Don't worry yourself, Josh, you will not require that device until the trip back; by then, it should be ready. Keep it in the back of your mind. There will be much more you will see of our technology. Jura, Todd, please charge the Asgardian federation account the credits for the upgrades and travel," Todd and Jura nodded in acknowledgement.

"Now that this business is complete, may I interject?" asked Che. "Josh, the fate of your planet may well rest on your shoulders. And Lady Kili, what is your report?"

"Yes, Master Che, It appears the planet has, as you suspected, emitted several signals across the galaxy and the Maku have caught on to some of those signals and initiated a low-key invasion of the planet so far. But aside from the dragoon we encountered, there is not much occurring. What can you tell us about the current threat?"

"Well, the threat is physical, but the enemy also intends to take primary control of your cyberspace to establish dominance, the human-technology is in its infant phase compared to ours, yet it has almost reached the point to bio-integration. Your analysis of their signal technology is correct, we have picked up many communication signals from the planet your kind call Midgard. This has indeed aroused the Maku's interest, though their leader at this location or the exact intent is still a mystery to us. I also sense a strange power in the land, something ancient and powerful. It was left there long ago, millennia before humanity got to where it is now. Yet, it lays dormant and would require a massive catalyst to awaken," said Che.

"So, do we know where to look?" asked Josh. "And how does cyberspace play into this?"

"Well, if you have weapons of mass destruction, it is much safer to control them from a distance when you use them. And more intricate weapons require more complex controls and signals to operate. Entire nations have waged war before from the other side of their galaxy, safely away from the aftermath. They completely obliterated other nations by simply having that superior technology. That's what's so important about cyberspace, the more elaborate it is in your planet, the more the capabilities of your weapons," said Kili.

"Josh, I believe there is more to you being here than merely your ancestry. Your background in your world; it places you in a position you may find the threat," said Che.

"What do you mean by this, Master Che?"

"Just Che, my dear, you honor me, but we are children of the same life force and its Creator," Che slowly gravitated towards the window of the room. It was a large glass window, floor to ceiling, looking outside the building. "Josh's world has just entered the digital era, and with it come cybernetic threats. I believe whatever is triggered by the Maku will initiate in your cyberspace. It is the closest thing I could find observing your planet, as it is the closest thing you have to my dimension."

"What do you mean, your dimension?"

"Bro, it's trippy!" said Jura, "You know how you can see him, but he's all made of light and what not? That's because Che is enlightened; he exists in this 5th dimension of virtue that develops insane talents and fine-tunes the skillset in people to the max. Notice right now everything feels super calm and clear? It's cause his aura radiates, clearing neuro signals and thought patterns, and just maximizes your potential. Just imagine having a symbiotic life with him man, it's gotta be insane!"

"Symbiotic life? You mean he occupied people

before?"

"Yes and no, Josh," said Che. "My kind does not physically exist in the same plane as yours, and so we take no additional physical space should we occupy a human, but we do add to the brainwaves. Small amounts of bioelectrical current generated by the brain. That little bit of extra information and the life force the individual generates. We co-exist within that, augmenting a person's inherent abilities."

"So yeah, bro! He creates superhumans!" said Todd. "People of your species way more talented than normal. Haven't you ever wondered about anyone that's super gifted and thought, 'Whoa, man! That's Trippy!' No way this guy is human! Well, you're partially right. Guys of Che's species probably merged with them at birth and are giving them that extra juice! The host even resembles a little the being that's inhabiting them. Most of the dudes in your species like that lead some kickass lives!"

"And most of us sadly have hosts that end those lives too soon," Che's golden aura and his very being transformed from a bright gold to a somber blue. It was as if the being was recalling a sad memory, feeling a deep sorrow at the thought of the loss of his host. "We're meant to be a gift of enlightenment to our hosts, bask them with knowledge of what we have seen and allow them to benefit their kind greatly, and in return, we see the world through their eyes and gain more to benefit other worlds, but unfortunately, that does not come without a burden. And thus, one more light goes out in the sky of a million stars."

"I'm sorry, your host must have been a great person; what happened?" asked Josh, not fully understanding the concept but acknowledging the loss of life in Che's host.

"His host was one of your famous musicians; he revolutionized music for a whole generation, but the flow of thoughts can't be stopped, the strain is great on emotions, and so Che's host ended his own life," said Kili. "I heard about that tragedy across the galaxy. It was a true loss to your race."

"I'm sorry... I mean, you guys keep tabs on us that much?"

"We gotta make sure you guys don't turn out too crazy, bro!" said Todd. "There are several planets with similar species to yours that may even have been able to breed with your species if it hadn't all gone wrong! We gotta make sure your kind is ready to move to our level, but that takes a long ass time, so we just kinda nudge here and there, you know?"

"Long time is an understatement. You must be capable of entering the intergalactic trade, diplomatic, and socio-political policies of the universe," said Kili. "We cannot have a bunch of monkeys shouting at us pointing nukes every time something is unfavorable to them."

"You're rather fond of calling us humans monkeys, aren't you Kili? But I see your point; we do have some crazy politics," Josh admitted.

"And your tech is not up to par with us, bro, you guys gotta step it up!" said Jura.

"Enough on those matters; we must act before the threat becomes more elaborate to your world," said Che. He had returned to his usual golden glow. "You must make your way to Kili's world and acquire the means to protect yours, it won't be an easy journey, but in the end, you may yet preserve the light of this young world as it flickers on an uncertain fate."

"Very well," Kili said. "We are ready Master Che."

"You honor me again young Asgardian, but I am merely a child of the same force that gives you life," said Che, "there is one matter at hand still requiring our attention, the statute of secrecy, we will of course, make all reasonable attempts to maintain it as such, but should things become too large an event to contain..." Che faced Josh directly as he said his next words. "Be prepared, Josh; your world may change vastly."

"We understand Che; we will try our best to resolve the threat reasonably and to delay that inevitable event. The human race may not yet be ready for such a change," said Kili.

"Very well. Jura, Todd, take them to the transport, ensure they have a smooth journey home."

"Yes, sir," said Jura excitedly, "and we just rigged it up to your world too!"

Josh and Kili followed Jura and Todd out of the building through the same elevator Josh originally came through. Once out of the building, they walked across multiple platforms. The city was as decorated and brilliantly designed as was the structure they had spent the last few hours in.

Golden pillars were leading to lightly stained-glass ceilings and strange vehicles stopping at every platform. The spaceships resembled trains back on earth but were intricately decorated and could fly in and out of an atmosphere with complete grace.

"You like that? Your first earth trains were fashioned after these mass transports. The initial engineers needed a design, so we kinda sent it to them a little subliminally," said Todd.

"But how? How does an alien species send ideas subliminally without people being suspicious?"

"Che's species, bro!" said Todd. "His species comes with a certain degree of advanced information when it merges and enhances the talents of the human it inhabits. Symbiotic life, man! It's freaky cool!"

"So, Che's species simply occupies a human? How have our doctors not caught a being inside a person yet?"

"Because bro…" said Jura, "Like I said before, Che doesn't even exist in the same plane with the same form as us! He's made of photons in our world, of pure light energy. As he said, all that does to a member of a biological species is boost their life force a bit. It just makes a human be born a little smarter or a little stronger or just overall more talented than the rest of his species. Che is ethereal so that he can occupy a biological species, and no one would ever know. Hell, only his species recognizes another of his kind inside a host, and they typically don't chat much in this plane."

"So, you mean to tell me, there are other planes of existence? Like life in another dimension?"

"Well, yes, but it is not exactly the way you think. All life supposedly began as it did in your planet, as have all dimensions; Che's is the fifth dimension, a world of enlightenment. However, before achieving that form per se, his world went through all the events and processes all worlds go through. So, for one of Che's kind to cross over to our plane of existence means he is doing us a great service as he is helping all species in this world come closer to an existence of true enlightenment," said Kili. "It is as if God himself switched on the light. The enlightened ones were all that remained."

"So, if he is from the fifth plane, what happened to the previous four?"

"Well, the Maku wiped some out completely, the energy dispersed elsewhere and are basically worlds of voids, and some are simply at varied stages of existence. There is 122 total on record at the moment, but getting that knowledge is difficult even for Che's species; once they take a form that leaves their plane, they are in here permanently," said Kili.

"Sounds like a one-way trip out of a happy world," said Josh.

"Well, it is, once you achieve their level of enlightenment, you are pure energy and information, you affect the world around you by sheer will. Just think, nearly a day has passed in the way your species counts time, and yet you do not feel hungry or tired," said Kili. "Che's aura fully supplies and nourishes the body and mind in most species just by radiating the energy you need to function."

"You're… you're right!" Josh stared at his hands astounded; he was neither hungry nor tired after traveling across a solar system and on his way to God knows where. He did feel a warm, stimulating feeling when in the same room as Che, similar to the feel of having a small cup of coffee in the morning with a balanced breakfast.

"Yeah, but don't count on your Buddha high to last forever, bro!" said Jura. "It wears off like a regular meal to your species; you'll be hungry and sleepy when it's over, assuming you don't find some other fix."

"Kili, he said we must prepare in case the statute of secrecy is broken, that my world would change vastly; what did he mean?" Josh asked.

"It means maybe we can finally hang out, bro!" said Todd excitedly. "Your world might open to all foreign species and me and Jura here can swing by, have some drinks, hit the gym on earth gravity, and check out some human chicks!"

Kili glared slightly at Todd for his comment.

"I mean," Todd caught the glare, "you know… responsibly. Your people must be prepared, nay welcome, to changes and to the introduction of other species. This will affect technology, socio-cultural and economics in your planet," finished Todd choosing his words carefully.

"As the Grextrasapiensporus explained your kind must prepare itself for the idea that it will co-exist with many other species in the galaxy and universe and prepare accordingly. Should the statute of secrecy be considered broken beyond repair in this mission."

"Wow! I haven't heard that term in quite a while!" said Jura, "like since friggin college more or less."

"Well, here we are!" said Todd.

They arrived at a building that was different from the usual gold; the structure was made of what looked like dark blue precious stones. The doors made of crystal opened smoothly, as did every door Josh had been through. Inside was a large round room with pools of what looked like liquid metal, perfectly round on platforms leading to what looked like a giant computer, the ceiling was made of glass, and light came from the walls in a way you couldn't identify where the wall ended, and the lights began.

"Alright! Step right up!" said Jura as he motioned for Josh and Kili to step on the large circular platforms. Large navigational computers around them were smooth as a marble table with multiple touchscreens and holograms protruding slightly from them.

In the center of the room, a hologram of multiple galaxies with a bright blue dot was indicating their position. "Since this time you'll be traveling from an intergalactic station, you'll both be landing simultaneously at your destination. Thank you for flying comet sphere!"

Josh and Kili stepped in the round platforms; the substance inside the venue, to Josh's surprise, was solid until he heard Todd and Jura begin typing instructions on the computer. Suddenly the liquid metal rose and encased Josh, forming a perfect sphere made of silver, surprisingly clear on the inside, and Josh could see outside his traveling vessel perfectly.

Next to him, Kili's vessel had done the same,

forming a perfect silver sphere around her.

"Well, see you guys next time you come by," said Todd as he looked at Josh. "Ready, bro?" asked Todd as he looked at Jura. The glass ceiling above them opened smoothly, revealing the clear night sky.

"Hit it!" said Jura.

"See ya!" said Todd as he hit the button and saw both vessels blast off into the sky.

CHAPTER 4

To Asgard

Josh again saw his feet leaving the ground quickly, before he could count to five, he was already in the air and leaving the planet's atmosphere. He found himself again flying fast but felt no gravitational force. He was floating inside a bubble soaring through the universe at light speed for the second time. This time however, Kili was also floating right next to him, he could see her sphere next to his flying just as fast. Different planets of different colors soared by, and different spaceships, at seemingly much slower speeds, ascending and descending into the planets. Finally, Josh's ship seemed to be headed straight to a planet, it shined in a light blue hue, similar to earth but lighter. Josh braced himself for impact but again, felt no indication there would be any. His sphere turned his feet smoothly towards the ground as it rushed towards him. Again, Josh attempted to land on his feet but took a knee instead, he was still not accustomed to the landing in these vessels.

"Get up you fool," said Kili as she landed gracefully, "there will be plenty of time for kneeling before the All Father."

"You mean Odin?" asked Josh. "So, you're telling me all the Norse stories are true, and he really exists?"

"Not exactly verbatim and not all the stories are exactly true. Your species' account of events is based on your understanding of what actually happened. Like being a human before the age of flight and seeing a spaceship or a smartphone. They don't necessarily grasp the full concept of what it is exactly, so they try to translate to the closest thing in their era. But yes, he does exist, and all human folklore aside, the stories are true to an extent. Except none of us ever understood human sacrifice as tribute, we appreciate the gesture from your ancestors, but don't understand. It is sort of like circumcisions."

Josh chuckled at Kili's last comment. He had always believed certain religious practices were a little ludicrous but that particular one, even Pete back on earth, questioned a few times. Josh couldn't wait to tell him there was no point in it at all.

Josh and Kili had landed in a massive round room, on two round platforms similar to the ones they used for taking off from Zion. The room was intricate, gold embedded in crystals and stone around all the walls. Similar, if not the same, computers he had seen in Zion stood by some of the walls and likewise a large hologram displaying galaxies in the center of the room. Everything seemed completely integrated into the building itself, and at the only doorway stood a tall figure. It was clearly male, white crystalline skinned with dark blue outlines of tribal symbols, massive in stature, with a helmet with two massive ram horns and armor that was a mixture of leather and steel, elaborate as it was functional in protecting the massive alien in combat. The alien held a large spear that appeared made of bronze if not for the glowing golden runes that shined in intricate patterns through the design.

"Welcome to Asgard," said the massive figure. He stood at least seven feet tall. "I am Heimdallr, watchman of the gods and guardian of the Bifrost."

Heimdallr looked directly at Josh with his bright blue glowing eyes. They were not as human eyes as they shined blue completely, but Josh could feel his gaze upon him clearly.

"Hi! Umm, I'm Josh… army veteran and Colorado College student," said Josh in reply, not knowing exactly how to introduce himself.

"Come on then, let us make our way to the palace, and knock it off Heimdallr!" said Kili slightly annoyed. "He is clearly not of this realm and has never seen an Asgardian in true form before."

"Apologies Lady Kili," said Heimdallr. "Welcome, army veteran and college student! We have been expecting your arrival. The All Father and the others await you in the main Hall." Heimdallr motioned with his hand for them to pass, and they did so, Kili with somewhat of a hurried pace as Josh gazed upon every detail of the intricate structure they left.

The massive bronze and gold room gave way to a bridge of stone, leading to a palace that seemed to emanate its own bright light. It seemed made of pure light as it shined brightly like a mixture of marble and crystal, enormously tall of a structure and intricate in detail. Josh and Kili made their way to the front doors of the main castle.

The massive doors were wide open as they walked through. The inside of the palace looked as incredible as the outside did. Josh could see giant dining room tables with human-like aliens eating at them. The aliens were large, each one taller than both Josh and Kili, light skinned to slightly darker shades of red, blue, white to gray, green and purple, and dressed lavishly in white and gold clothes. As Josh and Kili passed, they raised a cup to their return, some greeting warmly with "Hail" as they passed. Kili would nod in acknowledgement of the greetings. Josh began to do the same and nod slightly. Kili led Josh to the main court. It was a large room with what seemed like thrones surrounding the center of the room. On the center throne, at the rear, sat a tall figure, light blue skinned shining with light literally emanating from his body, with hair and beard that shined in a pale gold light and wearing golden robes. The figure stood as Josh and Kili approached to meet them.

"Greetings my son, I am Odin, leader of the Aesir of Asgard, known by your people as the All Father," said the tall figure. He was much larger now that he stood, over nine feet tall, and with a body proportionate to his height. Odin radiated a calming aura of wisdom much like Che but had more of a powerful presence as he did so. Like Kili, he had several outlines of tribal markings over his light blue skin, except his markings glowed faintly in a gold color as his hair and beard did. Aside his golden and crystalline appearance he looked much like the depictions in books of mythology. The alien was missing an eye, yet Josh had a feeling that, much like Heimdallr, Odin could still see far better than any other being in the room. Kili kneeled before him and urged Josh to do the same. Josh did so immediately, following Kili's lead as she said "All Father" to acknowledge his greeting.

"Stand my child, let us set aside the formalities at this time, we have much to accomplish, and my ravens bring much news, some of wonder but many disturbing ones."

"Well, looks as though she found the human

she sought faster than anticipated," said the figure on the far right. "I am Baldr, son of Odin, overseer of environment and atmosphere at Asgard. Your people may know me as the God of light, joy, purity, and the summer sun." He stood and made his way towards the two. He was shorter than Odin, his beard likewise shorter, and golden hair slightly curly, but still bore the same shining hue, his skin a crystal light blue and golden outlines. As Baldr stepped down from his throne and walked closer to Josh and Kili, Josh could now feel his aura, it was a rather light and jolly sensation. It appeared all the beings in the room radiated some sort of aura or presence.

"Obviously the boy can tell who we are," said the figure to the left of Odin. This one was female, her skin a shade of slight red instead of blue with white outlines of tribal markings, her hair a greenish gold hue. She was gorgeous, but taller than any human and equally large as the rest of their species, almost as tall as Odin himself. Odin chuckled slightly as she spoke. "In the meantime, my dear, do away with this human façade, show us your true colors." She clicked her wrists together gently and waved a hand with a faint glow, and Kili's disguise faded as she stood. Her skin was light blue as well, although slightly darker than the others in the room, her hair golden blonde and shining. She was dressed in lavish white clothes with blue embroidery that fit her form, useful for both combat and elegance with a cloak that could easily wrap around herself. She was shorter than the other Aesir, but still tall for a human, over six feet and easily as tall as a basketball player with a body very proportionate to her height. The Norse runes tattooed on her skin glowed in a more orange hue than gold, unlike her other counterparts.

"Ha ha! Very well Frigg! This one needs no introductory tour of the leaders of Asgard; we are in your mythology books after all!" exclaimed Odin loudly. "Baldr, outfit the mortal with our technology, let us begin his preparations for the coming battles."

"As you wish, All Father," said Baldr as he faced Odin. He bowed slightly and led the two out of the main hall. They made their way through a lavish hallway into the back courtyard. The garden was intricate between sculptures of black and white stone and plants. They arrived before a dome, made of black and white stone, inside a large machine, a pillar of stone with two crystals to its left and right. One pitch black, pulsing a dark purple light from inside faintly, one silver white, pulsing a golden light. On a table nearby were objects that looked like tattoo machines with a small tank attached.

"Bdellium and Onyx, shiny semi-metallic rocks when separate, but put them together with a living organism…" Baldr clashed both wrists together, the tribal markings glowed for an instant and a sword made of pure light materialized on his right hand, a shield made of light on his left arm. "And they are more effective than the mightiest steel!" Baldr clashed his wrists again, this time forming a longbow and an arrow. Baldr aimed the bow made of pure energy at the outside of the open dome door and fired it at a black horse sculpture on the courtyard a few yards away, with pinpoint accuracy. The arrow hit the sculpture in the head and exploded into a burst of light. The shattered pieces turning to a black tar-like liquid as they hit the ground and returning to the sculpture, reforming the same horse's head again perfectly. Baldr's bow vanished as quickly as he had created it.

"No wonder you guys don't need that many soldiers!"

"It appears simple, but it does take a lot of training," said Kili. "He must concentrate in creating the weapon as well as aiming and firing while maintaining the form of the weapon. The weapon, in all reality, only truly exists in his mind, so the biochips make the contents of his mind reality by reading the data in his mind, effectively digitizing the data and materializing it into reality. Takes time and concentration to learn, the metal alloys integrate to your nervous system, but it's you who must know how to use it."

"Ok, and how do I learn that? I take it we don't have that long to learn and practice until my planet gets destroyed right?"

"Time is a relevant construct, as one of your human geniuses once said. And here in Asgard, we make the best use of this relevant construct," said Baldr. "Step to the stone pillar and brace your back against it, extend your palms to the crystals. This should feel just like getting your people's markings on earth."

Josh did exactly as Baldr said, bracing himself against the pillars and extending each hand, palm outwards, towards the crystals. The white golden crystal to his right and black-purple crystal to his left shined brightly. Both Baldr and Kili grabbed one of the objects on the table. Kili stuck the needle of the device on the white crystal, filling the reservoir with a golden liquid. Kili began drawing a design on Josh's right wrist just as Baldr did, doing the same with his left with a glowing dark purple fluid. The material in Kili's needle turned from gold to white. Baldr's material from glowing purple to black, making the same markings and pattern Kili and all Celestials seemed to have. Kili and Baldr then touched the crystals and light shot straight into Josh's wrists. Josh felt a sensation of hot needles poking into his skin, like getting a tattoo with a needle that was just recently sterilized. The light faded, and the sensation went away, but

Josh's wrists still felt slightly tender. Josh rubbed them feeling the spot where he now had two perfect small diamond square shaped tattoos on his wrists, the same as all Celestials had.

"It's a good thing we perfected the process centuries ago," said Baldr. "Our first timers were not so fortunate."

"Baldr himself is a victim of that," said Kili. "We went from your earth's hammer and needle tattoo to this method once we managed to code the metal properly and make it act the way it is intended to."

"What do you mean code it?" Josh asked.

"Well, in case you haven't noticed, all these incredible feats we have done aren't by magic or accident," said Kili sarcastically. "It is all through a very superior nano integrated quantum biotechnology. We use elaborate integrated quantum bio-computers the same way I have seen your kind rely on your 'smartphones'. Difference is we are millennia ahead of your kind. But like all electronics, we must code our own technology. We've had a few millennia to perfect it, and so we are able to do all these things. And those 'tattoos' on your wrists, as you would call them, are the first step in all that."

"Well, I gathered your technology is far superior, I just didn't know it followed the same rules as our technology and programming as on earth."

"We do not follow your ways as we precede

your kind," said Baldr. "The way of technology is that everything is coded, and your kind are just beginning to understand that with their technology, we did not originally develop this way, we merely perfected it, as have many other Celestial species."

"Basically, superior technology and mastery of carbon has advanced us into biological immortality, and traditionalism has kept order in our planets. The leaders of those who have followed that, and prospered past millennia, have gained the title of Celestials regardless of species. Our specific race is Asgardian, and Celestials within our race are known as the Aesir. Your race may be familiar with this name, but basically, they designate Celestials as Norse gods, Greek gods, Egyptian gods, so on and so forth. We simply opted not to refer to our order as such because the term denotes a level of divinity we do not claim to have," said Kili. "So, we are simply the Aesir Celestials of Asgard."

"So, you guys watch over earth and keep things going in the universe?"

"Not just earth, many planets require our attention to ensure they continue to prosper. The idea is to have every planet in this world reach our level, a task that's proven difficult. On many accounts we have failed. That's why it's so imperative that we train and equip you and send you and Kili back to earth to advert catastrophe. A member of the race in question, and a member of the Celestials to guide that individual. That has always been our way. In the past we attempted to do so, but your race was not yet ready. So, we waited for your species to evolve to a new age," said Baldr. "Speaking of which, it is time to begin your basic understanding of your new abilities." Baldr looked at the skies attentively as they walked outside the dome and into the garden. "Thor! Son of Odin and God of strength and thunder, come forth and grace us with your presence!" shouted Baldr. An object in the sky suddenly began shining brighter. Suddenly, lightning began to dance across the sky from that point. A lightning bolt shot the ground near where they stood, from the lightning bolt appeared a figure. He was kneeling as he landed. The figure quickly stood to greet them. He was as tall as Baldr and light blue with reddish blonde hair, the same markings as all of Odin's species seemed to have in outlines of golden orange, holding a massive hammer and wearing a winged helmet and metallic armor with a dark red cloak.

"Greetings friends, I am the mighty Thor. I take it you know of me already."

"Yeah! I mean, yes," Josh replied. "You are legendary to this day umm… sir?"

Thor laughed a thunderous laugh. "Well then, there is no need for introduction or formalities! Come, let us feast to your new technology and begin your training soon after. Surely you are hungry after such a journey and training will be more productive with a belly full of mead and some boar!"

"I vaguely wondered when we would be less serious about this whole ordeal," said Baldr chuckling. "Even I was having a hard time keeping this freaking serious attitude. To the main hall it is brother!"

Thor led the others to the main dining hall, where all the nobles had previously been congregating as Josh and Kili passed by. The food looked remarkably similar to that of earth, and the mead was likewise, a similar drink. The tender boar meat was juicy and delicious, and the mead was sweet but strong, Josh ate his fill, which in comparison to the Celestials, was a portion appropriate for a small child. Thor and Baldr took massive mugs and filled them to the brim with mead, laughing as they celebrated and commented on their recent feats and issues they dealt with. They were almost like knights boasting about achievements, only they were across the galaxy instead of just within the kingdom.

"And the fool released the massive beast on me! I singed its whiskers with a lightning bolt on one side, it couldn't stand straight after that!" said Thor, laughing as he told Baldr a tale about a recent battle with what appeared to be a giant Cat of some kind based on his description. "This will forever be known as the Battle of the unbalanced beast!" replied Baldr equally jolly.

"They are always this way," said Kili laughing. "They start all traditional and serious, and then they take you for a drink and let loose."

"Sounds overall a pretty good way to welcome people," Josh answered. "I mean, they all had me going. I've been asking questions and trying to take note of what to do the whole time. It's astounding how little we actually know on earth, and we call ourselves an intelligent species."

"Oh, but you are intelligent, not as a whole species. You can be irrational and frankly crazy as a whole, but your kind does produce amazingly intelligent individuals. Look around you, there are servants and nobles, yet no one is truly suffering in life regardless of status, it is because we know balance. Unlike in your planet where there are issues with poverty and famine. We do our best to help planets achieve the harmony we have here, because the goal is perfect harmony in the universe. Make no mistake, everyone here is free to choose their destiny, to defend their home and to come and go as they please so long as they have the resources, but their basic needs are met. The rest is all up to them in how they intend to live their life," said Kili, "but this does not come absent effort, the same efforts we are applying to your species now. And already an enemy waits for the opportunity to bring it all down."

"Question is, what took you guys so long? You could have shared your knowledge anytime, why now?"

"Oh, we have shared!" said Kili. "We shared plenty! You are not the first of your kind we have taken to Asgard and shared our tech with. Your ancestors simply did not have the mind to master it at the time. Nor is this the first earth incident. It is just now things are crazier than usual as you move into your twenty-first century. It's like entering adolescence; that is where your kind resides now. So now we must pay more attention and make sure you do not screw up."

"Teenagers? We're teenagers to you?"

"Early teens but yes, relax! It gets fun from here! But there is lots of work so make sure you are well nourished. Thor works better when he had a mug… or five." Kili chuckled. She was starting to show signs of drunkenness. She was normally the easiest to talk to out of all the Celestials Josh had so far met, and her way of talking was becoming increasingly more outgoing and relaxed. She was a different person in the comfort of her home environment.

"Alright then!" Thor slammed his empty mug down on the table. "We have eaten and drank our fill, on to business. Follow me young lad, let us begin making a warrior out of you."

"Well, next time I see you, you might have a

proper weapon to fight dragoons with. Good luck Josh, try not to die." Kili and some of the nobles who sat at the table laughed at this last remark. Josh followed Thor somewhat nervous. This time they walked up the stairs to one of the towers. Josh occasionally looked out a window as they passed it on the way up and caught a glimpse of the kingdom of Asgard. It was a lush green land with mountains and lakes. Massive waterfalls and what looked like a sea connecting it all in the distance, lakes connected running from near the palace to the end of the kingdom as far as the eye could see.

"Majestic, is it not?" asked Thor. "I love this world. The land in which I was born. It is considerably smaller than yours, but it's beautiful. I could only hope that all my efforts, all the battles that I have fought for peace in the universe, lead to a world as beautiful and prosperous as my own home."

"It's incredible. But you guys fight to keep the peace in all planets?"

"It is not as simple as that. Some planets require aid, some require warriors to defend them, some a mere negotiator. The council you saw decides who to send and what action to take, based on what information we gather or is provided and who asks us. And depending on the section of the universe and nearby allies, sometimes we send different Celestials. Sometimes Olympian Celestials provide aid, sometimes the Greys. It all depends on what section of the universe and what the needs of the planet in question are." Behind the warrior God who likes to drink and engage in combat set a wiser and much more reasonable Celestial than he appeared. "We take action that is appropriate and necessary. Some of us are simply better and more accomplished diplomats. Others, more military action."

"Which one is Kili?"

"A bit of both, she is a technological specialist who can both negotiate diplomacy and engage in battle. She's swifter at the sword than many and excellent at improving technology and tinkering with gadgets as well as gaining new information. She is very talented, but she is also still young by our standards. She was born a while after we left your people to fend for themselves. Only about six or seven hundred years ago."

"Yeah, because you know most people live that long in my planet, so surely that's young!" Josh laughed. Thor began to laugh at that as well.

"Our kind age different. We are very good at longevity, especially us Celestials."

After a long flight of stairs, they arrived at the top of the tower. It was a large round room that contained several platforms with nearby computers like the travel room. In the center stood a holographic globe. The globe was blue with glowing landmasses, different shapes from the continents of earth, but Josh knew what it was no less.

"That is what you will connect to. Valhalla!"

"Valhalla? Viking heaven? This machine is Viking heaven?"

"It is a server in which the world of Valhalla was created. Your quantum physicists have just grasped that concept. All beings that live have a certain amount of bioelectrical energy in their brain; it is generated by them, their soul if you will. When their body dies, the energy and information returns to the universe containing their conscience, we collect that conscience, and give it a new home, if the person's essence is agreeable to the data," Thor sounded much less like a Norse god and more like a quantum physics professor. "They must meet the criteria, ranging from virtue to their very own consent to come to Valhalla. The Valkyries then escort the data given that the people have consented to it."

"Agreeable to the data? You mean you ask the dead if they want to go to Viking heaven?"

"It is not as simple as that, first they must be chosen, and then they must say yay or nay to the Valkyries. If both conditions are met, they enter Valhalla. Death itself works with us on this, he is a Celestial in his own right, although a vastly different one from the rest of us. The dead are existent in another plane parallel to this one. It is a rather complicated concept to explain. Think of it as the flip side of a coin. We merely salvage and keep the chosen ones as data in this one and give them the perfect Valhalla they dreamed of. Without an afterlife, your soul merely travels through the universe and returns to the Creator where he decides what is next. He has bestowed upon those with the power to do so the responsibility to guard certain members among the fallen."

"I see. Are all afterlives like this?" asked Josh.

"At least the ones guarded by Celestials, yes. But the criteria to enter is very high; most people simply reincarnate or follow the will of the Creator. It's not just the mighty who enter Valhalla, but the truly virtuous in life. You must be data worth saving in order to be saved. Or your energy simply merges with the universe and your essence, your soul if you will, reincarnates either into a new life form or whatever the Creator has in mind for you. The Creator himself has bestowed upon us Celestials this sacred duty, so that the species would have faith and belief and not simply see death as an end to a biological process. Faith is incredibly important especially in the eyes of the one who has made it all as only he may open his kingdom to the best of us living beings."

"So, you mean to tell me, aside all Celestials, there is a real God? That we are intelligent design?"

"My dear boy, of course there is a God, and we

love, worship and respect him above all else just like your own species. He gives us sacred tasks to watch over his creations because we have proved ourselves worthy, and he gives all life the freedom to do as they will. He is sentient, but not in the way you and I are, not in the way you imagine. He does not succumb to anger or ever become annoyed with us but loves his creations unconditionally. And yet, in his ineffable plan, he does not tell us everything, but allows us mostly to discover for ourselves the path. Few of us have ever even seen him even though many have heard his voice and felt his will, but those who have attest to the truth and have faith the most. That is the Creator. Odin himself can tell you that. Now, shall we begin your training?"

Thor motioned for Josh to stand in one of the platforms, it faced the floating globe directly. Josh entered the platform; this one was different from the traveling stations, no silver substance anywhere nearby, just a white platform with what looked like grid squares underneath. Thor likewise stood in a platform next to him. The platform lit up with a bright white light and suddenly, Josh and Thor were floating a few inches off the ground.

"Brace yourself, first log-ins are sometimes a little rough." The light shined even brighter. "Close your eyes," said Thor as Josh did so, still floating inside the platform. "Log in," he uttered commands in a strange alien language, it sounded like an incantation, almost musical to hear, and suddenly Josh no longer felt as if he was floating inside a room at all.

Josh felt the sensation of traveling through a tunnel at high velocity, the walls made of every color imaginable. Wherever he was, Josh was moving fast. Finally, Josh saw the light at the end of the tunnel as his body flew fast to it. Once past the light, Josh saw a lake, and fields, the only issue was, he was still falling at the end of his tunnel. Josh screamed at the top of his lungs as he fell right into the lake, splashing loudly. He quickly recovered from his plunge and swam to the edge of the lake, climbing out of it soaked. A few feet away from him a light shone brightly, and Thor landed perfectly on his feet next to the lake.

"Told you, first log in is kind of rough," Thor chuckled.

"Yeah, no shit. This thing landed me in the middle of a lake!"

"The program has a protocol for safety once it makes a profile, since we are not dead, our profiles are temporary. This is a virtual image of yourself. To the dead, this is home permanently if they desire, to the living, a training tool. Worry not, this realm is here strictly for your kind, hence I look more similar to your kind here," Thor's appearance resembled a large muscular human now, with reddish brown hair, same armor and hammer in hand.

"Well, you're still huge compared to a normal person."

Thor chuckled at his words and shook his head. "You'll need appropriate attire."

Thor pointed his hammer and fired a blast of lightning. Josh braced himself as he expected to be fried, but instead his clothes changed, his jeans turned into training pants made of a rough material difficult to tear. His shirt became a sleeveless martial arts top made of likewise a strong material with a short sleeve undershirt, a blue Jiu Jitsu belt around his waist. Josh looked like a classic anime character now in training clothes.

"Could have warned me first before you just zapped me with your magic hammer!" Josh eyed his new clothes. Everything was a dull grayish black except the belt.

"Relax friend, not even my mighty hammer Mjolnir can kill you here. You're already at the realm of the blessed fallen, you cannot fall twice."

"Well good to know, immortality huh?"

"Eliminates the inconvenience of only being able to engage in battle once if you lose. Allows you to keep at it until you get good at winning. Don't get me wrong, pain is very much real here, but death is impossible. And all the information gathered here, goes right back in your brain when you log out." Thor raised his hammer to the sky, his hammer shined bright and like Josh's, his clothes changed to an appropriate training attire as well. A dark blue colored martial arts outfit. His hammer receded into his arm forming a perfect Tattoo of itself on his forearm.

"Let us begin. We shall initiate with a nice run to the great falls where you will climb, then we shall train you at the spear, swords, bows, battle-axe and shield. You must learn to master wielding all those traditional weapons before summoning anything with your biochips."

Josh and Thor ran for what seemed like hours, the plains gave way to a forest, which they followed a beaten path to hills. The entire place seemed to have a nice path made of stone, similar to a well-cared hiking trail. Josh was astounded his shoes appeared to be merely thin leather shoes, but he ran smoothly. Finally, they arrived at a massive waterfall coming off a rock wall. Josh struggled quite a bit despite not having his real body doing the run but kept up with Thor adequately. They climbed the rock wall without ropes, Josh almost plunging to what would be his death several times, until they reached the top. Before his eyes stood a large platform.

Warriors from all over the world sparred at the platform. It was large and round as a plate directly above the waterfall, a massive palace behind the platform and several courtyards with likewise warriors from all over the world training in various weapons. Some fought unarmed, some firing bows and arrows, some fighting with swords, axes, spears, some with more modern weapons that Josh recognized. All weapons imaginable and all forms of martial arts were being used and practiced. Valhalla was a forge for amazing warriors. One of those warriors approached Thor and Josh.

"Greetings, welcome to Valhalla!" said the man. "Mighty Thor, it is an honor to have you among us as always."

"Bjorn, thank you," said Thor. "This one is not yet of this world but a visitor, he needs training to learn to fight properly."

"I will be happy to help," said Bjorn. "Newcomer, I will be your partner for axe, sword and shield. Wallace will teach you the long sword and the bow. And Tyberious the spear and javelin. Thor will teach you to summon your weapons."

"Right, well, I have seen you and Kili do this motion," said Josh as he placed his wrists together, nothing happened. "Ok… no magic words were uttered though, why do my tattoos not work?"

"It's not as simple as that, sit down mortal," said Thor as he sat cross-legged next to him. "You must picture in your mind a light, like a force, and feel biochips react to it. Then, touch them together and picture in your mind your intent, exact your will into reality. None of these weapons truly exist, they are but a creation of your mind, the biochips, or tattoos as you refer to them, code and material- ize what your mind creates."

Thor slowly put his wrists together. Both the designs on his wrists lit up in a bright white light, shooting from his palms like a flashlight. Josh at- tempted the same, his tattoos lit up slightly, shooting a light from his hands but much lesser than Thor's. Josh attempted several more times. "Good!" said Thor. "Excellent! We will practice this every night. Meanwhile every day we will train you in real weap- ons!" Thor stood up excitedly. Josh followed suit just before Bjorn handed him a sword and shield.

"We begin now, prepare yourself," said Bjorn as Josh quickly fastened the shield around his arm. It was round and heavy, made of steel on the out- side with a lining of wood and cured leather on the inside, a strap of leather as well as a handle on the inside fastened the shield to Josh's arm. Josh fas- tened the leather strap, and so they began their first sparring match. Bjorn was more or less Josh's size but was much stronger. He attacked fiercely and fast, but to Josh's surprise, his body moved rather precisely when blocking Bjorn's blows. It was as if Josh's body knew just when and how to parry and was adequate with the medieval weapons. He him- self was slightly surprised as he felt his body cor- rect itself several times when blocking a blow from Bjorn. "Hmm," said Thor as Josh and Bjorn continued to spar. Josh defended himself adequately but within a few minutes Bjorn plunged his sword through Josh's leg. Pain shot through Josh, real stabbing pain. He screamed horribly as he looked down at his injury. Bjorn wasn't simply sparring with him, it seemed this was a match to the death. He was surprised one more time seeing that he did not bleed massively when Bjorn pulled his sword from the wound, and it healed almost instantly.

"I told you newcomer," said Thor as he observed the match. "Once in Valhalla you cannot die twice. The pain is real to make you strong and teach you lessons in real combat, but the wounds do not stay, neither does the pain. In here, you may battle for all eternity."

"Yeah, but ouch though! You could have stubbed my toe or cut my finger to demonstrate."

"Where's the fun in that?" Bjorn chuckled as he charged forward again. Josh tried his best to fend off the attacks, again his body seemed to make slight auto-corrections by itself again. Josh was somewhat astounded at the unusual talent behind his motions. It felt slightly unnatural, like something was assisting him the entire time.

"Fight back!" said Thor. "Strike him down if you can, this is combat training for you! Real combat! In the world out there, you can die and if you can't fight a powerful enemy and win, you will!"

Josh bashed Bjorn with his shield, the blow

pushing him several feet back.

"Well, there is a warrior in you after all!" Bjorn chuckled.

"I feel strange though, it's like my body is responding to every move even when I mess up."

"I did notice a few times you moved unusual for a novice," said Thor. "Show me your forearms."

Josh approached Thor as he and Bjorn took a break from the sparring match. Thor examined Josh's arms carefully noticing a faint blue symbol on Josh's left forearm. The symbol looked similar to a snowflake, several tridents protruding from a center ring.

"That sly, crafty Kili. She coded a Helm of Awe on you when she and Baldr embedded your chips," said Thor.

"What do you mean?" Josh now noticed the faint blue Norse sign on his arm.

"The Helm of Awe in your planet is an ancient symbol, some even call it a spell of invincibility. They said the wielder had the power to strike fear in the hearts of their enemies and was nearly invincible in combat. This all derives from the helm's true nature. To us Aesir, it's a rune that's coded as an assist to your neurological system, perfecting your hand-eye coordination along with other senses. Basically, anything you intend to do, but your body lacks in response time or coordination, the Helm of Awe compensates and auto-corrects.

Thus, making you a much more skilled warrior by default."

"So essentially it corrects my movements and lets me fight perfect?"

"Not exactly," said Bjorn. "It makes you a much more skilled warrior, but not invincible. It simply auto-corrects as it reads the intent in your mind then compensates your blocks and parries slightly, and I imagine in ranged weapons makes your aim almost perfect. It is active at all times unlike most abilities, but you still have to take action first for it to work."

"Yes. That is how it works, it is only present to make minor corrections, but goes a long way. All Aesir have it," Thor showed his Helm of Awe. It was a darker blue and much more visible. "Then again we have all mastered the art of combat, so the helm seldom does anything for us anymore."

Josh fought for days. At night, he trained on summoning from his palms, and he could make basic shapes but nothing substantial. For the most part, merely light came forth from when he used the rare metals embedded on his skin to materialize objects. Josh feasted at the halls of Valhalla, only to return to training as the other warriors most nights rested when they pleased. Some, like Josh, merely returned to training, and some feasted, male and female warriors alike. As Bjorn had said, Josh was handed down to a different instructor for different weapons. Each day was a different kind of training and challenge, and despite all the training and strain, Josh did not seem to tire or require sleep.

"An inch over your knuckle mate," said Wallace. "You can hit anything if you aim properly. Of course, your energy weapons don't account for gravity, and that helm there keeps you on target, but it's good to learn the fundamentals."

Wallace was taller than Josh, trained him in longbows and weapons of marksmanship. He alternated between powering his weapons with the biochips and firing normal longbows regularly. Once powered up, the arrows flew straight and indefinitely but also vaporized on impact, detonating their target in a show of light. Josh attempted several times to mimic that effect only to have the tips of his arrows burn or melt slightly on impact, setting a target on fire more than once. His luck with spears was much less as he had a hard time powering a larger projectile with energy.

Every day, he trained in every weapon imaginable. Days passed, which led to weeks, weeks led to months, and months led to what seemed like years. Finally, Josh became proficient enough to win at some of the sparring matches against the permanent residents of Valhalla.

"Jolly good!" said Thor as Josh landed a shield blow flattening Bjorn on his back. "I believe you are ready."

"We have been here for a considerable time. It has been years, hasn't it?"

"Time goes by differently here," said Thor. "A few years here is a little over a week, you have nothing to concern yourself with. And since your body is in a consistent sleep while here, you need not rest."

"I still can't fully summon a weapon out of the… what do you call these things?"

"It's an integrated bioelectronic transmutation system. It turns your will and thoughts into reality through a quantum bio-computer, to an extent. The chips in your arms are like processors that interpret what your mind pictures and turns them to reality with photons, or essentially light particles. You can just refer to it as biochips, it's how the rest of us have gotten accustomed to calling them."

"Yes, because bioelectronic whatever you said sounds ever so casual in conversation, so far all I have is a flashlight," Thor laughed loudly at Josh's remark.

"Well, I'm glad your time here has not robbed you of your sense of humor. Let us return to Asgard, there is still much to do. Josh, to be able to summon full weapons, you must continue to train daily. To make your bioelectrical discharge more proficient, think of it like working a muscle into being stronger. Your shield is a good start. It will keep you from harm and is the easiest shape to will into reality."

Thor raised his hand to the sky, the hammer tattoo on his forearm came to life and materialized into Mjolnir back on his hand as it flashed lightning all around him.

"Stand next to me, we are leaving," said Thor.

As Josh did so, he could feel Thor's commanding presence. Thor's aura could be felt from afar, but it was nothing like standing next to the God of thunder himself. Josh felt strong, rejuvenated, confident. Thor raised his hammer in the air, and pure lightning shot down on it from the sky. Then, he spun his hammer in his hand by the handle and hammered the ground with shattering force. A circle formed around the two of them with runes, and they were quickly flying off from the ground and back into a bright light.

Josh woke up abruptly. He was back in the room with the platforms and the globe in the center. He gently floated back to the ground till he had solid footing.

"Get some rest, we shall test all that you have learned later. Change into night clothes, the maidens will wash and care for your current ones." Thor led Josh to the dormitory. They arrived at a simple but elegant room with large beds on wooden frames. Josh emptied his pockets and changed into the clothes that were left for him on the nearby chair; a sleeveless shirt and a pair of shorts, simple attire to merely sleep in. He looked at his phone to check on the update Jura and Todd had worked for him. The same upgrading screen with the bar at half full showed. He laid down and fell asleep almost immediately. He slept better than he had in a long time, his dreams mere recollections of the events that had passed. All the events that had happened were amazing. Josh dreamed of his time in Valhalla, of the feasts he had and the training. When he awoke, a handmaiden was opening the curtains to the large dormitory.

"Good morning my lord," said the maiden.

"Good morning. How long have I been asleep?"

"Nearly six days, my lord. Lady Kili expects you in the courtyard after breakfast." the maiden laid out Josh's clothes on a nearby chair. Josh took a good look at her as she brought the tray of food to the nearby table next to his cell phone and wallet. She was blueish white skinned but lacked the markings or the crystalline look of the others and did not glow from her blonde hair like Kili. She was also dressed rather simply in comparison to her highborn counterparts. Her figure was elegant and attractive, similar to a human save for the obvious difference in skin color. Clearly their species was similar to humans in physique.

"Do I please you, my lord?" the maiden smiled. "I could always return when the day is done if you like, assuming you're still here."

Josh blushed slightly and smiled back a bit awkwardly. She was also smaller than the Celestials, same height as Josh, not a Celestial but clearly of the same Asgardian species as Kili. It seemed the appearance of power and aura was limited to only the Celestials themselves. The maiden smiled at him again as she clicked her wrists together and the tray of food that sat on the end table by the window assembled itself gracefully at the feet of Josh's bed. All members of the Asgardian species seemed to have that technology.

Josh leaned over and grabbed the first plate near him, it looked like sausage. On the other plate there appeared to be bread. He was right on both accounts; his breakfast, even in an alien planet, was tasty and easy to recognize, even if Josh was sure boars in Asgard were somehow different in size and looks and the possibility of sausage not being made from pork in that planet.

"Wow! This is amazing!" said Josh as he took a bit of the sausage trying to change the subject. The maiden was a bit forward about her intentions as he ate his breakfast. She wasn't bad looking even from a human standpoint, but Josh was unsure how any of the Celestials would feel about him taking an approach that Pete was more likely to take about how to spend the nights on this planet.

Josh ate heartily and drank what tasted like beer

with coffee out of the mug. He got dressed in his usual clothes, only they felt different, they looked slightly darker, the material felt rugged, stronger, the signs of wear and tear on his jeans were gone. Clearly something was done to improve his clothes as they cleaned them. After he changed into his regular clothes, the maiden led him downstairs to the courtyard where Kili stood with a bow. She was in her true form, and her aura giving off a feeling of sharpness and total concentration. Josh could easily feel her intense dexterity as she fired arrows at a target fifty yards away without missing a shot.

"Ate your fill I take it, and it seems the maidens are quite taken with you. They've been gossiping for quite some time," said Kili as the maiden took her leave, smiling once more and winking at Josh, who smiled back awkwardly.

"Yes well, I'm not sure how to even respond to that," said Josh blushing slightly again.

"Think of it as the continent of Europe in your planet; have fun! As long as he or she is on board with it. I see no issue here; too bad you shall not be staying for long. We need to test what you learned in Valhalla, there is a certain loss of information when all the data transfers back to your mind as your consciousness goes back into your body. We need to gauge how much data loss you had."

"Wait, he or she is on board with it?"

"We don't judge here, although I'm almost certain you prefer women. The dwarf leaves me questioning sometimes."

"No, no, he likes women too… a little too much sometimes," Josh laughed. "Kili, why do my clothes feel different?"

"We took the liberty to add a few modifications to your clothes, make them more resistant. I noticed they have been suffering quite the wear and tear over time. We sprayed them with a nano repair that leaves the material more resilient to damage and tear. It is not the same as materializing a shield, but it should provide you with a bit more protection."

"I get the feeling you guys use nanotechnology to improve pretty much everything."

"It's the best technology to use for most minor details. You can control it well if you know how to, it does what you want and improves a lot. It's quite convenient. We have also mastered carbon. As I stated before, so material production through nanotechnology has completely advanced us to where we are and well beyond coming up short of any resource."

"So basically, you guys can produce anything in this planet?"

"I wouldn't say anything as some elements are not carbon based; but most materials, yes. Pretty much almost all materials found in the universe. To master carbon is to basically be able to produce any carbon-based material in chemistry. That one has been a particularly tricky one the All Father figured out in the early millennia of our time. Moving on, we must test your skill set, some of the data from training may have been lost when you returned from Valhalla."

"You mean my skills may be watered down? Am I still able to fight though?"

"Yes, but you are not quite prepared to engage a Celestial yet. Your muscles have also gotten developed to an extent due to some of the energy transfer from Valhalla into your nervous system, but you need to develop yourself more. Let us begin with simple marksmanship. This bow is just regular wood with arrows, Thor told me you cannot fully materialize yet, so let us start with enhancing the arrows. Apply as much energy as you can to the arrowhead."

Kili handed him the bow and an arrow. The bow was a longbow, six feet long and the arrow also large, suitable for the weapon it was being fired out of. Josh clicked his wrists together and aimed the bow, he put all his focus on the tip of the arrow. The tip began to glow brightly. Josh was surprised at how strong he had become, able to draw such a massive weapon without much strain on his body, his muscles had likewise adapted and developed despite not being physically training per se. He took aim at the same target Kili had aimed for, he focused, and his vision seemed to zoom in on the target slightly. Josh released the arrow, it hit the target, exploding a piece of it in a small burst of light and scattering chunks across the courtyard. The pieces immediately melted into a metallic liquid and began to flow back to the target, reforming it. The arrows remained shattered to pieces on the ground.

"Not bad, it is a start. You have enough juice to fire a generic blast with a projectile, but it's not enough to vaporize your projectile or your target completely. It's a hell of a good start though. We will need to work on your precision."

"I hit the target though, dead center, how much more precise can I get?"

"It's not your marksmanship that requires precision, it's your will and energy control. You can blast a target but it's no use if you can't pierce it or completely vaporize it." Kili picked up another bow from the weapons rack nearby and an arrow, manifested her energy on the tip of the arrow, it was a different glow from Josh's. It did not radiate outward like a light but glowed brightly in one spot at the tip of it. She fired her arrow, the arrow this time going into the target almost all the way to the feathers.

"I can explode that shot at any point of impact, but this time I simply decided to let it penetrate, you must be able to enhance all aspects of each shot."

"Kili, why a bow and arrow? Why not materialize a machine gun or a missile?"

"A machine gun is a projectile weapon that sus-
tains rapid fire, yes, but imagine the strain on one's
mind in making that kind of fire, or at materializing
every little intricate detail of moving parts behind
a mechanical weapon such as that. You wouldn't
be able to sustain a highly engineered weapon like
that while maintaining all other biochip functions
or control the shots and would merely fire shiny
pellets at the enemy's general direction. Highly in-
effective. Besides, the machine guns of your planet fire many projectiles to hit one target; we can
eliminate the target with one shot. And you haven't
seen the laser, rail, or proton canons. We have super weapons far more advanced. So, to try to materialize an engineered weapon with multiple moving
parts would be not only strenuous on the mind but
a complete waste of time."

"So, you do use weapons other than the biochips then?"

"Yes, we have them and use them for war if
absolutely necessary, but we have outgrown the
necessity for such weapons for the most part. Besides, we do have super weapons; Thor uses the
most popular one of all! A design of his own with
the aid of Hephaestus. But imagine the kind of
damage we could cause if we used our weapons of

war freely in the universe. There are laws in place against that, specifically for that reason. There would be no planets left," said Kili.

Josh thought of Thor's hammer Mjolnir, the hammer that allowed him to fly, and could fire lightning at multiple enemies, vaporizing them instantly. Truly no weapon the human race had even came close to that. Thor could shoot lightning or the hammer itself surrounded by lightning like an artillery shell, and it would simply return to him after hitting its target immediately ready to be fired again. The Celestials truly were centuries ahead in their technology and their super weapons were no exception.

"Thor gets away with it because Mjolnir is the first of its kind, and coded to Thor specifically, only him and a few worthy and properly attuned to the hammer can even lift it off the ground. Not to mention he has an official position permanently as a peacekeeper in the universe. But even lightning war hammers such as his are strictly regulated and in most instances forbidden. One can wipe out an entire planet in a few hours with it if used improperly."

Josh spent the rest of the afternoon practicing; his arrows went from exploding smaller blasts to penetrating almost the entire head through the target. At night, he feasted with the Celestials, the handmaidens offering themselves occasionally to him in the dormitory. Josh politely declining for the most part. Finally, the day came for his return to his planet.

"Come on then, Josh. The Celestials wish to bid you farewell," said Kili.

"Do they normally give formal goodbyes to all visitors?"

"Ideally no, but you are to assist in the saving of a new planet and its first guardian, the Celestials are traditionalists. All Celestials that have survived through the ages are. Discipline is the foundation to a culture surviving, and so all of our kind are highly disciplined traditionalists."

"Makes sense. Although all our modernization sounds counterproductive by that logic," said Josh.

"Indeed, the greatest challenge will be your new world nations in your planet. Unlike your regions known as Europe and Asia, the western part of the planet was not officially guided by any Celestial culture. They had visitors on many occasions, but no direct Celestial influence was established after the continent was split. And now your nation is the world leader as we see it. Your planet will need to develop much discipline, a lot can go wrong, and I do mean a lot."

"No wonder we're so messed up, we really don't have an official traditional culture per se."

"And we have established many, each with its own lore. The size of the regions says something about what our expectations were of your population and culture. In that regard, you have exceeded our expectations. Your population has grown larger than expected and our cultures shared with you have expanded vastly."

Josh and Kili made their way to the main hall. The Celestials sat on their thrones as usual, save for Thor's empty throne and now Baldr's who was also empty.

"You have come to us, a common human with an effort to save your planet," said Odin. "You now leave us a champion! One who has a chance of accomplishing such a feat. Kili will accompany you. As Thor has made me aware, you have not yet mastered your skills completely. Yet, you stand today a hundred times stronger than the first day you stood before me. From this day until the end of your days, you shall be a guardian of your race. Now go forth and repel the threat, restore the peace, and prosper."

"Thank you, All Father. I will do my best with the powers bestowed upon me."

"Ha ha look at you!" Odin laughed thunderously. "A few days in Asgard and you even speak formally as we do! There is hope aplenty for your planet after all, Josh Gunnar!"

"Let us proceed with your departure, time is not our ally in this instance," said Frigga. "Lady Kili, you know where to take him. Take appropriate action and secure the new world, should the statute of secrecy be broken, report it to the Universal Council for review."

"Yes, Lady Frigga," Kili made her way towards a throne in the corner. This was different from the other thrones, it was smaller, not like the traditional look of the other thrones, and this one contained several gadgets and instruments that seemed to be for electronics. Kili touched the right arm of the throne and one of the gadgets sprung to life and stood on four small legs. It looked similar to the gadget Kili left on earth with Pete. The gadget walked from the arm of the throne to Kili's wrist where it settled and turned into what looked like another ordinary smartwatch.

"Proper attire," Kili uttered to the device as she stared at the screen. The screen complied as she commanded and the wristwatch turned into a strange fluid, metallic and flowing as if with a mind of its own. Quickly the fluid covered her entire arm, then body. When it receded and turned back into a wristwatch Kili again resembled a human from planet earth as she had before.

"That's better. Now we may go. Josh, what's the status of that upgrade on your electronics?"

"I even forgot about that!" Between traveling to Asgard and training in the halls of Valhalla, Josh had only checked his phone once. His cell phone was still undergoing an upgrade since Zion. "It's still upgrading," said Josh as he looked at the screen, a bar almost completely full now at the screen.

"Expected, as the greys stated, the upgrade may take a considerable time," said Kili.

"Very well, may your journey be safe, and best of luck," said Odin.

"Thank you, All Father," said Kili as they bowed slightly and left. The palace was as impressive as ever. Walking towards the Bifrost, Josh could see several figures sparring in the air. They wielded swords, spears and shields, some a sword in each hand, clashing as they flew, most on two but some would materialize as many as six wings. Josh watched as they would protrude large wings and recede them as they shot up in the air with what looked like jet thrusters from their backs.

"Valkyries," said Kili. "They train openly in aerial combat around the palace. Bit of a show-off, but it comes as a warning to potential invaders."

"Why do they thrust up like that? Why not just fly up with the wings?"

"Wings do not mean flight automatically if your body is simply too heavy along with anything you may carry. The wings are really only made to glide through the air, but to go up, you need thrust. They do have stabilization with the wings and complete flight control. But the boost is essential for altitude gain until they pick up an air current. Just like on your planet. Despite all our technology, physics still plays a huge part in flight."

They made their way to the chamber of the Bifrost, Heimdallr stood at the door as always.

"Welcome to the Bifrost, state your champion, destination, and your cause," said Heimdallr.

"Kili the… you damn well know it and Josh Gunnar, college kid. We're going to planet twelve sixty-eight to grab some additional technology to resolve the coming threat of the Maku."

"I thought we were going to earth?"

"I need to make a pit stop and grab an extra gadget. The planet we're going to specializes in this sort of thing, they're among the best at what they do. Although it will be a bit strange for you."

"Strange how?" asked Josh as they stepped on the platforms. This was now beginning to become more routine for Josh.

Heimdallr made the signs in the air with the tip of his spear. The mandalas that lit in front of him lit up on the platforms under Josh and Kili. They were again encapsulated in the silver spheres only they could see through.

"Farewell travelers," said Heimdallr. "May the Gods grant you safe passage in your journey."

Josh and Kili again shot in the air, destined towards yet another planet.

CHAPTER 5

Extinct by Kindness

Josh and Kili landed on a desert just before a city. Before them, buildings and structures that looked weathered and destroyed. On some of the buildings you could see the metal frames, rusted and decaying. A bird of prey flew high overhead looking for something to eat, going in and out between the city and the desert. Josh and Kili walked to the city and made their way to what would be downtown.

"Kili, have we landed in the right place? This place is in ruins."

"Only on the outside. The labs and production buildings are all underground. This planet is a key example of when and how things can go wrong for mankind."

"Mankind? So, this is inhabited by humans?"

"A twin species to the humans in your planet, yes, but it wasn't war that killed them off, it was actually their technological success. They developed artificial intelligent beings so elaborate that in the end AI replaced human interaction completely. This is why we so strongly caution you about the technological development of your race. This planet's dominant species was genetically identical to the humans in your planet in every way, but they progressed in their technology faster than your race due to politics and socio-cultural aspects being vastly different here. Their progress was unhindered by many historical events that slowed technological advances in your planet."

"So, they achieved creating full androids? And they killed us?"

"For a lack of better terminology, yes, but not by war or assassination. The machines never raised a hand against mankind in war. Instead, they replaced every aspect of human interaction and fulfilled humanity's every need a little too well. They were the perfect partner in every way. So, humans stopped becoming personally involved with one another."

"Sounds a little impersonal, having nothing but machines to keep you company all the time. I couldn't imagine that."

"Imagine a partner that does what you want, presents a valid argument but acknowledges your point as valid and, in the end, agrees with you. Great conversations, no arguments ever, it simply apologizes if you're mad at them, and consents to pretty much anything you want anytime you want it. Soon you'll find yourself less and less trying to debate with humans or pick up a partner to have a relationship with. The machines did exactly that until mankind became less and less capable of procreating. Governments of the world attempted to resolve the issue with mandatory social gatherings and mandatory births by state, but by the time they noticed, it was simply too late."

Josh and Kili reached the entrance to a structure, despite of the state of abandonment of the streets and most buildings around them, the doors to the structure looked freshly painted. It looked like the entrance to a subway station. At the door stood a figure, it resembled a male, only it had a completely mechanical body that was painted green. Clearly it was what Josh referred to as an android.

"Welcome!" said the android in a foreign language to Josh. Kili appeared to understand him perfectly. "Please, right this way, Masters."

Kili replied likewise in his language as the android opened the doors at the bottom of the stairs and led the two down a flight of stairs. It looked like an underground train station like the ones in major cities on earth, but was actually an underground city full of computers, screens everywhere showing diagnostics and lines of code. Machines as far as the eye could see performing different functions. Josh did notice half of the machines and robots simply

stood still. Androids everywhere that were not performing some task stood silently by as others with
a task made their way around them. Some plain
colors as the one that received Josh and Kili, others more elaborate and dressed as casual males and
female humans, with perfect resemblance. Occasionally Josh saw an android make its way towards
what looked like maintenance stations, chairs with
spaces for hands and fingers, scanners, and tools
with service bots on standby. But aside from essential functions, there was no extra movement in
the station. The androids which more closely resembled humans usually simply stood by until Josh
or Kili came near them while their conventional
robot looking counterparts would perform many
functions around the city. It was a bizarre display,
as there was so much movement in one massive
location but no life anywhere you looked.

"Don't mind their language, we'll get you a
translation module here as well, so you're not lost
anymore traveling through the galaxy."

"Will I be able to understand all languages in
the universe?"

"For the most part yes, an argument can be
made for some of the most primitive variants of
dialogues but those are mostly matters of interpre-
tation."

"Welcome!" greeted a female android warmly
as Josh came near her, this time clearly in English

as Josh understood her. She was wearing a lovely white summer dress and looked indistinguishable from a human being save for the fact that she was perfectly still, priorly staring into nothing. "Is there any way I can assist you, Master? Would you like some company on your way to your errands?"

"Ummm… no thank you…" said Josh awkwardly to the female android. "Kili, what in the world is going on here? Why is everyone so creepily nice? And how come she suddenly speaks English?"

"They are doing exactly what they were originally designed for; to please their human masters. She speaks English because the first initial automatons we interacted with gathered that we did not speak their native language, so they shared that information as public information across their network and switched to your earth's English. Your language wasn't placed in your planet by chance you know. Most of the intergalactic council implemented its derivatives into it slowly until it evolved into English. It is after all one of the seventeen universal languages in the Intergalactic Trade Federation."

"So, you mean to tell me you guys invented English?"

"Not us Asgardians specifically, but yes. The original language was implemented by another species similar to yours and was widely accepted for trade due to its ability to adapt, sounds that were easy to make by many species and its smaller overall quantity of words required to communicate effectively. We guided your race in that direction by merging and implementing different languages through an elaborate linguistics technique we implement to teach nations normally. In the end, it all worked out and your species developed the language. That one of your nations would make it so spoken for the purpose of trade was a coincidence. Now here, stick your hand here and let's get you an adequate translator."

They arrived before a machine that stood about as tall as Kili. Josh hesitantly did as Kili said and placed his left arm in the crevice of the machine. Through a looking glass he could see it was surrounded by sharp instruments that looked as though they could easily perform open heart surgery. A computer suddenly came on and the instrument began moving. A mechanical arm grabbed Josh's arm inside the machine and Josh felt a tinge of panic as he was suddenly trapped by the contraption. A few feet behind him, Kili crossed her arms and looked slightly amused. Josh suddenly felt as if he was getting another tattoo on his forearm as some of the instruments moved closer and further touching his skin for a brief moment.

"Relax; they're coding the translator into your bio chips. It won't hurt much, and it won't take long. Try not to move."

The mechanical arm suddenly released Josh as the instruments moved away from his arm. Josh pulled his arm out and examined the spot the machine had touched. There was a new symbol in a slight shade of red; it looked like a small bird, similar to a parrot on Earth.

"So, this will let me understand alien languages?" asked Josh.

"Yes, the initial 17 universal languages are coded into it, but you will begin picking up more languages as you attempt to speak to people. It will also enable you to translate more of your human languages over time. To normal people you'll simply look unusually talented in terms of linguistics."

"And you had to make it look like a parrot?"

"That parrot as you call it can mimic just about any language, it's only appropriate those who designed the sign give it due credit. That and the makers of the app encoded into your skin thought the parrots were… well… cute birds," Kili grinned. "Now on to the next task we have at hand."

Kili instructed the android that was guiding them to lead them to their next objective. They made their way further into the city. There were no cars but plenty of walkways where androids, much like them, simply walked their way to perform whatever task they were assigned. Josh and Kili passed another group of female androids who were somewhat forward about their intentions of keeping them company. Josh politely refused again. Kili mostly ignored them altogether.

"It never ends, does it? Their solicitation?" asked Josh. "It's unsettling!"

"Well, that's because you didn't grow up with them making your life too easy or convenient. Those female androids were designed to resemble perfect human companions. Look around you, all of them on standby look like humans in their prime, as attractive as they can possibly look by human standards, and they are amazingly pleasant to chat with. Lovely automatons, but they are also the reason mankind is extinct here. They can detect we are biological by our heat signatures, and they sense our pulse when we come close enough, so they activate automatically. But since they have no master, they simply activate and follow the first directory; serve the dominant species. In this case us." They reached a door that slid open smoothly. "Go ahead, touch the one inside this room and tell me if you can tell the difference between that and a real human female in your world."

Josh and Kili reached a room with a large machine that looked like a giant three-dimensional printer of sorts but with additional tools; like a whole robot assembly line in front of them. Inside the large chamber was a small figurine, it looked like a samurai armor that was slightly smaller than

Josh's hand, painted red and incredibly elaborate for its size.

"Greetings, Masters," said the android working on a computer screen. "I am KY3LXE, I'm finishing up patches of code for the AI integration, and the final patches are loading and should be ready shortly."

"Thank you, Lexi," said Kili. "Please approach me and my companion."

The robot immediately abandoned the loading screen before her and approached Kili and Josh, standing just a few feet before them.

"Extend a hand in formal greeting."

The android extended out a hand at waist level, palm down, as if a lady shaking hands to greet a gentleman.

"Go ahead Josh; see if you can tell the difference. Greet her, touch her hand."

Josh reached out and touched the android's hand. It was more or less the same temperature as his, warm to the touch, felt like real skin, she was likewise petite in form, slightly shorter than Josh, dressed as a laboratory technician, lab coat over a sleeveless shirt, mini skirt, dark brown hair and blue eyes. She was made to look as attractive as possible, less like a real professional and more like a movie star playing the role of a scientist in a movie.

"KY3LXE, or Lexi as I call her, was designed

to fulfill basic engineering functions and coding as well as entertainment. She kept the nerds busy, when they were alive anyway. Get closer, even her breathing is similar to humans."

Josh came closer to the android, almost nose to nose as he held her hand and moved it aside. There was simulated breathing, the air coming in and exiting her body slightly warmer.

"She's liquid and air cooled, the air she breathes carries out the heat from the cooling system, there is of course one instance in which they do up the tempo…" Kili smiled. "Go on then, Lexi, give him a kiss, and make it passionate."

"What?" asked Josh, but just before he could react the android placed her hands over his face, pulled him in and kissed him passionately, as if she was a lover who had not seen her significant other in a long time, Josh felt her body press against his, felt her lips and her tongue, even felt her breathing intensify as she kissed him. She pulled back immediately, her breathing still elevated as if she was deeply in love with him. Kili laughed as Josh had a look of mixed confusion and enjoyment in his face.

"Stop," said Kili, "return to work."

"Yes, Master," said the robot as she immediately turned away from Josh and returned to handling the computer casually as if she were a human. Her breathing and expressions were immediately back to normal the moment Kili gave her the command.

"Pete would really enjoy this planet!" Josh chuckled.

"Yes, well, she is made to imitate everything attractive about a female human. They analyze patterns and match accordingly to simulate emotion; she's always perfect for her partner in every way. And if any aspect of them bothers you, you can always change it. Lexi, my name is Kili, do not address me as Master, and address me as Avocado Kili."

"Yes, Avocado Kili," said the android.

Josh laughed.

"See? She can easily replace a human girlfriend and keep you entertained for hours on end. Lexi, disregard last command."

"Yes, Master Kili," said the android. "The rendition is complete, as you requested, samurai build, thermal sword. Reinforced armor."

The doors to the large machine opened, a tray slid out revealing the small figurine. Kili quickly grabbed and examined the figurine before placing it in her pocket.

"Terrific. Charge the credits to the Asgardian Federation Republic. The usual account," said Kili to the android.

"Yes, Master Kili," replied Lexi as she made her way to another console.

"Kili, what exactly is that you just picked up?"

"Call it a contingency. In the event we need more warriors to fight, this will be the backup we can use."

"That thing is a robot?"

"More like an automated suit of armor, all it requires is an AI that is powerful enough to control it," Kili pointed at her wristwatch.

"I see, so basically it's an android bodyguard, but why a samurai suit?"

"A compact one yes, it gives us another highly capable warrior on the ground without calling upon a full army. I figured it would be a good idea since we do not know exactly the threat. And well, samurai have always had a code of honor that gives them unquestionable loyalty to their master. This applies to their coding here as well. And they are precise in all they do. Personally, I find them impressive, so I picked up a samurai build for this mission. Echo 336, lead us out to the transport," said Kili to the robot that stood at the door.

The android at the door came to life and replied positively before leading them out through the underground lab. They did not go through the stairs they originally went out through, but a different set, one that led into a glass building, a tinted glass Josh and Kili could see the outside through. They climbed the stairs and found themselves at another transportation room. This one only had one circle on the ground as opposed to two.

"This one sends us one at a time; we'll land more or less in the exact same location. The technology for interstellar travel was established at the end of mankind on this planet, so naturally it is a bit new and not very elaborate for them."

"I take it not a lot of people travel to and from here."

"Correct, to be exact, no inhabitant of this planet travels from here as none of them are technically alive and thus do not feel desire nor have any reason to travel. Occasionally peacekeeping agents like me drop by for some technology, but the planet is pretty much autonomous and always on standby for the visit of intelligent life. Remember, we have to keep secrecy on earth about this. Do not tell anyone about this mission against the Maku. Make stuff up if you must in case things get crazy." She motioned him toward the platform, "You first Josh, I shall be right behind you."

Josh stepped on the platform and Kili gave several commands to the androids who immediately began the takeoff procedure. Kili waved goodbye to Josh as he took off from the planet in a silver sphere.

Kili followed soon afterwards, and upon her exit, all androids simply stopped, the last one in the room uttering "Farewell, Master. Until we meet again," just before he stood still. The entire planet returned to minimal function as their planet no longer had a dominant sentient species to serve.

CHAPTER 6

Are We Back on Earth?

Josh believed he landed on planet Earth, but for some reason he did not recognize it at all; it was a dark night, and he landed on the rocky shore of a very small beach. The beach ended at some rocks and a large castle nearby. On Josh's side, an elevated sidewalk, raised high by what looked like a seawall meant to keep the tide out of town. Josh called out for Kili but to no avail. Over the sea wall facing the beach, he saw a bright light shining from the sky some distance from him, somewhere in the town. Josh decided to follow that light assuming it was Kili. As he climbed the steps from the sea wall to the sidewalk. Josh checked his phone again, the upgrade was almost complete, but the phone was still useless. Josh rushed into the street as fast as he could, the buildings were made of bricks and the streetlights were rather artistic. But the streets were empty. Not a soul in sight as far as Josh could see. Josh made it to the central plaza to find a mandala on the ground similar to the ones from all their landings; it was made of a little bit of sand over the stone bricks that covered the ground of the plaza before a fountain. Kili had definitely landed. Out of the corner of his eye, Josh caught a glimpse of someone moving fast into a nearby alleyway to his right.

"Hello?" Josh followed the movement into a dark alley. "Kili is that you? This isn't funny! Are we even on planet Earth?"

There was no response. Josh caught movement up ahead where the alley forked into two and walked in the direction of the movement he saw. It was a dark alley indeed, leading down between two of the brick buildings. A tall figure stood facing away from him as he approached it.

"Kili, what the hell happened?" Josh approached the tall figure. "I thought we were landing back in my town before we broadened our search for the…" But Josh stopped just a few feet away only to realize this was definitely not Kili. The figure turned around and Josh saw the horror, it was a man, pale and dark haired, his mouth full of blood and with sharp jagged teeth. He was holding what looked to be a dead soldier, his neck bit wide open by the man's terrible teeth, blood still pouring from the wound soaking his uniform and dripping on the ground.

Josh fell back as the man hissed at him aggressively. The man dropped the dead soldier on the ground and began walking towards Josh, smiling menacingly as he reached for him with one hand, his long nails sharp as claws and black at the end of pale fingers, blood still dripping from his jagged teeth. Josh quickly got to his feet as he turned to run but saw another soldier standing at the beginning of the alley where he had come from.

"Get down!" shouted the soldier and Josh did just in time for the soldier to fire. A hail of bullets hitting the man square in the chest as he shrieked loudly like a monster. The soldier continued to fire at his chest as he moved forward until he was at arm's reach of Josh, placing his last shot square between the eyes on the creature, who dropped on the ground lifeless. Its body somewhat melting where the bullets hit, no longer maintaining a solid human-like face but a somewhat charred and melted corpse on the ground.

"Vampire goat-drinker killed Vaz!" said the soldier. "What the hell are you doing out here at this hour?"

"I was looking for someone."

"And what the hell is that someone doing out here at this hour?" asked the soldier. He was clearly European; his accent was thick and very different from anyone in America. "Doesn't matter, come on, we have to get to an outpost, the night is young, and these undead freaks aren't going to stop hunting anytime soon. Follow me!"

Josh, not having any other option, followed the soldier. They walked quickly down the opposite side of the alleyway from the monster the soldier just felled, taking side streets to a one-story building. It was a heavy brick building like many in the town that didn't stand out at all except that every window was heavily barred and braced with wood and iron. The soldier knocked loudly on the iron door of the building. A voice from the inside shouted a question in a foreign language, the soldier replied in the same. Suddenly, the iron door in front of them opened letting Josh and the soldier inside. It was as plain on the inside as it was on the outside. The soldier walked over to a nearby ladder leading to a metal hatch, climbed halfway up the ladder and propped the hatch open slightly with a rock and lit up a cigarette.

"We do not see many Americans normally. You picked a stupid time for vacation."

"I'm Josh, and I'm not on vacation."

"No? Then what the hell are you doing on Dubrovnik at a time like this?"

"I've been out of town for a while, it's complicated."

"Well, surely you're not from around here. I sure as hell am not. I'm Sergeant Nikolai Astrov, French Foreign Legion chuteurs operationels. Here to eliminate this undead plague you saw take my comrade."

"Ok, and what exactly are these guys, Sergeant?"

"It's just Niko. We do not know; we heard the stories, the myths and lore. And we have heard of legionnaires bumping into them before during covert missions, but ever since this Corona plague hit, they have taken the opportunity to run rampant. So much that under the NATO treaty agreement they deployed us here to this place. It seems all those children's stories meant to frighten kids are true, and vampires really exist. They took this Coronavirus pandemic as an opportunity to seize towns for themselves. Everyone is either isolated in quarantine or infected by them already, fewer people around. They picked off people in the streets until it became a ghost town, and the local government has stopped doing anything to protect its people."

"Pandemic? Coronavirus? What do you mean?" asked Josh confused.

"Have you been out of town somewhere with no internet or media, too? It started in China, another respiratory virus. Spreads easy, feels like your common flu, kills old and sick people; caused quarantines all over the world and a lot of places to shut down. We suspect the leader of these vampires is in the local castle since it got closed off from the public after the virus. At first, I took you for an American tourist who got stuck here by accident; it happened a lot. This coronavirus spread so fast that the airports shut down and left a lot of people stranded," Nikolai finished his cigarette and closed the hatch. "Come, I'll show you the barracks and what we have going on in here."

Nikolai led Josh down a flight of stairs and through a hallway; it was wide enough for five men to pass at a time and occasionally had a gurney with an injured soldier laid out.

"What the hell is your business here, anyway?" asked Nikolai as they walked.

"Well, I can't tell you much, but I think this is exactly what who sent me was looking for. They told me to look for anything unusual, well, here it is."

"Well tell whoever sent you we need backup! We are running low on soldiers as they keep picking us off and only a platoon sized element was sent to contain this shit. Vaz over at that alley means we lost more than half our force. And Micah over there is wounded and leaving tomorrow by airlift. We're down to just over twenty men."

"Well, that's the bad news… it's just me and one more operative and we got separated."

"Well damn! What's the good news? Your partner has beer flavored tits?"

"Well, no, but I'm pretty sure she won't get killed by the creatures out there."

"Either way, you better be good with a rifle. Ammo is limited and we have to use these silver tip bullets. The vampires are allergic or something, the silver bullets work well; it melts their skin and bones and blood and makes a mess. It kills them well enough."

Nikolai led Josh to a wide room. In the corner, a soldier was packing ammunition. Nikolai uttered some words at the soldier in a foreign language, and the soldier grabbed a nearby tactical rifle and bulletproof vest packed with magazines and handed it to Josh. Josh checked the weapon, cleared the chamber and loaded a magazine into it, chambering a single round and placing the weapon on safe. Another soldier approached, he was more well-groomed than Nikolai and carried himself as if in charge. Nikolai snapped to attention as he spoke to the other soldier in a language Josh did not understand.

"Well, whoever you are, you look like you know how to use a rifle at least. This is commander Bordeaux. He welcomes you and all the help you can bring. Tomorrow night we raid the castle and look for your partner if time permits. Rest for now. Come, I will show you the mess hall, and we can have a drink and some food," said Nikolai.

Josh acknowledged the commander realizing he did not seem to speak English. The soldier who provided him a weapon and armor did not speak his language either, but Josh thanked him and followed Nikolai to the mess hall for dinner.

Josh and Nikolai spent the evening having dinner and wine. The dinner was a French ration of anchovies with a side of biscuits and pudding. This was not a lot of food, but it was far better than the ready-to-eat meals Josh had back in the days he served in the army.

"So, you see, we never bother with the plates here for the vest, weighs too much. Our enemy is fast but does not shoot, and they know how to avoid the vest and just cut our necks open. Our first five men died with the full kit on, it was completely useless. After that we just moved light and fast. So far it has worked, and we've had some close calls. But it looks like it ends tomorrow, one way or another."

"How long have you guys been here? It looks like you guys have been fighting for a while."

"Surprisingly, it's only been a few weeks. Little over five, I think. We were in Somalia before eliminating terrorists and local pirates, but when the virus became a pandemic, all the fighting died down and we got reassigned. My men were good men. Seventy-six scuffles with the enemy and not a scratch on my men; we land here, and this shit happens."

"How come most of you don't speak English?"

"Well first we are the French Foreign Legion! English is not necessary to join. Then there is the question of where people are from. The commander is actually from Belgium, so he only speaks Dutch, German and French, and poorly at French, you can tell a mile away. And most of our guys around here are from poor European countries and joined because they had nowhere else to go, myself included. So, we improvise on language."

"Makes sense I guess."

"How many languages do you speak?"

"Well, English is a given, I took Spanish in high school and Portuguese on my first college semester."

"In other words one, and then some. Typical American! It is time to rest, come, tomorrow we have big plans. Tomorrow, we take back the castle and kill those freaks, hopefully once and for all."

Nikolai led Josh to a big room, dimly lit by flashlights soldiers had lit up. Nikolai motioned for Josh to lie down on a cot. Josh did so, trying to fall asleep. Nikolai handed him a basic pillow and blanket. It was a fairly sleepless night; the events of that night reminded Josh of his past, of when he served in Afghanistan and had to treat the wounded in combat. Josh was not a stranger to blood and gore as he was only eighteen years old when he went to war, he served in the army for three and a half years and had deployed once before going to college. But the sight of the vampire, blood dripping from the jaws, soldier dead in his arms, it gave Josh a new set of bad memories aside the ones he had of fellow soldiers he had to treat, to take to safety and watch over as they were wounded. Now it was years later and another battlefield with a mix of normal weapons and his alien technology acquired somewhere else.

"Wake up, American!" said a random soldier to Josh. "Niko wants you upstairs. We have to prep for mission and send away Micah to the airstrip."

Josh got up and dressed as quickly as he could and made his way upstairs. "This way!" said the soldier as he led him to the back doors. They were double doors this time, a loading dock just beyond them as four soldiers carried the wounded man into the back of a van. The van was packed with equipment and medical supplies. Nikolai was at the side of the stretcher overseeing the process, giving orders to his men as the van drove away.

"Well, those two taking Micah will likely live," said Nikolai. "They have been told not to return unless they have backup. We cannot wait though; we pushed the vampires back from town for now and that gives us one opportunity. Tonight, we take it!"

The sun was just going down. Nikolai led Josh to the briefing room as the van disappeared and the back doors closed. The commander was already briefing the soldiers. There were only nineteen of them now. They listened attentively. The commander spoke in Dutch apparently, as that

seemed to be the language most of them understood. Once he was done, he addressed Nikolai
directly.

"Well, looks like you're with me," said Nikolai.
"Makes sense since only me and Joel here speak
your language."

They made their way rather quickly through
the streets. They moved fast but quiet, no vehicles,
just foot soldiers. They encountered a few of the
vampires hunting, some smaller pale creatures with
pointy ears walking on four legs. They resembled
what were once humans and charged fiercely at the
soldiers but were put down fast. Nikolai referred
to them as ghouls, as the common lore stated in
the region according to him. Josh was astounded
that his Helm of Awe corrected even the slightest
error in aim as he shot a vampire square between
the eyes three times in a row from fifty yards away;
the creature going down with a sharp exhale. The
other soldiers stared at Josh in awe as he felled the
creature.

"I took the sharpshooter course back in the
United States Army," said Josh, kind of embarrassed. The Helm of Awe coded into his body
truly did much more than just a little help. With
modern day weapons it perfected his marksmanship almost completely. Any minor mistakes he
made when he tried to aim, the helm coded in the
biochip system corrected, making him much more

skilled as a soldier.

"If your American army has a lot of soldiers who shoot like that, that is an army I would not want to fight," said Niko.

A few ambushes caused some close calls, but all the men were still mission capable as they reached the castle.

"Those ghouls are corpse eaters; they just eat whatever the vampire doesn't. They turned almost half the town into those and also turned quite a few people into vampires," said Nikolai as they approached the gate. It was a tall structure, a giant metal gate stood before the brick and stone road leading to massive doors made of wood. "Guess again," said Nikolai as Josh eyed the massive door, one of his soldiers lighting a welding torch and melting some of the bars, just enough to make a hole for the soldiers to pass. "We are entering through the side door leading to the kitchen. Less impressive, but quieter," said Nikolai as they made their way through the gardens on the side of the road, hiding behind bushes and small trees. Nikolai uttered some commands to the men, who attached silencers to their rifles. "You too, side pouch. Clip it on," said Nikolai to Josh, who did just that. One of the men approached the door. It was a heavy wooden door with an old lock. The soldier wasted no time and melted the locking mechanism through the large keyhole of the old door. Opening the door with just the creaking of the hinges after the lock was gone.

Inside they saw a large room leading to the kitchen; only the kitchen was empty due to the castle having become a tourist attraction. Old electrical lamps lit the halls dimly. Exiting the kitchen was a hallway, long with high ceilings. The team split into two groups of nine men and went their separate ways there. Nikolai's squad took the way up towards a tower, having to split again as they reached a staircase in a hallway. It was now Josh, Nikolai, Joel and two others. The first room they breached had two ghouls, which they cleared quickly. The silver bullets seemed to have the same effect on them as it did vampires. They weren't as lucky on the second room on the way upstairs as one of the ghouls managed to bite one of the soldiers badly on the shoulder. The soldier used the welding torch to melt the ghoul's face half off before the rest of the squad put enough bullets in him. Josh began administering first aid with what supplies he had in the soldier's aid bag attached to his vest.

"This is bad," said Josh. "It's going to get infected if we don't get him the right medical attention."

The soldier protested in his language, motioning that he was fine. Nikolai replied in the same. "We will get him medevac soon. He will carry on behind us," said Nikolai.

They continued to move towards the top of the tower until they reached the heavy wooden entrance. They tried the door handle and found that it was unlocked. Joel led the way inside, followed by Nikolai and the rest. It was a massive bedroom, a giant bed in the center, old furniture and decorations on the walls. A shield with crossed swords bearing an old family crest, paintings of nobles, the massive glass door leading to the balcony wide open with the curtains aside revealing the bright moonlight which provided some illumination. The team approached with caution but suddenly one of the team members flew into a wall at full force, pushed by a shadowy figure. The soldier slammed into the wall knocking a set of crossed swords and shield on the ground. He did not move afterwards.

The soldier with the wounded shoulder began firing in the direction of movement. "Get down!" shouted Nikolai as one of the swords went flying in the air towards them. Josh and the others had just enough time to react, but the soldier firing was impaled through his vest square in the chest. He died instantly and fell crumpled to the ground.

"You dare invade my quarters!" shouted a voice that echoed through the room. "You'll all pay with your lives!"

Josh concentrated, clicked his wrists together and a bright light shined through his hands. He aimed at the ceiling where he found the vampire.

She hissed angrily at him as her skin began to smoke and crawled quickly on the ceiling towards the open glass door, landing right in front of it on her feet.

"That's a neat trick," said Nikolai as the light faded from Josh. "We may need it again."

"Mortals, so feeble, weak…" said the vampire as she walked towards them. She was tall and pale, her petite figure masking the monstrous strength she had. "I am Lady…" she stopped dead as Joel fired two shots square on her chest. She had a look of surprise on her face as she fell to her knees, blood pouring from the gunshot wounds as the area began to burn in an amber color. Joel stood up and fired five more shots on her chest as she fell backwards.

"Who the hell cares?" said Joel as he fired one last shot directly on her head.

"Good man, let's check on Mark and Kevin before we move out of the tower," said Nikolai.

Mark, the soldier who was slammed into the wall was dead. His eyes stared blankly as Joel shined his flashlight on him. Kevin was slumped on the ground with a sword through his chest, clearly also dead. Nikolai removed the sword that impaled him and said a prayer for the men in their native language as he dropped the sword next to him, and they moved out of the tower.

"Bad luck to leave the sword that killed a man

still in him. Anyway, what the hell was that in there?" asked Nikolai as they made their way down the stairs. "Some kind of special flashlight?"

"It's a gadget my partner gave me before we split up. It creates light like the sun, I guess. Honestly, I don't really know how it fully works, but apparently it burns them."

"Best to make use of that gadget of yours. Whoever sent you, they have shit for organization. Giving you equipment but not telling you what it does or how it works."

"Well, it wasn't exactly made just for this situation. And as you've seen, there isn't exactly a lot of time to test the features."

They made their way back to the hallway where the tower began and continued down, they reached a fork again. Josh and the others turned the corner only to find a figure standing at the fork in the end of the hallway. It was another vampire, this one with ten ghouls around him; they were eating the rest of Nikolai's team that had split up. The vampire smiled at them briefly as the ghouls looked up at their new target. He wiped the blood off his lips as the ghouls charged. Nikolai raised his rifle swearing in his native tongue as he began taking down the ghouls with Josh and Joel, but before he could fire at the vampire, the vampire looked to his left with a look of panic as suddenly a burst of light, bright as the sun shined on him, burning him to a crisp instantly. Around the corner came an all too familiar tall dirty blonde female figure Josh had been looking for.

"Bloody creatures," said Kili. "They made a fine mess of things."

"Who the hell are you?" asked Nikolai pointing his rifle.

"Put that down you buffoon! I'm on your side!" Kili walked right past him. "Where in the name of Hel have you been?"

"I could ask you the same thing," said Josh smiling. "Looks like we got separated."

At that moment they all heard several electronic beeps. Josh checked his pocket; his phone had finally finished the update and was ready for use.

"Well whole lot of good that did," said Kili. "I would have found you a lot easier had that been ready to begin with."

"Well, this ensures it doesn't happen again. So, is this the threat we came to deal with?"

"No, this is something else entirely. I heard of their presence here on earth, but they never should have taken over to this extent, nor cooperated this much. Vampires are usually more solitary and secluded than this since mankind reached an age of technology."

"Vampires? So, this is legit? Not some old European legend?" asked Josh.

"Have you not seen the fangs and the weird

crawling around ceilings and the neck biting? Yes, they are vampires. A plague similar to rabies got released back in the eighth century that created this. It was some experiment by a mad genius from God knows what planet who wanted to mimic our biological immortality with viral treatment on your species. The ones afflicted were normally very isolated though. They usually secluded themselves and caught unfortunate humans by ones and twos, but this is rather ridiculous. And I'm not fond of the corpse eaters either."

"Well, I'm glad you clarified what they are, lady-who-knows-how-to-use-that-bright-light-gadget-better," said Joel. "What's our next move?"

"We find their leader and eliminate him. We also eliminate evidence he even existed. Lucky for you there should be no paper evidence in this ancient castle of any kind. So just burning the bodies will do," said Kili.

"And who the hell are you to give us orders! I'm the team leader here and I follow only my commander. You have no jurisdiction," said Nikolai.

"Very well Sergeant, I am Agent Kili Asgard of the British Secret Intelligence service." Kili flashed what looked like a legitimate ID to Nikolai; her accent passed for European enough for Nikolai to buy her story. "My partner and I were outfitted with her majesty's latest experimental technology and sent here to gather data; we had no idea things would turn out so bad. As it stands in the cooperation pact, your commander follows orders from NATO intelligence and myself being the senior ranking agent and the one with the most intel means I am now in charge."

"My apologies ma'am, I did not know. He is American though, why are you with him?" asked Nikolai. He did not like being told she had power over him just like that but did not bother to further press the question given the circumstances.

"He is part of the testing team for the technology, it was meant to be a coalition mission with the U.S. and European Union. We've been developing this technology and testing it together in order to create another special operations coalition force. Did you not get in contact with the French and German agents?"

"No ma'am, we only found the American dazed and confused. He almost got eaten."

"And I take it you lost the rest of the equipment and your credentials too huh?" asked Kili winking at Josh. Josh quickly caught on to what was going on.

"Uh yes ma'am, I landed by the small beach and in the whole run in with the vampire most of my gear was destroyed," Josh tried his best to sound convincing.

"Bloody hell! Stupid Americans! Don't know why we ever agreed to the coalition exercise with you," remarked Kili, putting on a show for the soldiers.

"No wonder your ass was so secretive, not only were you on a special mission, you were embarrassed because you screwed up." Nikolai chuckled.

"No matter, your primary gadget still works and we need to eliminate the threat. That's all the intel I can give you on these guys. I won't get into detail as to how the ghouls are made or how that virus spreads, let's just go and finish the job. Sergeant, I hate to be the bearer of bad news, but I passed five more corpses besides the ones here. If there are any left of your team, they are likely in a fight as we speak. Now once we eliminate their leader, the rest should be easy pickings especially during daytime hours, or they should disperse and go back to seclusion."

"What are we waiting for then, let's avenge the fallen and kill this undead bastard," Nikolai swapped magazines in his rifle.

The rest of the castle was rather easy to clear with Kili in the group. Apparently, Nikolai and Joel bought her lame story about a coalition mission perfectly well and were fully cooperative. Kili did not act like an agent or bothered to move quietly or tactically so much as walked in the direction of danger, grabbed their attention and lit them up with her bio chips. The intense light would burn the vampires and ghouls to a crisp instantly. Finally, they reached the staircase that seemed to lead to the dungeon.

"Kili, what the hell was that?" whispered Josh while Nikolai and Joel secured the rear. "Suddenly you work for British intelligence. How do you have an ID from them?"

"The nanotech I picked up in my planet researched agencies and printed me an ID. It's identical to the real thing, and I just researched while you were gone and came up with the story. I told you we needed a cover. Don't worry, I also printed you one. Like I said, this is not the Maku, we landed in a different part of planet Earth and it happened to have this going on."

"I guess we just roll with it from this point on?"

"Guess so. Don't worry, we'll get home on the next one."

"I hope so, for an advanced race, so far your traveling has been kinda faulty," Josh chuckled.

"I told you they didn't use the Bifrost much on planet twelve sixty-eight, so they aren't very accurate."

They reached the door to the dungeon at the bottom of the stairs. Joel began preparing a breach charge, but Kili simply stated, "Don't bother," as she clicked her wrists together and sliced the door's mechanism before kicking the door open.

"Whoever you are, whatever you think you're in charge of, kiss your ass goodbye!" stated Kili bluntly.

"Not how I'd have entered and approached that situation but hey, it works," said Joel.

"She has her way of doing things, and her gadget is working fully, so yeah," commented Josh.

"Well, it seems you have found my humble abode," said the figure sitting at the end of the room. He was taller than the other vampires, slouched forward as he stood, the two other vampires around him hissing loudly. "Forgive the manners of my brethren; we do not receive visitors often, not of their own accord."

"This is no social call vampire. We're here to end this!" said Kili as she walked towards him. The first vampire stepping directly in front of him as Kili approached preparing to attack as she quickly activated the same flash of light she had been using to vaporize him, catching the vampire behind him in the face slightly as he covered himself with his robes but missing the vampire in front of him as he quickly leaped out of the way several feet in the air, landing on a nearby wall. The vampire hissed loudly as his skin was still smoking before a hail of bullets from Josh, Nikolai and Joel firing all at once hit him. The vampire fell to the ground dead. The second vampire, seeing the first skirmish, attempted to escape but was caught in the face by a bullet from Nikolai. He hissed loudly as Kili blasted him with another intense burst of light, catching the master vampire in the light again making his skin burn and smoke even more.

"You will pay for this," said the third vampire, his face burned, chunks falling off, he burned different from the other two, clearly the light affected him, but he did not turn to ash despite being burned twice. "You will pay for this dearly… I am no mere vampire! And I have had enough of your species insolence!"

Kili took a step back, the vampire was somehow growing taller, horns were now protruding out of his head and growing, and his eyes were turning from the black of a vampire to bright red and focused with hatred. He took a bigger demonic grotesque form as he roared in pure rage. From the pale tall slouching figure, emerged a bigger body that was red with giant horns. He was now easily becoming twice the size of his brethren.

"Uh Kili… I think we have a problem…" said Josh, "nobody said we'd be fighting the devil."

"He is not the devil, I got this!"

Nikolai and Joel did not waste time; they emptied their magazines on the creature's grotesque chest, their bullets simply falling to the ground once impacting the increasingly bigger monster before their eyes.

"We're out of ammo comrade!" shouted Nikolai. "This is the end."

"I told you, I got this. He is no devil, just a

Surtr," said Kili as the monster was now twice their size, his head nearly bumping into the ceiling as he again roared with rage.

"You dare challenge me!" said the creature out loud. "I am death incarnate! None shall survive! I will destroy all of you! I am… wait… why am I upside down?" said the creature suddenly as he saw his body fall to its knees and finally down lifeless. Next to it, Kili had a sword made of pure light protruding from her hand.

"You are nothing but an ambitious little creature with a big mouth," Kili's wristwatch took a form similar to a canon. "Obliterate!" she uttered, the mini canon shooting an unbelievably powerful shot of energy, taking out the creature's body and head completely.

"Nooooo!!!" shouted the beheaded creature as his head and body were completely disintegrated, leaving nothing but a charred shadow on the side walls. The part of the room where Kili fired the canon at the creature's body and head was completely destroyed, revealing a cliff and the open sea.

"You know, you really should consider being more careful with that," said Josh.

"They will rebuild it, let us get out of here, it is almost dawn," said Kili as she made her way to the door. The others followed. Nikolai had several questions ranging from "Is that another gadget?" to "When do we get one of those?" as they made their way through the castle.

"Kili, what's a Surtr?" asked Josh.

"It is a fire giant. Basically, they are enemies of the Aesir in your human mythology. To Christians they are arch demons and typically command lesser creatures in secrecy. This one disguised itself as a master vampire and rounded a group to take over the city. They're very opportunistic creatures and use folklore to control small populations, but this one got greedy once he had a few vampires on his side."

"And vampire is really a correct term?" asked Josh.

"I told you before, yes. To us one only qualifies as human if they meet the human criteria. To be infected and mutated by that rabies-like disease and modify genetic material and properties beyond normal human parameters is to become another species more or less. Normal humans do not live eternally, feed on blood of other humans or have those teeth and claws for fingernails."

"I get that, it's just funny you refer to them as vampires when you normally have another explanation," said Josh as they left the dungeon.

This time they chose to take the main hall as they left the castle, which, when they approached it, Nikolai's commander and what was left of the soldiers greeted them as they stepped away from a pile of ghoul corpses.

"Here," Kili handed Josh an ID card that read "Central Intelligence agency." Josh took the ID card. "And don't you dare lose it again!" said Kili loudly as she winked at Josh.

"Yes ma'am," Josh winked back.

The commander greeted Nikolai and Joel warmly, Nikolai explaining briefly who Kili was. The commander nodded to her in acknowledgement.

"Looks like he called backup. They're arriving now," said Nikolai. "You guys want a ride? We can take you to the local airport and get you out of town, but the flight home is up to you."

"Sure, we need to get to the airport; we're taking a commercial flight back. No one can know we were here!" said Kili loudly as they approached the helicopter, the sun rising as the helicopter arrived, burning the ghoul corpses to ash and scattering the ashes near the castle doors as the helicopter landed. Kili and Josh climbed on board headed for the nearest airport. The flight was short. Kili and Josh turned some heads at first when they came in from a military aircraft, but soon people resumed their routines. Kili purchased two tickets to Colorado with a card her new machine "produced" out of the blue. To their surprise, they had to wear facemasks in the airport and for the entire flight.

"Relax," said Kili, "your currency is mostly digital. I simply hacked the system and added a few digits. These face coverings sure are bothersome though, I wonder what they expect to prevent with this."

Kili and Josh made their way back to Colorado after a long 18-hour flight. Once back at home, Josh rented a car to drive back to town.

"So those were legitimate legion soldiers? They were quite fearless compared to some of these local soldiers you have here in your city."

"The people patrolling around here aren't soldiers, they're police. They just enforce the law and establish order. And my hometown isn't much of a city as the one we just left; it's more of a small town."

"So, they are peacekeepers like myself then!" "Wonderful! Does their order also have command over military forces?"

"No. It works kind of differently," Josh tried to explain to Kili different aspects of government. The ride home seemed relatively normal if not for the extra precautions the world was now taking. Apparently, everyone had been wearing masks now in public to cover their faces, and stay at home laws were implemented, closing bars, restaurants, and public places. Josh was astounded Kili even invented a story as elaborate as she did on the fly since she seemed to lack so much understanding of governments in the human race still.

Josh and Kili were just arriving in town late at

night, they were back where they had started almost a year before, the temperature was cold and there was snowmelt on the sidewalks. Josh had just parked the car when they heard a loud bang by the dumpsters behind Josh's apartment. Josh and Kili exited the vehicle quickly and went to investigate the noise in the alleyway next to the dumpster. It was another dragoon creature by the looks of it.

"Oh, come on! Can we get a freaking break?" said Josh as the dragoon took notice of them. It was digging into the trash as they approached it and now they had its full attention. Its tail swishing back and forth as it looked at them. This one was smaller than the one they originally fought. It was shorter than Josh by a few inches, stood on four legs but did not have the terrible upper body the first one had and seemed to act more like a stray wild dog and less of a creature legitimately making an invasion attempt on their planet.

The dragoon roared loudly, ready to charge when suddenly a figure dropped down on its back from the roof of the apartment. The dragoon shrieked in pain just before the new creature snapped its neck and dropped the lifeless body on the ground.

The creature stood up as it stepped away from the dead animal and faced Josh and Kili. It was about as tall as Kili, had golden brown fur all over his body, seemed to wear somewhat torn shorts and had the head of a large cat, resembling some-what of a lion but bigger and without a mane. Kili prepared her sword to fight, but the creature raised a hand in protest. On its wrist was a gadget familiar to Kili, the nanotech device.

"Wait!" uttered the creature suddenly in a deep voice, sounding more like a growl. It began to shrink, its arms and hands became smaller, its form took a more familiar shape, one shorter than Josh and very familiar.

"I'm glad you two are back," said Pete, his eyes still glowing amber. "There is much we need to talk about."

CHAPTER 7

Much to Explain

"Freeze!" said Deputy Brady with his gun out pointing directly at Pete.

"Whoa! John, calm down! It's just Pete man!" Josh raised his hands in alarm.

"I don't know what I just saw but sure as hell it ain't just Pete! Keep your hands where I can see them! You two back up now! Hands on the wall!" said John as he motioned to Kili and Josh. "Dispatch this is Deputy Brady requesting back up!" said John as he pressed a button on his radio. The radio returning nothing but static.

"You need to understand Officer, Pete is not a threat, he seems fully in control of his mutation," said Kili.

"Shut up and don't move, back away from… whatever he is and put your hands on the wall! I'm not gonna say it again! Dan! Where are you? I need back up!" John pressed the button again multiple times. He had known Josh and Pete for years but none of the things he saw made sense, and he definitely did not know how to handle this situation other than taking in all 3 of them for questioning on the strange events happening all over town.

"John please! You've known me for years!" said Pete. "Put the gun down and let's talk about this."

"I said don't move!" said John, but Pete took a step forward at the wrong time. Officer Brady was completely freaked out by everything he had just seen. John fired his weapon twice as Kili stepped in front of Pete just in time. Two shots hit her right in the torso, the bullets stopping dead at the surface of her skin.

"What the…?" said John.

"Calm yourself human!"

"How did you do that?" asked Josh astounded.

"I keep a small portion of concentration into a total protection shield at all times, it's a trick Baldr made originally, I'll explain later. Listen officer, you can try to take us captive or kill us with that primitive weapon, but it will do you no good, or you can calm down and let us explain what you just saw. It's up to you, either way, I'm fairly sure I'm done playing this game." Kili materialized her twin swords. Josh now stepped between the two of them to intervene.

"Wait! Wait! John, put your weapon down man, she's not playing around! Kili, power down your blades, he is a friend and part of law enforcement! One of the good guys, you can't hurt him!"

"One of the good guys who just shot me twice!"

"He was trying to hit me!" said Pete. "Ok that doesn't make it any better, but Kili, calm down!"

Kili and John stared at each other eye-to-eye for what seemed like an eternity, finally John lowered his weapon slowly, Kili likewise powered her blades down.

"Listen, Dan is gonna be here any minute. We cannot tell him about Pete. He will put him down. Let me do the talking." John walked to the dragoon's body and unloaded his entire magazine on the creature's head. Josh and the others were still unsure if they could trust John at the moment. The police lights and sirens from Sheriff Dan's patrol car were right around the corner now. John walked over to Dan at a hurried pace as Dan left his car running, shotgun in hand.

"What the hell just happened?" asked the Sheriff. "I just heard a whole lot of gunfire!"

"Found another one of them weird gators. Trying to eat those three, got the drop on him and emptied a mag on his head. Seems like it worked."

The Sheriff acknowledged the three as he walked carefully past them, his shotgun now pointed at the dragoon's body, he unloaded three more slugs on the creature's body. "Just in case," said the Sheriff, "the last one nearly took my leg cause I thought he was dead. Good job deputy, you got lucky. Take a statement from them and I'll meet ye back at the station. We gonna start carrying more ammo now in the cars," said Dan as he greeted the three on his way back to his car, his radio going off the entire time. Josh and the others catching words about another 'mutated alligator' on the other side of town. "I trust you three can throw the body in that dumpster there. The folks at animal control already got a few of those in storage waiting for big government to come pick them up," said Dan as he rushed to get out of there.

"No problem, Sheriff, we shall throw him in there for you," said Kili.

"Thank you, lady," said Dan as he turned off his lights and drove off after hearing his radio dispatch one more time. He left in much more of a hurry than Josh and Pete normally saw any officer leave in this town.

"Looks like he got somewhere else to be and fast," said Pete.

"Yes well, you better start talking, it's not too late for me to change my mind and bring you in," John eyeballed Kili carefully. The two were still a bit tense over the situation.

"Come inside, John, this is gonna take a little while," said Josh.

They came inside the apartment and sat down. Pete as usual placed a six pack of beer on the table. John declined as he was an on duty cop, but that didn't stop the rest of them.

"So, you see, it appears I'm some sort of were-cat man now." Pete said as he offered Josh and Kili a drink. Josh was all too happy to be at home drinking with his best friend again.

"How the hell did that happen?" asked Josh.

"I'm guessing it must have been the first dragoon we fought. I told you his blood was a mutagen. I don't understand though. The mutation should have been mild, maybe even temporary. And the stabilization should have just kept you alive and sane."

"Oh, it wasn't mild or temporary!" said Pete sarcastically. "I started noticing changes, at first, your nano-gadget thingy began analyzing my blood. Mutagens increased gradually, so I began treating myself with the chemistry lab at the college campus after the pandemic."

"Well, have there been any more instances like this John?" asked Josh.

"Nope, we were keeping everyone away from these… whatchamacallits. Telling everyone they're mutated alligators and are dangerous. Animal law enforcement has been helping us handle them and even set up a temporary station at the Sheriff's department to keep a few bodies, waiting for big government to come get them."

"I am surprised you managed to contain them so far. How many have you encountered?" asked

Kili.

"About seven or eight not counting today. They've been keeping us busy, what do you call them again?"

"It's called a dragoon, and this is just a start. Josh and I saw something that has happened in another continent, things are going to get much worse from here. Tell me about this Corona virus pandemic."

"Oh, some virus originated in China and infected the whole world and now we all need to follow some stupid new public laws and a stay-at-home order was issued. John, you said seven or eight, yet the news shows nothing about them at all," said Pete.

"Folks have been told to keep quiet about this. Not to let the media near the bodies. Dan's been receiving orders from some bigger agency to just get rid of the bodies and guard the ones in the safe house 'til big gov gets here. Won't even tell me which agency is coming to get the bodies or when."

"That sounds awfully fishy, it is as if someone is trying to keep it all quiet," said Kili.

"But media manipulation in the United States? That's insane!" said Pete.

"Do not underestimate the Maku. Just because your nation is a world leader does not mean they cannot infiltrate and manipulate everything. They are masters of taking control of a planet and it all begins with disrupting communications."

"Well, we need to find out who is talking to Dan and giving him the orders then," said Josh. "They might be the Maku disguised as government officials."

"Yes, but we shall need to get to the station for that. I can get in the department's communications, but I need to be in range of it," said Kili.

"Whoa hold on a minute now. You talking hacking the Sheriff's department? That's definitely against the law lady!" said John.

"I mean alternatively you could let an alien species enslave and eliminate the entire human race, John," said Pete. "It's your choice, really."

"Ain't much of a choice there I guess. Ok, I'm in. But we ain't gonna do anything more than we have to on this!"

"Well, we'll have to do it soon, John. How long has the temp station been set up?" asked Josh.

"About five or six weeks, it's really just a big cooler with some dead dragoon bodies in it. It's in the back room. Dan had us set it up when we got the second one, we got two more in there and it stays under surveillance. The real catch is finding out who is telling Dan to do all this."

"Leave that one to me once we are inside," said Kili. "Meanwhile, Pete, tell me more about these newfound powers of yours."

"Well, I started to mutate after you left. Your nanodevice helped me come up with some means to stabilize it, but I had to get stuff from the university to do it. In the end I managed to get myself more or less stable."

"And you did all that with a college chemistry lab?" asked Josh.

"Well, I am the top medical school candidate in the county, and top of my class."

"Well done, Pete, that is all I can say," said Kili. "You took the issue you had and learned to use it for other purposes. Josh here is still learning how to use his newfound abilities."

"Yes, well it's not as simple as that," said Pete. "You've been gone for almost a year, and likewise I have spent a considerable time stranded in the wilderness like a wild beast! I had to learn how to change back in the end just to make it back home."

"But nobody tried to eat you, stab you, or drink your blood," Josh quipped.

"And all that's happened to you in this spam of time?" asked Pete.

Josh and John both looked at Kili, who nodded stating, "They are both in too deep now. I guess we also owe you two an explanation."

Josh explained to Pete and John everything that happened, from the visit to the Zion planet to training with the Gods of Norse mythology to the battle in Eastern Europe. Both John and Pete seemed as astounded at their journey as they were of Pete's new abilities.

"So, this scale I found…" began John.

"Is from a fully matured dragoon. Yes, and the charred scar on the road is my attempt at keeping it secret. I'm sorry we had to keep you in the dark about this John, I know they're your friends and that it's your job to maintain order, but we must maintain secrecy on my side of the world about these things."

"Y'all could have told me," said John.

"You tried to shoot Pete twice when you found out," said Josh.

"Ok, good point, sorry Pete," said John awkwardly. Pete nodded acknowledging his apology.

"So how does it work, anyway?" asked Josh. "Do you simply say magic words and turn super-cat?"

"I wish it were that simple. It feeds off my emotional state and body chemistry, primarily adrenaline it seems. Apparently, I need to feel severely distressed and focus on a cause to morph and fight," said Pete. "The first time was the most difficult. I had just stabilized myself, the readings seemed normal on the nanodevice, and then one of these dragoon creatures came after me on campus. I thought I was dead for sure but in extreme panic, I morphed. I killed it surprisingly easier than I thought I would, but then came the issue, I was stuck in that form until I went to sleep at night in the woods. Only weeks later did I begin to realize the triggers, and the way to turn back, and since you were gone and the pandemic hit, school closed temporarily, so I have been out hunting every night for more dragoons and they have been increasing in number ever since."

"Well, if the nanodevice has not found a way to reverse the issue, I can only deduce it shall be permanent. But at least you're stable, and now much more useful to help us."

"Yes, if you don't take into account the anguish of suddenly turning into something inhuman, the mornings of waking up in the cold woods and let's not forget, I've been fighting a one-man war all by myself for months now! Aside that, I am truly glad to have the ability to turn into a giant cat man… thank you for that statement."

"Bro, you're not the only one who came back special." Josh clicked his wrists together and powered the biochips, his empty beer bottle now floating away from him and towards the garbage can as he motioned with his hand, suddenly going up and down by a foot before dropping to the ground just before the garbage. Kili laughed as the bottle shattered to pieces.

"Very impressive," said Pete.

"Shut up, Pete!" Josh stood to get a broom. Kili motioned with her hand and all the pieces floated from the floor to the garbage instantly.

"He needs more training," said Kili. "This pandemic may play to our advantage as it gives us time to train. No crazy thing has happened yet in the world out there, let's take the time to prepare ourselves better."

"So, you mean the dragoons don't count as something going on?" asked Josh.

"No, they are a mere distraction. The first one we killed was one we would normally see in a full-scale invasion, but the smaller ones are more numerous and are simply a nuisance. They are created to deal with foot troops, but in this case, they are just being used to cause general mayhem and distract your species from their real plans. Besides, it has all been covered up by this so-called pandemic, I imagine this is to cause confusion both in your government and among the people as well. Pete, what changes have occurred since then?"

"Well, people don't really go out as much, public places are shut down completely, night life is virtually non-existent, and most professionals work from home now. The only people coming into the office are people who really have no other alternative."

"So, a population that gets isolated and has few very needed individuals up and about, that is quite effective," said Kili. "They can identify where to attack and who to follow this way. Not to mention with fewer eyewitness accounts the media literally tells them what to worry about."

"But like you said, nothing happened yet, no massive terrorist attacks, no plane crashes into government buildings, nothing lately," said Josh.

"Give it time, the Maku would not simply attack recklessly, they would create a massive distraction and infiltrate a system majorly. Although something feels amiss. Those dragoons would normally have a master who is of the reptilian race tagging along and directing them. But they are just roaming around."

"I guess the only thing we can do is keep killing them for now," said Pete. "I'm sure we'll find this reptilian person you speak of, eventually."

"Not exactly a person, you shall see soon if I am correct."

"Wait, reptilian? You don't mean like lizard people, do you?" asked John.

"Well, yes and no. Your 1967 account was actually correct about reptilians as they probed around the planet back then. But they learned to disguise themselves better and blend in your society. They are normally the infiltrators."

"So, all the conspiracy theories are true then?" asked Pete.

"Likely not, but they do exist, and most of them are part of a nefarious organization called the Maku, so if they are plotting something, this is just the beginning."

"Unfortunately, we don't have a lot to go on. So, I guess we just prepare for it however we can meanwhile, right?" asked Josh.

"And find out who is giving your superior these odd orders," said Kili to John, "but yes, unfortunately. At least with us three we can cull the dragoon population down and eliminate the reptilian in charge of them if we can find him."

"You mean us four, right?" asked John. "I mean I can help with these things."

"No offense, John, but you're rather ill equipped to handle the dragoons. As they grow larger, they get stronger, and your weapons simply aren't made to kill them. Besides, you take longer than we do to even get to a location when a dragoon appears. Just let us know if you encounter one and take the credit once we killed it to avoid mass panic," said Kili. John looked unhappily at her but nodded in agreement no less. He didn't like the idea that he, as an Officer, couldn't do much, but two of his deputies were on sick leave thanks to injuries related to the dragoons and were told to keep completely quiet about it, and he himself had a few close calls. So, all he could do was agree to play his part.

"Wait, he's taking all the credit for the kills? Won't that feed right into the Maku's plan to keep everything quiet?" asked Pete.

"And what would you have us do, reveal you

now can shapeshift into something not human, and let the people know there are creatures running around which most weapons are useless against? That would cause mass hysteria and only make things worse. People would completely lose their confidence that their government can keep them safe at all, it would be total anarchy and probably accelerate the Maku's agenda. Unfortunately, the only thing we can do right now is play their game until we discover who is behind all this and what do they truly intend to do," said Kili.

"Well, tomorrow night Dan is off duty. If you guys can get enough of a distraction going, we can look into Dan's computer and see if we can find out anything. Just don't get caught or you're all in jail and I'm fired."

"Tomorrow night it is then," said Kili. "We shall come up with a plan and go from there. John, meet us here at dusk."

"Yes ma'am!" said John as he finished writing their bogus statements on the events regarding the dragoon. As John scribbled the words "mutated alligator" he mumbled them aloud. He flipped his notepad closed and looked up to see the others gazing at him blankly. "Sorry, folks at the station are not used to those things' real names. Besides, they'll start asking where I got the name dragoon, so best to stick with mutated alligators."

"I think we've been a bad influence on the

Deputy," said Pete. Everyone laughed at his remark.

The next night they exacted the devised plan. They split into two groups, Kili stayed with Josh, and Pete would cause a distraction. John would begin at the police station but would eventually link up with Pete to buy more time.

"Ok, we are in position," said Josh over the phone. "Pete, start the distraction."

Pete fired several shots in the air as he left the body of the dragoon they killed the previous night behind on someone's property at the outskirts of town. Josh and Kili saw several patrol cars leaving towards the commotion and they quickly left their car and made their way stealthily to the back of the building. The door was propped open. Immediately, they ducked behind a desk once inside and saw John giving orders to other officers as they rushed out the door with more elaborate weapons than a normal Sheriff's department.

"Go! I got the station in case of secondary incidents! The dispatcher is here for when those big government guys show up anyway," said John to another officer who nodded and rushed out the door.

John walked over to the door, unpropped it and closed it. "You guys need to hurry, the department will only be out for so long. Josh, follow me to the freezer where we keep the bodies. Kili, you handle

Dan's emails if you can hack his computer. His office is to the right, has his name on it. Don't go too far or you'll run into the dispatcher." Kili nodded to John and headed for the office. They were very lucky this was a small department and didn't have surveillance cameras all around. Either way, once Kili made it into the office, she found Dan's computer surprisingly secured. She could easily bypass most security protocols and her system pretended well enough to be Dan, but there were a few tricky systems; Kili almost accidentally sent a confirmation text to Dan's cell phone when entering one of his accounts. Luckily, the nanodevice intercepted the communications and got the message from the system. Kili had it hooked to the computer as soon as she entered the office to access Dan's emails.

Kili read through the information quickly, she set the nanodevice to download the emails and all the contents from Dan's computer. On the other side of the station, Josh was almost at the cooler with the other nanodevice.

"Ok, the cooler is in here, there is no surveillance but they keep a guard passing by at all times. I took the shift since I sent all my guys to respond to Pete. Do we need to unplug the cooler?" asked John.

"Nah, Kili let me borrow this thing, besides, we just need to make sure we track where the bodies are going, not destroy anything," said Josh. He turned the nanodevice's clock face towards him, it looked like an eye attentively paying attention. "Ok nano, put a tracer," said Josh to the device, which turned into a strange object with a needle point. Josh was about to drive the strange looking needle into one of the dead dragoon's wounds when suddenly both him and John heard a loud buzz at the door.

"John! The big guys from the city are here for them alligator bodies man!" said the dispatcher through John's radio. John keyed the microphone to acknowledge.

"Stay here, finish what you're doing. I'll buy you some time," said John but a bit too late, as soon as he walked out the door he was face to face with the agents. They wore suits and ties, kind of like what you would expect of a federal agent or some sort of secretive organization. Josh dove inside the cooler to avoid being seen and finished injecting the body, but he suddenly felt the whole container move.

"Don't worry about the container, it's going into a refrigerated truck. It needs to remain sealed as a precaution. We were told strictly not to open anything until we get it to headquarters. I trust you guarded the bodies well," said the senior most agent. Something about his voice sounded strange, a certain deception to it. Josh could hear him through the cooler and his voice gave him the creeps.

"Of course, had a Deputy always by the door just as instructed by our boss. Here, let me get the door," John tried to be courteous, but the senior agent also gave him the creeps.

"Thanks," said the agent, smiling menacingly. Something about his appearance was off, he was too neat looking, kind of pale, and carried himself as if he just had a fresh cup of coffee despite all the agents being there just half past midnight. "The truck driver has some paperwork to be signed. Is there a place he can sit down and go over it with you officer?"

"Yeah, of course, come on in, we got a spare office we keep to talk to perps." John buzzed the front door to the station to be opened again.

"Wonderful, I will be in my vehicle, I have to notify Headquarters the package is secure." the agent walked past the front of the truck. The cooler had been loaded into a refrigerated box truck. Josh was already shivering as he exited the cooler and looked around him. The nanodevice gave him night vision again, but he was inside the back of a truck. He opened the door with his biochips from the inside. He was just about to step down when suddenly the agent appeared in front of the door inhumanly fast. Josh tried to react, but the agent moved faster, he raised a hand, his eyes glowed a deep amber color sinisterly, and Josh flew towards the back of the truck, slamming hard into the back wall.

"Enjoy the ride!" The agent smiled menacingly and locked the door.

Josh was still dazed from being knocked into the back wall of the truck but should have no issue opening the door of the truck from the inside, he had the nanodevice, but for some reason no tool he used seemed to work. The nanodevice tried to melt the lock from the inside, the door stayed icy cold, he tried to manifest blades and slice the door, the door did not budge. Josh tried using his chips to manipulate the lock into opening but this time the lock didn't move. It was as if the box truck ceased to be steel and became some harder material Josh could not penetrate and the lock was dead to the world. He could feel the truck was in motion. He was already on the road when suddenly he felt the truck start to move unevenly until it came to a dead halt. The door opened and Kili was standing there, staring right at him.

"Some nice ride you had, not part of the plan at all. What happened?"

"The agent, he's not human. I think we found the Maku we were looking for. He slammed me into the back of the truck; he was powerful."

"He probably thought you were destroying or trying to steal the bodies. Did he find the tracker?"

"Yeah, I'm ok Kili, thanks for asking. No, he

didn't get the tracker," Josh felt slightly annoyed.

"Well, it was not all in vain, we got the job done. Well done bud, besides, we rescued you."

"Yeah, about that, how come the nanodevice couldn't put a scratch on the door and the lock didn't react like the first time?"

"Someone hardened the lock and door with nanotechnology. It was made to react to certain energy signatures. And it nullifies biochip signals as well as resists energy outputs. This is advanced technology well beyond your species." Kili produced a vial out of her pocket and collected a sample of the nanotechnology. The nanobots looked like a liquid silver going into the vial. "I shall analyze this when I get the chance, let's get out of here before the driver wakes up."

"Oh yeah, what did you do to him?" asked Josh as they walked towards John's patrol car.

"Knocked him out and wiped his memory, he has no idea what happened in the past 5 minutes. He will wake up soon though, so move," said Kili. They went inside John's car as he drove off.

"Quite the rescue we had to do. As soon as I noticed you missing, I warned Kili and we set out after the truck. She shot out the tire from that box truck from my moving car with some kind of energy weapon," said John, "it was kind of cool!"

"Yeah, thanks guys. So, what do we do now?" asked Josh.

"We wait and see where the bodies go. Also, Josh, we need to load all the Sheriff's emails into your computer, I believe I found something."

John finished his shift and the group rested until the afternoon. John was all in this time on looking at Dan's emails, which was surprising as he had been straight as an arrow since he started working as a Deputy. Now he was rather excited about breaking some of the laws he had upheld for over two years.

"Did you guys get anything good?" asked John as he came in the door.

"A few emails from a company named Raytech. Seems they are a federal government contractor. They sent the security procedures for the Sheriff's department, but there's more to it, seems they also intend to update the department's technology. Looks like we got lucky getting all this stuff done, next time they may have full surveillance and more security behind it all," said Josh.

"So Raytech, what sort of organization is it?" asked Kili.

"It's a federal government contractor. A company that works for the nation's government. Basically, they made a deal and for a certain amount of money every year they do things and sell things to the government," said Pete.

"Sounds like that capitalism you spoke of before. How many people commit their 40 hours to them?"

"Thousands… eh… that's not exactly how it works but we'll go over that later. How's the tracking on the dragoon bodies?" Josh chuckled slightly. Kili seemed to take their explanation of capitalism quite literally.

"So far it seems to be stopped in a major city," said Kili as she touched the screen on her nanodevice, a hologram emerging from it showing streets and buildings, coordinates written on the edge.

"I can track the coordinates of it and narrow it down to its location. It looks like the address is a building owned by Raytech as well," said Josh.

"Ok, Raytech, looks like we gotta get in that. Too bad I got no power to get you in at all," said John. "I guess this is the part where I'm not useful at all no more."

"Well, you played your part," said Pete.

"And we still need this place safe, John, keep your AR nearby," said Josh.

"Doing that every day, it's in the patrol car right now," said John.

"He does have a point though. Keep us posted of any threats and if the dragoons are in fact growing in numbers, if you require assistance contact these two," said Kili.

The four spent another night having a few drinks at the apartment. Their research of Raytech showed the company was majorly involved with the government. Pharmaceuticals, experimental technology for military, cyber security and missile defense. Raytech was a major contractor for military and defense technology and would be the obvious target for the Maku. But aside some social discords due to the pandemic not much was happening. So, they turned to the next best topic they had for the night. They asked in detail how Pete gained his new form, his new abilities. Pete, in this opportunity, took his time telling his story. "Well, sit down and enjoy your drink. It's gonna be a wild ride and I assure you, you won't find entertainment like this in Hollywood," said Pete as he told his story.

The night had clear skies, Pete had just seen his best friend take off into the stars with a strange random alien lady that was taller than both of them, heavily tattooed in blue, and used crude terms referring to people. Pete walked to the car, adjusted the seat and mirrors. Lucky for him the car was a small economic model but somehow he felt like he had more reach than before. He felt taller, leaner, and as he saw his arm, unfortunately hairier. Pete was slightly concerned. Once he got home, he consulted the gadget Kili had left behind attached to his wrist.

"I know I'm probably talking to a machine, an alien machine at that…" said Pete as he looked into the screen, a blue eyeball staring right back at him through the screen, "but if you can hear me, if you can comprehend me, please, help me. What's happening to me?" To his surprise, the eyeball nodded and created a hologram. It indicated an image of pricking a finger and dropping a droplet of blood into the screen. Pete did exactly that as he found a thumb tack to prick himself with and dropped a droplet of his blood into the screen. The machine absorbed the blood leaving no trace behind. Suddenly it projected a hologram around Pete. It was a sphere, edges in blue and hollow, with Pete dead center of it. The device displayed the words "would you like to view a holographic sphere tutorial?"

Pete said "yes?" in a rather questioning manner. He was unsure how exactly the nanodevice operated. The machine prompted him as to how all functions worked, that while it could hear him, it did not have a voice module for communication by design as it simply wasn't programmed to do so, and how to navigate all features and the functions of the sphere. Pete quickly became acquainted with the system as the machine had finished his blood analysis. The nanodevice then suggested appropriate courses of action, proper stabilizing compounds and probability of success. Pete picked the highest probability only to find he needed more materials and chemicals. And so, the next day, he visited the College campus for his supplies.

Pete's new project required some secrecy. The

nanodevice performed some basic lab functions, but others required lab materials and chemicals you would only find in a laboratory. He often stayed behind after class hours during the free lab study time, so it wasn't unusual of him to be there. Very few other students had the interest he had on chemistry anyway, so he was often alone after class.

"Watcha up to Lage?" asked Chad, one of Pete's classmates who dropped by that day.

"I'm making a new type of drink. It's gonna make the alcohol tasteless but hit you like a train with just one shot," lied Pete.

"Typical Pete, works hard to party," Chad jested.

"Yes well, one must pursue his talents."

"Yeah, you better pursue it soon, they're talking about shutting down campus and making everyone take classes online man. The whole coronavirus thing is getting bad dude!"

"Yes well, hopefully it doesn't come to that. I'm rather fond of having equipment and a decent chemistry set available and if I can't have access to it, we can't party harder, can we?"

"Shit, you might not party at all if we get quarantined, yo ass will be having a drink and partying on video conference!"

Chad walked out of the lab with the bag he had left behind, leaving Pete back to his work. With no one there, Pete could open the hologram sphere and have full access to all his information easier. He took samples of the chemical he was making, along with some chemicals he questioned if he should even take with him and headed home.

Over the next few days Pete continued his work. Parts of the potion he was crafting required time for chemicals to set. Part of it required a few more lab trips here and there, but as the pandemic became worse, lab hours became stricter. Thankfully, he was done just in time with the final touches and decided best to use the chemical at home. He was taller now, hairier, he had noticed physical changes in himself in strength also, he felt more athletic.

As he made his way to his car in the parking lot, a homeless man was approaching him. It was just the crazy old homeless guy from the neighborhood. He often came to the parking lot around the campus and harassed students for cigarettes or whatever he could bum off them. Annoying, but not enough of a nuisance that campus police got called much. The students were largely at fault as they often indulged his requests and gave him smokes, alcohol and occasionally food. After years of being there he had pretty much been deemed harmless by faculty and since he had nowhere to go, they just let him roam free around campus even. The lot was mostly empty though and Pete did not see this as an appealing circumstance. He walked faster towards the car, but the man seemed intent on confronting him this time for some reason.

"The end is near! Repent and you shall be saved! Condemn those who have been punished!" shouted the old man. Pete mostly ignored him as he tried to head for the driver's side door. Before Pete could get inside the homeless man was suddenly at the rear of the car, banging loudly on the trunk with his hand.

"Excuse me sir that's my car and…" said Pete as the homeless man cut him off with another "condemn those born of defect! Those punished will not be saved! Demon! You walk upon this earth but are not of it!"

"Sir, please stop banging on my trunk and leave!" said Pete as the man came closer, blocking his way to the car door.

The man slapped Pete across the face uttering the words "devil monkey!"

Pete seized the man by the collar of his shirt, he felt strong, adrenaline going through his system, his teeth felt sharp like fangs "Leave! Now!" said Pete, not at all sounding like himself. His voice sounded rough, more like a growl than a voice. He shoved the man aside, who fell backwards with a clear look of panic as he ran away shouting "Ahh-hh! The devil is among us! He walks among men!"

Pete entered the car and looked in his visor

mirror. His teeth were sharp, his eyes were now amber, he was becoming more beastly. He decided to drink the potion he made then and there before any more changes happened. He pulled the stopper off the test tube and downed the liquid in one gulp. His potion was cold and tasted awful, like rubbing alcohol but thick like motor oil. Pete wanted to gag as he downed the potion. His insides felt cold now, made him shiver, tremble terribly. The sensation was like having icicles in your stomach. He curled up into his seat as the sensation got worse. Suddenly, he began feeling like his old self again. His arms returned to their original length, no excessive hair, his teeth felt normal. He looked in the mirror and his eyes were back to the normal hazel color they were originally. The only thing bothering Pete now was that he was hungry. It was after hours, and the cafeteria was closed but the snack bar stayed open late, so he drove the car to a spot closer to the campus entrance to avoid any more run-ins with the crazy homeless man. He decided to go for a snack, got himself a sandwich and a red bull, ate the sandwich and returned to the car having his red bull. On the way back, he heard a loud banging noise by the dumpster area a parking space away from his car. He was startled by it, but curiosity got the best of him as he decided to investigate the noise.

"Hello?" said Pete as he approached the now continuous strange noise "crazy homeless guy? It's me, the devil monkey. You ok in there?"

Pete saw a dragoon head pop right out of the dumpster, looked right at him, and screech to his horror. He made a run for it towards campus as the dragoon gave chase, leaving the dumpster somewhat clumsily, a bag of trash stuck to its leg as it tried to free itself while chasing him. This one was smaller than the one he originally fought, ran on four legs but did not have the upper body with the hands and torso, yet it still had sharp claws and fangs versus an unarmed now again normal sized dwarf.

Pete locked himself behind the plexiglass door, the dragoon running face first into it. He took a breath as the creature looked around for a way in. It stared through the glass as if examining it. It was armored everywhere, blue scales and built like a crocodile in armor but slightly taller. Pete had little time to keep looking at the creature as the creature impaled the glass with a claw. "Oh shit!" he said as the creature began breaking the plexiglass, tearing several chunks off the frame of the door.

He ran as fast as he could towards the chemistry lab, looking for something to defend himself with, a weapon, an acid, a chemical. He found just what he was looking for in the back towards the burners, two oxygen tanks still full. He knew he only had a few minutes before the dragoon came for him, so Pete put together the tanks and stacked them with the propane tank that sat under one of the chemistry tables, lit up a burner and placed the nozzle in front of the oxygen's opening valve, where he opened it facing the other tank. He then ran for the window as the dragoon bashed into the room at full speed. Pete had just long enough time to fall out of the window before the tanks exploded with the dragoon still inside, the creature screaming as it burned from the explosion, he looked over the window just to see the dragoon get itself up from under several collapsed desks.

"Oh, come on!" he shouted as he pointed the nanodevice on his wrist at the dragoon. "Incinerate." But the device merely beeped twice while flashing a red light at him. "What?" he exclaimed as he looked at the screen. The words "No ordinance/ammo, please integrate bioelectrical discharge system" flashed across it. "What the hell is that?" thought Pete as he ran as fast as he could.

The creature was wounded but not dead, it came after him still, although at a somewhat dazed pace now, stumbling with several burns on its hind legs. Half its head and a good chunk of its body had burn marks from the explosion and it seemed to be missing a few claws on its front paws. But it was now just more determined to get Pete for it. Pete ran into the automotive shop class hoping to find something else to explode on the dragoon, but the dragoon caught up to him first, breaking the door behind Pete and knocking him flat on the ground as it made its way forcefully into the room. Pete began to crawl away as the creature approached him slowly, savoring the moment of the kill. He had nowhere to go, and no means to fight. "I'm gonna die!" was the only thought in his head. "I'm gonna friggin die!"

Suddenly he felt a surge of strength inside him, his arms were getting longer and his body leaner, his teeth were getting sharper, fur was growing out of him, no longer just body hair but thick fur. Pete stood and found himself now towering over the dragoon. Sharp retractable claws at his fingertips, powerful as if made of steel. The dragoon shrieked as it leapt forward but Pete simply swatted it away like a basketball. The creature landed back first into an engine hoist, its back making a nasty cracking noise. It tried to scratch at Pete with its claws but to no avail. Pete raked it across the face with his new claws, grabbed a chain from the engine hoist and wrapped it around the dragoon's neck before kicking the hoist back full force, taking the creature with it and snapping its neck with a nasty crunch as the hoist hit the back wall.

Pete made a run for it before anyone could see him like this. He was now a wild animal. He ran for the woods behind the campus where he found a safe place out of sight to re-evaluate his situation. He was now over seven feet tall, had retractable claws, and a powerful body. As he felt around his face, it seemed to resemble somewhat of a lion or big cat of some kind. He had fur everywhere. His shirt had torn off completely, but his jeans thankfully held as he transformed, although they became shorts apparently. He was still wearing the nanodevice, which stared back at him as he looked at it and immediately began displaying a status screen. Pete was undoubtedly concerned but also tired, and since there apparently wasn't a creature alive that could challenge him at that moment, he simply laid himself down and slept right where he was in the woods.

Pete woke up the next morning back to his normal self again; no fangs, no claws, no fur… just his usual dwarf self. Except for the torn-up jeans and no shirt. He made his way to the parking lot avoiding people like the plague, which was fairly easy considering the police and fire department were on the other side of the building with students and staff clustering around observing the situation. The October morning air was cold on his skin as he was nearly naked. Apparently as a result of the battle, some of the campus was still smoldering while the fire department finished extinguishing the remaining fires.

Pete quickly got in his car and drove off. Making it home as soon as possible. At home, he checked himself up and down. He was back to normal and, judging by his torn-up clothes, this was definitely not a dream. He had turned into a werecat of some kind to put it simply. He showered, changed clothes, and went on to find out what was going on with him. He used the nanodevice, which had been recording his status for changes in heartbeat, metabolism and chemical imbalances. Pete read through the data thoroughly and theorized the stress and extreme panic had triggered this response, causing his transformation. He had to test his theory, but how? He asked himself over and over until his phone rang and he picked up. It was Abby, one of his classmates who normally invited him for parties.

"Hey Pete, you busy?" asked Abby.

"Somewhat, what's up?"

"Well, since they shut down campus due to the fire and the coronavirus thing, we all took a beer cooler and are going to Paradise Cove, you in?"

"Maybe, I got a few things to get done around here."

"Ok. What's going on with Josh anyway, I tried calling him and it went straight to voicemail. Everything ok?"

"He's fine, he's just taken a little trip. Something going on with his family."

"I hope everything is ok. Did you hear about the fire on campus? Someone blew up the chemistry lab and apparently there was a weird alligator in the auto shop. Crazy stuff!"

"Yeah, this is the year for crazy apparently with all that's going on. Listen, I gotta get going, just shoot me a text and let me know what you guys are planning. We only got so many days left of good weather before it gets too cold so I'm kinda down but got a lot to do."

"Ok, will do. Say hi to Josh for me when you get a chance ok? Bye!" said Abby as she hung up.

Pete thought that was the perfect idea, Paradise Cove was a known spot to cliff dive from some of the lower rocks, and he never touched the bottom or came close to it from there, but it still scared him shitless to jump from tall heights. He decided best to wait for his friends to leave the cove and then try to test his theory. He needed to maintain his social appearance but also keep his secret safe as well as cover for Josh, who suddenly left at the end of the semester. Pete opted to take the summer courses just to have something to do but now things were getting complicated. He decided best to put off being social with his fellow classmates for later after he got more of a grip on his situation, so he opened himself a beer and watched some TV until dark.

Pete drove to Paradise Cove and looked right at the nanodevice on his wrist. "I don't suppose you can give me the night vision thing again, can you?" he asked hopeful. The device nodded in reply and shined a bright orange light right into his eyes. "Oohhh, ouch! Ok! Thank you!" said Pete as he adjusted his eyes to his newfound night vision. He changed into his swim trunks and headed for the cove.

Paradise Cove was quite the walk, a nice hike between two massive rock formations through a wide corridor of grass, a stream that runs along and a nice goat path until you go up the rock formation at the end and there it is, Paradise Cove. A water bowl perfectly round in the bottom, about ten feet deep, surrounded by massive rocks. Pete had been there plenty of times, but during the day. Jumping the cliffs at night, even with night vision, brought a whole new element to it in terms of excitement and adrenaline.

"Ok, here it goes… nano, monitor me while I do this," said Pete to the nanodevice. The device complied by flashing a thumbs up across the screen.

He took the first jump, a jump he normally takes, twenty feet into the water, nothing. He looked at the screen and checked the status, felt all around his body and face for change. No changes. Pete climbed on the second rock, a little further from the water than he liked, but still a possible jump, more or less thirty feet, and jumped. Mild excitement which showed different levels on his screen, still no relevant changes. "Well, I suppose the only way to change is to have real distress," he thought as he climbed to the very top of the biggest rock on the stone formation.

The rock Pete intended to jump from was over sixty feet above the tiny round pool at the bottom. He could see climbing hooks where climbers would clip ropes to descend into the pool. The nanodevice began beeping as it displayed a higher level of adrenaline for Pete. And Pete himself was starting to feel a change, he felt bigger, stronger, his teeth sharper. He took a deep breath before he leapt from the ledge.

In the air he suddenly regretted his decision; too late now as he was falling. His adrenaline kicked in, his body grew larger and transformed as it had before. He hit the water and swam out quickly, shaking himself dry. He stood and looked at his reflection in the water, the moonlight doing little for light, but he could still see his reflection clearly. His body had transformed completely, he was back to his werecat form as he kindly referred to it.

And despite being bigger and heavier now, he swam to the edge of the pond nimbly. Pete climbed up the rocks again by leaping on each crevice a good ten to fifteen feet high off the ground at a time. His claws gripped easily, and his body reacted swiftly. He jumped again but landed on a nearby boulder this time on all fours making no noise whatsoever. Pete looked at the nanodevice still on his wrist and studied the change. He was in complete control of his body and yet here he was morphed into a beast. He decided to run across the field before the gorge and test his climbing abilities some more and found his physical prowess amazing. His perception had also changed, he could see clearly in the dark, could hear and sense every life form around him. This was not the artificial night vision the nanodevice gave him, but his natural vision was extremely sharp, as were all his senses. His only issue was, he did not know how to turn back.

Pete repeated the same experiment several nights after without knowing exactly how to morph back into his normal form. Each time he morphed he spent the night in the woods. He began bringing a tent and setting it up to have a plausible excuse in case someone caught him in the morning. Finally, he managed, with difficulty, to somewhat control turning back and forth between human form and cat form.

Pete began transforming closer to town. He found two small dragoons during his experiments over the next few weeks. The first one shrieked and charged right at him. "Come to papa," said Pete before morphing and tearing the dragoon apart. The second he caught by surprise as he landed on the creature from a rooftop, snapping its neck afterwards. They were becoming more common and increasingly bigger. Pete tried to burn the bodies of the dragoons only to find that the nanodevice lacked the means to create that flamethrower device which somehow Kili used before, so he made pyres in the woods and lit them up the old-fashioned way once he piled enough of them.

He often wondered when Josh and Kili would return. He was increasingly better at morphing, but he still needed a catalyst. Summer gave way into fall and winter, and back to spring, until on one night Pete decided to check the area around his neighborhood. He used treetops and rooftops to scout. His sense of smell could pick up any distinct scent, which when he heard a loud clang near his apartment, he picked up the alien scent of a creature digging in his trash. Pete leapt from treetop to rooftop until he ended at the roof of his quadruplex. On the street level, he could see Josh and Kili preparing to engage the dragoon. Pete leapt…

"… and then there we were!" said Pete raising his mug of beer.

"I came by a bunch of times to ask you about stuff and hang out. You were at Paradise Cove the whole time?" asked John.

"Either that or lost in the woods, but pretty much, yeah."

"Well, sounds like you've been busy," said Josh.

"Quite productively if you ask me. But did you ever understand why the nanodevice's weapons did not activate when you commanded it?" asked Kili.

"Something to do with an integrated bioelectrical discharge system powering the core of the firing capabilities. I'm not exactly sure what that means, but it appears you have some technology that adapts to it."

"It is the biotech chips Josh is using; they power the weapons module. All our technology is integrated. Without it, the nanodevice is just a very capable AI system. But it does not have ammo to fire weapons. It is essentially just an AI core you can interact with and gather information."

"And it allows you, in your case, to make canons and flamethrowers apparently," said Josh.

"Well, it gives me more tools in my toolbox," said Kili. "Using the biochips for all abilities and more intricate tools is difficult and takes time to code and create new weapons."

"Hence my constant training," said Josh to Pete, "and I'm still not all that great at it."

"You are better than you were when you started, that is what matters. Either way, the dwa..." Pete looked at Kili disapprovingly, "I mean Pete is ahead of the game, he can use his abilities well, which reminds me, mind if I get my nanodevice back?"

"Have at it," said Pete as he extended his arm. The device leapt off his wrist on the table, sprouted legs and walked over to Kili's left wrist, where it attached itself, leaving Kili with a smartwatch on each wrist.

"You know, folks normally only wear one of those," said John.

"I shall adjust accordingly," Kili looked at the device on her right hand. "Search the web and find proper disguise." The screen in the device nodded and began disguising itself, turning into a flowing liquid metal on her right arm before receding and taking the shape of a medical looking bracelet.

"Seems medical is the easiest to pass through all checks," said Kili.

"Except for the part where the bracelet says, 'delete internet browsing history', which might raise an eyebrow," said Pete.

"What? It's a good conversation starter," said Josh laughing.

"It's your internet that suggested it, why do you delete your browsing history in a medical emergency anyway?" asked Kili.

"You don't want to know Kili, some questions are better off unanswered," replied Pete.

Days passed as they monitored the web for anything unusual. John had gone back into the work routine but didn't call often about dragoons. The tracker on the dragoon body they had planted never moved from its position, which implied the beast stayed in the same building. They couldn't quite find anything unusual besides restrictions increasing due to the pandemic and cyber-attacks

began to make the news more often as crypto cur-
rencies were more popular now.

"I don't get it," said Kili. "They said it would be obvious, but in all reality, not even sightings of the dragoons are reported."

"I feel like that's a big cover up," said Pete. "I killed one on campus and left the body dangling by an engine hoist. They called it a mutated alligator like the rest of them and the campus kept quiet."

"Well, there is all these cyber-attacks...," said Josh. "Wait, cyber-attacks! That's it, everything is controlled by computers nowadays! What all does Raytech do?"

"Experimental military technology, logis-tics, missile defense, cyber security!" said Pete as he looked through his smartphone. "Raytech is the newest defense contractor for tactical nuclear missile defense and mobile defense systems! That definitely is something noteworthy, but who do we know that would even remotely work with com-puters like that?"

"That one's easy! Alex!" said Josh.

"Sorry, who?" asked Pete.

"When I was leaving the army, my old super-visor was entering an IT firm when we were leav-ing. He had a top-secret clearance and entered cy-ber-security. We still keep in touch."

"Well, now you just need to find out what he is up to. And enter his company," said Pete. "We'll need to build you a résumé."

"Well, Kili, can you get me online certificates registered to the system?" asked Josh.

"I can certify you… as soon as I learn what these certificates are," said Kili.

"We have been a bad influence on her since she landed on this planet," said Pete. "Brilliant teachers of how things go, but terrible influence as to how to go about them."

Over the week Josh established contact with Alex. Josh and Kili met him at his apartment first since most public establishments were temporarily closed. Josh had a rather impressive résumé, but they also brandished a false CIA ID to give Alex a good reason for Josh to suddenly be so interested in his company. To all their surprise, Alex did in fact work for Raytech. At that point, the plan to invade the company and building began.

"Well, that's perfect, we can go in and check it out for ourselves!" said Pete.

"Alex isn't a stupid man, he will definitely question all three of us going in," said Josh.

"I'll stay in the car then, you guys check the building," said Pete.

"I expect our access will be limited," said Kili.

"Well, he barely bought the CIA agent story, let's see how much we can push it. Maybe we can see where the dragoon is," said Josh.

"Assuming he even has access to the body.

Didn't he usually work weapons systems from what you told me?" asked Pete.

"Good point, either way, we'll be in Raytech, there's gotta be something there," said Josh.

CHAPTER 8

Raytech

"And the mainframe is right over there, with the servers in the server room," said Alex as they walked down a corridor with a window view of the server room showing the system working and maintenance personnel walking around checking the many machines in the room. The temperature was kept generally cooler inside the server rooms to keep all machines in optimal conditions, but it made for a slightly chilly and uncomfortable atmosphere for Josh and the others since they were dressed for summer.

"I gotta tell you, that decryption program you gave me is actually a bit dangerous," said Alex. "Three out of five algorithms I used it against actually did break the code, and it only took a few hours. Is that what we expect out of the Chinese now?"

"It's expected out of someone, the nation is not specific," said Kili. "The prediction of the threat is confirmed, the point of origin is not."

"Yeah, could be Eastern Europe, they have the capabilities. China just has numbers," said Josh trying to maintain the topic. "So, you said you manage nukes?"

"Oh yeah! Dude! It's super cool!" said Alex excited. He always surprised Josh for a senior leader with his outgoing personality and excitement. "Come on I'll show you."

"There's two firewalls that keep all diagnostics and procedural systems safe and in check, one is here, the other one is in the mountain site. Originally launch controls had two keys that had to be turned in symmetry, but now this new system is way more advanced and secure than even that!" said Alex as he walked them to a row of lockers next to a door labelled "restricted". Alex placed his cell phone and smart watch in one of the lockers and the others did the same before entering through the door. The room consisted of several cubicles with people behind computers. Alex guided Josh and Kili to his office, which consisted of walls made of glass on a separate area.

"Dude, I love this office!" said Alex. "And the system lets me monitor everything. I oversee all the projects, but this one is my favorite! It even tops the basement project!"

Alex logged into the system and showed Josh the live video feed of the nuclear program, and the firewall system along with status checks of half the bay systems. Josh could see the firewall protocols working on the screen and several other live status reports about the nuclear missiles. A camera feed showed a small silo bay with a missile inside. Diagnostics screen showed temperature and other stats.

"Alex, is that a missile? Where is it exactly?" asked Josh.

"Exactly, I don't really know the exact location. It's somewhere in the Cheyenne mountain facility but yeah! It's one of the new weapons the company has, small tactical nuke, made to take out aircraft carriers and massive armored ships. This thing can level a city!" said Alex.

"And what is it you do with that thing again?" asked Kili.

"I mean, my team is in charge of the firmware. We make sure it's un-hackable while going to the target since apparently a few missiles went rogue in Sudan recently due to hackers. We also oversee the input of some of the launch commands if we ever were to fire it and make sure it always gets the best communication with the base. Like I said, man, this new system is way better and has a lot more fail safes since the President can launch it from a suitcase. This thing can go three thousand miles out and receive real time commands, so it needs to be on the ball about communications at all times. Right now, it doesn't do anything except send and receive signals to make sure everything is working perfectly since you know… it's a nuke, but it's a new generation, smart weapon technology. It's literally different from any other warhead we ever had though. Yeah, we can guide it, but it also detects heat and energy signatures on the target for best impact. It sends the information back in real time to the operators and it has auto-targeting. It's super precise!" said Alex still sounding excited.

"Kili, you thinking what I'm thinking?" asked Josh.

"This is definitely a weapon they'd be interested in," said Kili.

"Sorry, who is they?" asked Alex.

"Alex, do you have any guys who work for you from outside your normal group? Somebody you hired recently? We think someone may be interested in stealing this weapon," said Josh.

"Well, I mean there's one dude who transferred from the biolab but that's ridiculous though!" said Alex. "This thing has controls at the main facility, plus this place has a security back up, and they would go to prison for life if they even managed to get the missile to move!"

"Even so, we believe someone is after it, someone who works for a dangerous organization. Who is your new person?" asked Kili. "Is he here in this building?"

"Yeah, I mean he is right over…" said Alex, when suddenly the screens began to flash red as every computer in the room began beeping loudly.

"What the hell? That's never happened before!" Alex began typing frantically on the screen as he tried to get a hold of the situation. Suddenly he ran outside his office. "Did the primary firewall just go down?"

"Yeah, we're trying to get it back up! Someone apparently shut off all the security protocols and fried the secondary systems," shouted a guy in the back. "Hey! What the hell are you…" said the same employee as he looked next to him, but too late. The guy next to him seized him by the neck and flung him several feet across the cubicles, towards Alex and the others.

"What the hell man?" said Alex.

"Oh, I'm so sorry, my fingers must have slipped," said the man as he walked down the middle of the room. "Run," said the figure to one of the employees who stared at him terrified. Before their eyes the man's nose receded into slits and his ears became rounder and more attached to his head. He had a reptilian look about him as his pale white skin gained a greenish hue. "I'm glad you figured out my plan Asgardian, unfortunately you're too late."

Even the employee who was thrown out of the cubicle had ran out of the room by now. Only Kili, Josh and Alex now remained. The reptilian clicked his wrists together and materialized what looked like a crossbow, which fired a lightning bolt at the trio. Luckily Josh materialized his shield just in time to block the bolt of energy.

"Trained your pet human well, I see," said the reptilian man, "but not well enough it seems."

"Spare your concern with my companions, I shall do just fine to handle you!" said Kili as she materialized a bow with her biochips. Kili fired arrows of pure energy mercilessly at the reptilian man, but he managed to block all shots with his shield. Kili materialized wings on her back and swords at each hand. She charged the reptilian man full force, knocking them both out of the window of the building into the parking lot.

"You guys aren't really with the CIA, are you?" Alex turned to Josh as they stared at the large hole now looking out into the horizon.

"You know, now might not be the best time. I'll explain later."

Josh barely had any time to grab their equipment as they ran out of the building through the stairs and down to the parking lot where the two warriors had landed. Kili was fiercely engaged with the mysterious reptilian man. Both had dual swords drawn and fighting, moving incredibly fast. Kili was fierce but somehow the reptilian seemed to have an advantage. He seemed to have manifested slightly smaller swords than Kili but blocked and deflected every blow smoothly.

"What the hell happened?" asked Pete as he ran towards them from the car.

"Well, we found the threat!" said Josh as they caught their breath. "He was in Alex's office, and now Kili is trying to kill this guy."

"Well, she needs backup," said Pete as the reptilian looking man kicked her several feet back. Kili materialized six wings this time and turned a longbow made of pure energy on the man again, who instantly blocked multiple blasts with a shield. Pete morphed and charged but the man simply slapped him away like he was nothing, sending him flying in his full werecat form into a car in the parking lot. He morphed back into his human form when knocked unconscious.

"I've had enough!" shouted Kili as the biochips began generating an overwhelming amount of energy. Kili's skin had now turned blue, the outlines of symbols on her skin now full glowing glyphs in bright orange. She ditched her disguise completely for her full form and power. The reptilian man now turned a darker greenish grey with scaly skin, revealing his true form as well. Kili charged forward locking hands full force with the reptilian as they clashed, the force of their impact creating a massive shockwave knocking Josh and Alex on their asses.

"What the hell man!" said Alex as they got up.

"I'll explain later!" said Josh as he tried to wake

up Pete who was still somewhat dazed but coming to.

Kili was pushing the reptilian man back; he was visibly struggling. She snapped one of his hands back and quickly materialized a blade ready to strike him down.

Kili looked down in surprise as suddenly all her power was gone. A sharp dagger quickly stabbed her right in the chest. The reptilian dealt a final blow with his tail. He had hidden that limb and the weapon the entire duel for this opportunity.

"The thing you forgot, my dear, is that the Maku do not fight fair, especially us Nephilim!" said the reptilian as he kicked her several feet back, landing her on a nearby car.

"No!" shouted Josh as he ran toward Kili, Alex helping the somewhat still dazed Pete move towards her as well.

"Mistletoe…" said Kili, "it's a mistletoe… dagger… it's lethal to Celestials…" Blood poured from the wound and the sides of her mouth. She bled in a semi-transparent blue color. The severity of the wound was clear to Josh. "Baldr's armor… can't stand… mistletoe… Josh… run… call for back-up… don't fight… you're not strong enough…."

Josh abandoned all reason as tears rolled down his face. Not only was Kili the best hope his planet had, but she had also become a dear friend to them, a loyal comrade. He did not listen to Kili as

he powered his swords. This time they materialized as solid blades; bronze colored with a golden
glow around them. He charged forward full speed,
attacking fiercely, but the reptilian enemy easily
avoided his attacks, dodging as if he was being
chased by a small child. The reptilian whipped his
tail at Josh's arms just before he managed to land
a blow. Finally, he kicked Josh behind his knee and
materialized a blade at his neck as Josh fell off balance and on his knees.

"Impressive!" said the reptilian man as he held
a blade to Josh's throat. "Very impressive! They
have trained you well it seems! But you're a mere
human boy, and I am one of the Nephilim! Spend
a couple more millennia in training and you might
stand a chance!"

The reptilian kicked Josh flat on his back, extended his blade until the tip pressed against Josh's
chin.

"I should kill you. End this here and now. But
watching you along with your entire useless race
simply fall to its knees and serve my kind for the
rest of your existence is far more satisfying."

The reptilian powered down his blade. Turned
away from them and with a powerful thrust he
leapt from the ground and landed somewhere beyond their sight. Still recovering from the ass kicking he just got, Josh crawled his way back towards
Kili. He felt her pulse, it was weak and growing

faint; she was dying. She handed the contents of her pockets to Alex and instructed him to safeguard one nanodevice as it morphed from its disguise and transferred over to his wrist.

"Josh… take this…" said Kili as she picked up and handed Josh the nanodevice he dropped near her as he charged the enemy. "I told you, do not engage… he is part of the Maku, but he is a Nephilim… they are as powerful… as we are."

"What do we do then? You can't die! I can't do this on my own!" said Josh as tears rolled down his eyes.

"Do not… concern yourself… go to Asgard. Call for backup… the Gods are always on your… side…" Kili closed her eyes. And just like that, the daughter of Loki was gone.

Kili could see everything shrouded in grey mist, but she could see her body, laying lifeless with her friends mourning her passing. She was in a realm a mere veil away from the living world but had no effect upon it. She saw that she no longer maintained her human form but was in her true form. The dagger made of mistletoe still plunged in her chest. Josh had just removed it after checking her pulse and confirming, she was indeed dead. they mourned her passing; the dagger was a fine and ornately designed weapon. The blade was constructed of mistletoe infused steel, it was a true killer for any Celestial as there were few artifacts that could do it so easily, fewer even who knew how to craft one in all the realms.

"It is time," said a booming voice behind Kili. She turned around and found herself face-to-face with Death. The figure had a hood that covered his skeletal face, tall as she was and holding a scythe in one skeletal hand, dark wings protruding from its back.

"I figured as much. Was I good in my time?"

"No. I was told you were the best. Your return to the light is welcomed, Celestial one." Death extended his hand. Kili took it and he began to float, dragging her gently by the hand when suddenly they stopped. Kili grew heavy, as if cinderblocks had just been tied to her feet. Death continued to pull at her hand but he could not lift her any further. She began to descend back to the ground. She saw her physical body suddenly begin to glow in the chest, a golden orange glow from a bright sphere.

"I see…" said Death. "It is still not your time… it may never be…"

Death released his grip and faded away into the grey mist that shrouded this realm. Kili walked over to her body, quickly being turned to ashes as the glowing orb at her chest shined brighter. On the world of the living, Josh and the others watched with wonder at the glowing orb that emanated from where Kili's chest was.

Kili's remnants disintegrated before their eyes, the ashes falling to the ground, but the glowing orb stayed where it was, gently floating a few feet from the ground. Josh gripped the orb gently with his hand, it felt warm to the touch, like a ray of summer sunshine on the palm of his hand. Josh placed the orb on the nanodevice's screen. "Analyze" said Josh as the orb was absorbed by the screen. Immediately changing the screen to a fiery orange.

"And what do you expect to analyze, my soul?" said an all too familiar voice.

"Wait, Kili?" asked Josh.

"In the flesh! So to speak!" Kili was suddenly behind the screen of the nanodevice. "It appears I cannot die yet, but neither do I have a body. We need to get me one."

"And how in the world do we plan on doing that?" asked Pete.

"Do you mean the little samurai figurine?" asked Josh.

"Do not be ridiculous, that armor would fry in an instant from this much power. Whatever happened to me is creating tremendous amounts of energy, the nanodevice can barely contain it. We need a more Celestially crafted artificial body. There is only one deity I can think of capable of making such a thing. And he is not a Norse Celestial."

"Hephaestus," said Alex. "You need to see a

Greek god to get you a new body."

"Wait, you know about all this?" asked Josh astounded.

"I have a top-secret clearance, my man!" said Alex smirking. "I thought some of the more unusual emails I got were a hoax or just another phishing scam but apparently it's all legit. That and I studied mythology and theology in college."

"Well, you were ahead of the power curb this entire time!" said Pete. "I hardly touched those topics for two semesters until I needed an elective credit."

"Can we focus?" asked Kili. "We need to reach their world, but we will of course need an emissary. We cannot just appear with a human wielding our technology, a mutated human and a Celestial stuck in a wristwatch!"

"She actually referred to her invention as a wristwatch," said Pete laughing. "Oh dear Kili, you have been down here in our little blue marble a little too long."

"When I get out of here, I shall kick your ass Pete," threatened Kili.

"Forgive me if I don't appear overwhelmingly concerned, my lady. It's just seeing you in a smartwatch screen and not towering over me as you normally do is kind of… humorous," said Pete.

"Well either way, looks like you're stuck in the nanodevice, and Pete is coming with us this time," said Josh.

"Absolutely not! How will we even explain this mess to the All Father?" asked Kili.

"How will we explain how you got killed?" asked Josh.

"I… Very well. I shall set the portal for two. It's how many the nanodevices could normally transport, anyway. You, Alex right?" Alex nodded. "Keep the other nanodevice on you at all times. If anything unusual begins to happen, combine it with the suit of armor I handed you, the small one. It won't defeat a Nephilim, but it should do against normal enemies and buy you enough time to get away."

"Well, what do you mean by 'devices could normally transport'?" asked Josh. "Are we out of fuel?"

"No, we're simply not going to use the nanodevices this time. Josh, you have a phone that can call any entity in the galaxy, call the greys and have them patch me to Heimdallr. We should be able to bounce off Zion and right into Asgard," said Kili.

"Ummm Kili, I don't have phone numbers for grey aliens in another planet outside our solar system. That might be an issue…"

"No you idiot, we don't use phone numbers to communicate. There aren't enough numbers in your numeric system to even accomplish that. Check your smart phone, there should be an app with their contact," said Kili, and sure enough, she was right. Josh scrolled through all his apps until the very bottom. There was a new icon with a new app under a strange name written in an alien language. Josh clicked on the app and suddenly the screen displayed a galaxy, Josh's galaxy to be exact. All planets appeared labeled and seemingly in motion. Josh moved around in the screen until he found the Zion planet just on the edge of his Galaxy and clicked on the planet. A list of known contacts appeared on the right of the screen. Josh only had two options, Jura and Todd. Josh clicked on Jura's photo and the phone's camera activated, it was apparently a video call.

"What's up bro?" said Jura as he picked up. "First intergalactic call with an alien, huh? Whoohoo! Hang on, lemme patch in Todd, too." Suddenly the screen split into two and now Todd was also on the video call.

"Well screw me in zero G, right?" said Todd. "You get one first contact and you do it with this guy?"

"I uh… yeah?" said Josh not knowing how to reply.

"I'm just messing with you, bro! Anyway, what's the situation down there?"

"Well… Kili is dead, kind of, we need to talk to Heimdallr and go to Asgard immediately. Can you patch me to Heimdallr?"

"Oh yeah that guy!" said Jura. "Yeah man, you might get picked up off the bat so whoever is going hold hands or something, no homo. I'm sorry about Kili by the way. What do you mean kinda dead?"

"Like her soul is in the nanodevice but her body is gone, it's complicated," said Josh.

"Weird, ok, I just messaged him for ya so back away anyone not going. You should see a light in a minute," said Jura.

"Thanks guys," said Josh.

"No prob, later dude!" said Jura.

"Later," said Todd as they both ended the call.

"Well Alex, it's been nice to meet you," said Pete as he walked closer to Josh.

"Good to meet you, too. Good to see ya man!" said Alex to Josh. "Come hangout sometime, nothing like a good party after you save the world, right?"

"Likewise man, but it's not over yet. Keep an eye on the other site. Whatever the Maku plan next will happen soon," said Josh.

"Well, you know my number. And clearly calling is no problem for you so, keep me posted," said Alex as a bright light began to surround Josh and Pete.

"Will do," said Josh as he and Pete were quickly encapsulated in a silver sphere and shot through the stars.

CHAPTER 9

To New Worlds

Josh and Pete landed abruptly at the platform in Asgard. While Josh landed on one knee, Pete landed flat on his face with a loud "Umph!" They had briefly stopped at Zion just long enough to see Jura and Todd waving as they left immediately, as if they simply bounced off the planet and took off for Asgard.

"And I thought I was bad at landing on these trips," commented Josh. Even Heimdallr chuckled a bit before greeting them.

"Welcome to Asgard," said Heimdallr "Do you require guidance to the main hall?"

"No thank you Heimdallr," said Kili from the nanodevice. "I can guide them."

Heimdallr looked taken aback by the holographic image of Kili coming from the nanodevice but complied and stepped aside as it was his duty. Josh and Pete made their way quickly through the kingdom and into the main hall, where all the Celestials awaited them.

"What happened?" asked Baldr. "Kili once had a body, now she's a pocket watch!"

"Hey!" said Kili in protest.

"Well Kili, he is right," said Josh.

"And what's with the mortal that stands before us? You recruited a Dwarven scholar to assist you?" pointed another Celestial who was now occupying one of the previously empty thrones. He had silver blonde hair and was missing a hand, the deity pointed with the knub where his hand used to be.

"No lord Tyr," said Pete "I am a scholar of sorts on my planet, but me being a dwarf is not a question of race, it's a mutation. I've become quite gifted with those lately."

"It's just Tyr, dear boy, but your scholarly studies have taught you well of our race I see." the Celestial replied.

"Silence!" shouted Odin, the halls seemed to shake with his booming powerful voice "You all speak and ask so much all at once, neither Josh nor Kili have had a chance to explain anything. Let them have their say!"

"Well go on then, dear," said another Celestial. She sat next to Frigg and had been at gatherings before but this was the first time Josh heard her speak. "Tell us your story."

"Well, we found the Maku, he was disabling security and tampering with a new kind of nuclear weapon. Those are the strongest kind of weapons of our planet," said Josh.

"We're well aware of your nuclear power. It's actually in baby phases in your planet believe it or not," said Thor. "Go on."

"Kili engaged him at first, she seemed like she was going to win but…," said Josh.

"But then it turns out a Nephilim has joined the Maku. Pete, the dagger," said Kili's hologram. She had opted to appear this way now as it gave her some semblance of a body. Pete had been carrying the dagger in a simple backpack; he opened his bag and showed the dagger to the Celestials, some of which gasped as they saw its green shine.

"Mistletoe! Preposterous! How would the Maku acquire such a thing?" said Baldr.

"Well, as I said, this was done by a Nephilim, an ordinary Maku would be easy to eliminate. But as you all know they despise all other creation, and usually are involved with chaos, but it is certainly a surprise to have one join the Maku. Anyway, he used the mistletoe dagger to kill me. Death's reaper himself came to claim me. But somehow, he couldn't carry me into the afterlife, so he just left me behind," said Kili.

"Well, there was this strange glowing orb on her body's chest, we put it in the nanodevice and somehow she lives, kind of," said Josh.

"Let us see this orb," said Tyr. "Perhaps it will

shed some light on this ordeal."

Josh pointed the nanodevice's screen upwards, Kili's hologram faded as the orb slowly receded from merely showing on the screen to a floating fiery orange orb from the device. It glowed and felt warm to the touch, an almost perfectly spherical orb.

"Hmmmm…. her soul remains intact inside this little vessel. Her body is long dead and gone, turned to ash by the sheer power of this vessel, but her soul is of this realm," said Odin. "It is not a thing we of the Norse are familiar with."

The orb entered the nanodevice again, and Kili again formed herself as a hologram emanating from the nanodevice.

"Yes well, I need a body, we will figure out this fiasco later. I require an emissary to accompany us to the Olympian world."

"Very well, you shall have one," said the same Celestial who had never spoken before. "But you have another form," she spoke to Pete, "a more useful form. Reveal yourself." Freya's eyes flashed an orange glow and Pete instantly turned into his werecat form.

"Freya, at times it would behoove you to simply ask nicely," said Frigg chuckling.

"Sorry, I do not get to participate much in these meetings," said Freya. "Anyway, this one can be useful in a different way, take him to Cernunnos.

Arm him properly and train him the best you can. When you return, he will be a better aid in your journey. As for the dagger, either destroy it or lock it in the vault."

Pete nodded to Josh, still in cat form. Tyr climbed down from his throne and motioned for Pete to follow, which Pete did as he handed Tyr the dagger.

Baldr climbed down from his throne as well. "Shall we go then?" He asked as he led Josh to the Bifrost for a new destination.

Josh had landed in unison with Baldr in this new planet. Its climate was different from Asgard where everything was lush and green. It was more similar to Colorado except for the sea nearby, islands sat everywhere on the horizon. Some close, some far, and the structures were different from anything on planet Earth. Machinery integrated into rocks serving many functions, some looked like giant computers, others were clearly robots with specific purposes, such as the giant metal robot at the edge of town holding a spear and shield. It looked perfectly like a statue representing an ancient Greek soldier with the exception that it faced all ships coming into the town and seemed to look directly at them. Josh briefly gazed at the mechanical marvel as its head turned to face a new arrival. Baldr led him through a town walking with ease as locals from the town conducted business. Each pausing for a moment to stare at Josh and Baldr as they passed by with interest. "Do not worry yourself, the Olympians are an ally to us!" said Baldr merrily. "And they welcome most races with open arms. The only reason they sent me as emissary is because there really has never been an earth representative among us Celestials. Tis but a courtesy."

Baldr led Josh to a sailboat, he spoke in a strange tongue to the man who owned the boat. He was human-like in features and certainly larger than a normal human, but unlike any of the Norse gods, his skin was a metallic bronze. The captain of the sailboat set sail with Josh and Baldr off the bay, passing the bronze giant as it stared at them, its eyes a bright blue color.

"It is a city guardian," said Baldr as Josh stared at it. "It protects the city from any threats, performs scans of energy signatures and identifies vessels and their business here. It is quite the elaborate system for an ancient looking statue."

"Do all cities have one on this planet?" asked Josh

"Yes. There is a reason we took you here specifically. The Olympians have a lot of specialized automatons, and they are some of the hardiest and most capable. That, and Hephaestus owes me a favor."

Josh and Baldr were approaching a smaller island just off the mainland they came from. The island contained a large temple, statues of mighty heroes at the entrance, and atop the temple sat a crest of a hammer, an anvil, and blacksmithing thongs. "Thor is filled with envy of him," said Baldr "He can craft some powerful weapons and does some smithing, but nothing compared to Hephaestus. Thor was always more of a warrior; he lacks the patience for fine details"

"Baldr, who exactly are we seeing?" asked Josh

"Hephaestus. The smith of the Gods. In our world, many crafted different accessories, tools and weapons for their ends and purposes, Kili crafted those nanodevices herself hence only she uses them. But both in this world and when you need something that can endure a beating in any world, Hephaestus is the man to go. He crafted everything for the gods and shared a lot of his knowledge with men. There are still a few things you can go only to him for. This is one of them,"

As they entered the temple Josh could hear the forge work. Hammers beating steel and entities moving materials. They seemed similar to the Androids in one of the previous planets Josh visited, but with a few more artistic details to them and some more elaborate tools they could produce out of their bodies for specific functions.

"Automatons," said Baldr as he noticed Josh staring. "He crafted them to work for him, Zeus disapproves of it to this day, but tolerates it as long as he keeps them on the island. He is the only living entity in here."

They reached the center of the workshop. Hephaestus sat on a bench hammering on a piece of steel. He was easily twice the size of any of his artificial creations, Bronze skinned and dark haired with golden eyes.

"Greetings Hephaestus," said Baldr. "It appears we require some assistance."

Hephaestus grunted as he stood to greet them. He was slightly taller than Baldr. He beat the steel piece he was hammering towards the edge of the table. Sparks flying at Baldr's chest piece and bouncing off him before making any real contact.

"Your father always had the talent for making the best defenses," said Hephaestus as he eyed Baldr, he stopped just short of the Norse God's companion. "His hammer boy still getting good at smithing?"

"Not nearly as good as you!" replied Baldr smiling. Hephaestus laughed loudly with Baldr and hugged him warmly.

"Years Baldr, years where in Hells have you been?" Said Hephaestus as he walked towards what looked like a small bar.

"Well, I have been busy you know!"

Hephaestus motioned for one of his creations to pour them wine. The Automaton poured one human sized cup for Josh and two massive mugs for the two of them.

"Ah Balderdash! You could come by more often! Who is this now?" asked the massive Celestial as he handed Josh a cup of wine "Go on, tell me your name, little one."

"I'm Josh sir, Josh Gunnar."

"Ha! A Human! I have not seen one of you in two millennia! How is my fine land of Greece? Ah what a shame we had left that planet! We had to. They were too primitive, but there was so much potential." Hephaestus was jollier than Josh expected, and it seemed Baldr was a very good friend of his.

"Zeus still giving you grief over these automatons?" asked Baldr. "I see they are quite advanced, They even look somewhat human."

"Eh, he dislikes robots. Says they take from the occupation of our people. I get it but crafting is my trade, and crafting the help makes sense from my standpoint. But enough on that, what is it you need?"

"Well, Kili is… Take a look, sir," said Josh as he turned the nanodevice screen up. Kili transformed again into the glowing orb and floated a few feet from the device.

"That girl always amazed me with her ability to craft tiny things," said Hephaestus. "I can craft yes, but with her attention to details and her functions, she may be more skilled than Thor himself."

"Don't let Thor hear you say that," said Baldr as they both laughed. Hephaestus eyeballed the orb with interest, he tried to nudge the orb with the tip of his hammer, his hammer was singed slightly by the orb.

"Well, this thing holds a lot of power," said Hephaestus.

Hephaestus picked up a golden statue about as tall as Josh, it had a female form, smooth and seemed made of pure gold. "Try to contain it in this body."

The orb floated into the center of the statue and gave it life. Giving it an appearance similar to Kili, still completely gold colored and resembled Kili's body as opposed to a simple smooth golden statue.

"Well, that's much better than being in the nanodevice," said Kili in her new golden body. "Now we can proceed with our mission."

She clicked her wrists together but to everyone's surprise her entire body lit like a living flame, she was no longer golden but bright red and radiating an intense heat. Baldr stepped in front of Josh to avoid getting him burned to a crisp.

"Power down! Power Down!" shouted Hephaestus as Kili did just that. Smoke still coming from her body.

"What the hell happened?" asked Kili, her gold body now smoking from her display of power.

"You released too much power," said Hephaestus "This body should have been able to handle all your might but somehow that orb is too strong. Too powerful, too hot!"

"Well, is there anything we can do?" asked Josh stepping out from behind Baldr.

"Any suggestions?" asked Baldr.

"I can only think of one," said Hephaestus "Go back to the mainland and climb the volcano closest to my island. There you will meet the one who powers my forge from underground. Her name is Fyra. She is an expert in anything that generates heat and power so perhaps you will have more luck there than with me in finding a clue to this little powerhouse Kili's become. That intense fire, it feels just like my forge but alive. As if fire made flesh."

"Very well, thank you Hephaestus," said Baldr.

"And come visit more often will ya? It would be nice to see you more than once every few decades!" Hephaestus laughed thunderously. "Give me back my statue, I can still use it for a lot of things if you haven't fried the inner workings."

Kili receded the glowing orb from the statue and floated back into the nanodevice. "Well, I'm still without a body!" said Kili on the screen.

Josh and Baldr said their goodbyes as they took a boat back to the mainland. Once on the mainland they made their way up the nearest volcano. It sat atop a massive mountain, dwarfed only by Mount Olympus, which could be seen miles away. The mountain had a lush vegetation at the bottom and a stream running right next to it. As Josh and Baldr climbed however, the area became dryer and the air hot. There was a well-made pathway made of black rocks along the side of the volcano. The pathway led to the top then cut right into the volcano. Josh and Baldr made their way inside and across a stone bridge leading to a platform suspended hundreds of feet above lava with a single house in the center of the crater.

"Don't fall in," said Baldr as Josh looked over the edge "The lava is so hot I doubt even my armor would go unscathed."

Suddenly a fire bolt struck Baldr on the back. He took a few steps forward off balance. A massive bird made of pure fire flew overhead, breathing fire on Josh and Baldr. Josh materialized a shield, which became much stronger with Kili's assistance as she used the nanodevice to make a physical one around them. Baldr simply regained his balance and stood his ground as his impenetrable defense caused his armor to cover him from head to toe, creating a helmet, chest plate and gauntlets. His armor simply spreading automatically, covering his whole body. The fire bird landed just before them and morphed into a tall, magnificent woman. She had red skin and flaming red hair and stood almost as tall as Baldr.

"Who dares invade my lair?" said the fire lady. "So, the Norse gods wish for combat now?"

"No no no!" said Josh "You got it wrong, we're here because Hephaestus sent us!" shouted Josh quickly before she could engulf them in flames again.

"She is not listening to reason, get behind me!" said Baldr as he was still fully armored. The Phoenix lit up brightly and fired at Baldr like an intense flamethrower. The flames bounced off his armor as it materialized a shield for him on his left arm, the rebounding flames scorching pieces of rocks around them and turning them to charred dust.

"We just want to talk to you Fyra. It is Fyra isn't it? Listen we are not here for a fight!" said Baldr.

"Lies!" said Fyra "The last one of you who visited me shared my bed, tricked me! And took my child!" She had materialized an armor made of fire and an eagle's head. She was glowing in an orange color like a sun as she walked towards them radiating heat and firing off fireballs. Baldr deflecting the fireballs into the walls of the volcano with his shield as she continued to fire mercilessly at them. Josh could feel the intense heat even behind Baldr's protective armor. It kept Baldr safe from harm but Josh wasn't so sure how much of that protection would keep him from getting burned to a crisp soon.

"We're sorry about the acts of one of our brethren, whatever they may have been. But we are not them! And we know nothing of this!" said Baldr as she walked towards him. She was furious, hell bent on destroying the two.

"Bring me the head of your Trickster, your father of lies! And I shall consider not incinerating you alive!"

"Wait, Loki visited you?" asked Baldr "You're this mad because of Loki? He has been banned from Asgard! Doomed to suffer for all eternity until Ragnarok!"

"Then bring me my child!" said the Phoenix, Scorching the ground around them as she stepped closer to them.

"Baldr, what child is she talking about?" asked Josh

"I know not!" said Baldr "But we better think of a way out of here fast! She is immensely powerful, and I doubt even I can stop her if she keeps this up."

"Wait! Intense fire! Fire made flesh! I think I know what she's talking about!" said Josh.

The Phoenix began to glow red; she extended a hand out pointing her open palm in their direction. Out of her palm, a small orb began to glow, the orb burned bright orange as a mini sun, and began to get bigger. Suddenly Josh stepped in front of Baldr and raised the nanodevice to his chest, Kili left the nanodevice as a glowing orb and floated out in front of the two, several feet in front of the Phoenix's hand. The Phoenix suddenly stopped, the sun she was creating in front of her began to get smaller until it vanished. "My child," she said as her eagle head morphed, revealing the face of a woman. Tears, blue as the oceans, rolled down her cheeks as the orb slowly began to float towards her. "You're back! What have they done to you?"

The Phoenix stepped forward and gently embraced the fiery orb that was Kili. She then began to glow bright red and radiate an intense flame. The flames so intense Josh and Baldr had to step back and look away. When the flames receded Josh and Baldr rested their eyes on Kili, fully restored and embracing her mother.

"Your trickster God came to my realm," said Fyra. "Shared a bed with me, for many a night, in the end, I had a child. I did not think it was possible, but sure enough, it happened. An egg of fire. The egg was naturally smaller as it was a half-breed child. He left in the night with the egg before I awoke. I searched everywhere but could not find him," said Fyra as she poured them some wine. They were at Fyra's home in the center of the crater. It was a lovely Spanish Villa style home with the exception that it was made of the same black magma rock everything else seemed to be made of there and was suspended by massive chains dead center in a volcano. Despite that the climate inside the home was quite nice, not the scorching heat you'd expect, but a breezy summer temperature.

"So, this entire time, the reason I never knew my own mother was my father's fault?" asked Kili.

"Oh, my darling, yes. Your father as you know is the trickster, he has had many children, some good, some terrible, but none as unique as you," said Fyra.

"So, this explains the small orb Loki simply appeared with centuries ago. When asked about it, he refused to provide any information besides to place it in a great pyre and set it ablaze. Told us none of the Gods had any business meddling in his affairs due to our own lewd behaviors. Then he was banished for the crimes he committed and all the insults he gave us that very night," said Baldr. "He was always one for avoiding questions regarding his children."

"And what has become of the trickster?" asked Fyra.

"Oh, you know… bound somewhere with a serpent pouring venom from its jaws on him. Punishment for multiple killings, severely insulting and affronting the Celestials and an attempt on my life. Typical All Father punishment, very poetic," said Baldr sarcastically.

"I feel not an ounce of pity for him, centuries I searched the realm, I could not leave the planet as it is my duty to keep the forge fires lit for the Celestials here, but every corner of it I searched, every planet I communicated with, yet nothing. Until finally you arrived. How was I not informed of this egg before?" asked Fyra "And what has happened that led you to regress to your egg? Who is this mortal that stands before us?"

"The All father decreed that Kili's existence be kept secret until she was of age to all outside Celestials. Being Loki's daughter, the child would be in danger as many of Loki's children have been hunted for his deeds, so we raised her and trained her as one of our own, yet few knew she was even Loki's. No one knew she was your child. There are no Sacred Beasts in our kingdom anymore," said Baldr.

"I was defeated in battle mother," said Kili "By a Nephilim. I thought for sure I would die, that I was dead, but Death could not take me as the egg began to glow."

"Oh, that poetic idiot!" said Fyra laughing "He could not tell a Phoenix egg from a chicken's! Death tried to reap you? He can never reap a Sacred Beast such as a Phoenix! So, the human? Why is he here?"

"I am Josh ma'am, and I was chosen by… well… them," said Josh not knowing how to address a Phoenix. Ma'am, your honor, your fieriness? Josh had met so many entities he believed to be just myths and legends he simply did not know anymore.

"Well at least you have picked a respectful one among their kind. Speak freely child, I am a Sacred Beast not a judge," said Fyra.

"Pardon me but what is a Sacred Beast?" asked Josh. Fyra laughed at his question as she stood from her chair.

"Once upon a time the great Creator bestowed upon the world immortal beasts, we were among the first but were not considered Celestials. We aided in shaping some of the realms, or planets as you call them, in accordance with the Creator's will and assisted the first once-mortal races with the creation of the technology that gave the Celestials their divine abilities. Abilities you seem to possess yourself now to a lesser extent. Some of the beasts sacrificed themselves for this world. Some like myself gained sacred duties, and some still roam free to this day. We have since come to be known as Sacred Beasts. We are part of creation itself and are duty bound to some of the Celestials as the Creator has decreed, All of us are biologically immortal without any technological aid. To us beasts, death is but a mere temporary and transitional stage. And all of us have unique gifts, powerful ones at that! Follow me child, allow me to bestow upon you one of my own," said Fyra as she approached Josh. She motioned for Josh to follow her, they stood before a massive mirror bigger than the two of them. Fyra simply walked right into the mirror, passing through seamlessly. Josh followed her into the strange mirror, entering what appeared to be not just another room but another realm entirely. Josh looked around him and it was as if the universe had simply encased them. Stars could be seen in the distance but otherwise it was a void of black with the mirror still standing behind him as if an open door, showing Kili and Baldr on the outside still enjoying their wine. Suddenly letters and numbers began to flow out of the doorway and around them in a gentle orange glow.

"When the Creator tasked us with assisting the mortal races, he taught us the coding of the universe itself. You might have heard of coding with your biochips, it's similar as you can directly code abilities and simply pass a complete product to another individual. It's just in our case the coding is much more massive, and is in the universe's coding language," said Fyra. The letters and numbers were matched to strange symbols from varying alien languages, they were beginning to look like sentences as they circled around them, like lines of a computer code.

"So, you mean to tell me the entire universe is like a computer code?"

"Well, yes and no. The universe came first as the Great Creator made time and space. Everything else followed afterward and mimicked his grand design. Your so-called computer code is just another imitation of that. To you humans, it's still confined to your computers and robots sometimes. To the Celestials and the advanced races, it's in their biochips and all their technology, but we Sacred Beasts have actual access to the coding that is responsible for the fabric of the universe itself. It is a gift bestowed upon us by the Creator himself, but he has also bestowed upon us the duty of watching over it and making only the most minute changes when absolutely needed. We are duty bound and cannot break our vows to the Creator."

"So, if he created time and space, how was time and space before him? What was it like before then?"

"It's difficult to explain that. He has always existed, even before time in a measurable way existed, so he has existed in the past, exists now and in the future all at once. And in every place even if he is not seemingly present. As I said, difficult to explain. Now, where is it?" said Fyra as she looked through the lines of code. She touched and moved line after line as if looking for a specific sentence in the midst of the floating text around them.

"I'm sorry, what exactly are you looking for?" Asked Josh.

"I wrote a special line millennia ago for an occasion like this, a gift of my own abilities. But of course, while millennia have perfected my craft it also left me with a lot of extras. That's why my home is so stupid elaborate inside a volcano and somehow physics allows it. With this coding I bend time and space just slightly, a privilege the Great Creator allowed me for never abandoning my sacred duties. Ah, there it is!"

Fyra grabbed a piece of code and moved it closer to her, the lines began to move in a circle at the palm of her hands.

"Kneel child and take off your shirt. This will not harm you, but it will feel warm for a second," said Fyra. Josh did as she said and kneeled. She touched him on his back just below his shoulder, and the lines of code flowed from her hands to his back. Josh felt hot, like getting a sunburn that became more and more intense, he could hear whispers in a strange language in his ears as the heat intensified. His back was now glowing bright orange, he was about to scream in protest when suddenly the glowing lines on his back cooled. Fyra took a step back as Josh stood up.

"Take a look," said Fyra as she waved her hand into a random space, creating a full-sized mirror. Josh stood before the mirror and turned himself sideways so he could see where the code had embedded itself in his body. The bright orange letters took the shape of a large orange bird seemingly made of fire. It was an impressive design.

"Art imitates life. The more elaborate the art embedded in the code, the more powerful the ability your biochips will have available. It's done. You now have some abilities inherent of a Sacred Beast. For a normal human, you are the very first of your kind," said Fyra as Josh admired the design. It was indeed a very elaborate design, the tattoo on his back appeared alive, like living flames of a real Phoenix looking back at him.

"What exactly is it you did to me?" asked Josh. The artificial mirror that was created by Fyra faded away. Fyra motioned for Josh to follow her out of the mirror's dimensional room. Josh followed her, still in awe at the amazing room behind the giant mirror.

"I bestowed upon you some of my abilities. To your technology I basically coded my powers into your system, which means you should be able to use them assuming you know how to."

"Does every power that gets coded mark me with a new tattoo?" asked Josh

"Of course, it does!" said Baldr chuckling "Why do you think we Celestials have so many marks? This system is bio integrated, and your body is living flesh in which data can be stored and your skin a mere shortcut to where it can be accessed faster than the blink of an eye! So, every time a new ability is coded properly, a new mark appears. Your basic abilities are beginning to show, haven't you noticed?" asked Baldr as Josh took a good look at himself. Indeed, Josh had faint glyphs on his arms, almost invisible but he could see a slight outline on his left and right forearms. A shield glyph showed near the now much more visible helm of Awe, a sword and bow with an arrow on his right arm. Josh was slowly acquiring more blue glyphs as he became more proficient in his abilities.

"The firebird on your back is my mother uploading the coding of her abilities into your system. The glyph on your left forearm is your shield, and the other glyphs are your sword and your bow," said Kili.

"So, each ability I learn and use shows a new tattoo?" asked Josh as he put his shirt back on.

"Yes, that is the way the system registers you have a specific ability and quickly accesses it and materializes it. Humans have mimicked us for centuries with their tribal tattoos," said Baldr. "The difference is yours will show as you become proficient in the ability, and it simply allows the biochip to load the ability faster and more proficiently, making it stronger. Think of it as the desktop on your computer, but instead installing the icons and shortcuts on your skin."

"I simply loaded the full code into your system. Those chips aren't magic young man. They are an actual fully integrated bio-computer you have, and the results of the programs are made reality by the chips. When they embedded them in you, they loaded more than just two chips on your arms, they loaded a full system into your entire body. And the ability to make the tools you need into reality," said Fyra. "An idea that was created by some of the first Sacred Beasts to share the knowledge and power of the universe with the rest of the races."

"Fyra, how come you don't have bio chips?" asked Josh

"Simple, I don't need them," said Fyra. "I was made fire and flesh by the Creator himself, and my abilities are inherited and coded into my very being. I am limited to my specific powers therefore, but they are not dependent upon bio integrated nano technology."

"The biologically integrated nano technology we have was created mimicking the powers of the Sacred Beasts. They have been born with the already existent coding of life that provides them their abilities. But then how come I did not have those abilities initially if I am born of a Phoenix, mother?" asked Kili as she stood up.

"Oh, my dear daughter, how much time have you missed away from me, and how much you could have known. Firstly, you're only part Sacred Beast. You're the offspring of one with a former Celestial. Second, the offspring of Sacred Beasts are always late bloomers. The only reason your ability matured at the time it did was an extreme circumstance was met. You had to almost die to manifest them. And it took an extreme source of fire to awaken you and rebirth you," said Fyra. "Just imagine how long you would have been roaming the universe a mere egg had you not found me here by chance!"

"So had you not powered up and embraced me I would have stayed an egg forever?" asked Kili

"Yes, unless someone had the sense to build a large pyre or throw you into a volcano," said Fyra. "There is not much on us Sacred Beasts in the books as we precede even the Celestials. But as we do, we also precede the Nephilim," Fyra gave Kili a faint smile as she said that.

"Well, that makes me feel ready for round two," said Kili as she clicked her wrists together, this time her body lit up like her mother's as her swords manifested. The swords were also different, an amber glow around the blue hue of the blades now appeared. Her intense aura now radiating around the room. Kili quickly powered down cautiously.

"Easy!" said Fyra. "You have received an upgrade to your abilities, and a powerful one at that. Remember, you are now much more powerful than before. After all you are part Celestial, part Sacred Beast. And the powers that exist in me now reside in your very being as well."

"Well, this is gonna play out very different for round two I guess," said Josh. "But how come Loki managed to have a child with you? Aren't you two different species?"

"Well, yes, however, most of the biologically immortal beings, to include Celestials, have a genetic compatibility. Especially us Sacred Beasts. You must take into account when we were created, there were not that many living beings around. And the Celestials were among some of the first initially mortal races made immortal. So, the great Creator gave us the ability to breed with many different races and create powerful offspring."

"The Maku will never know what is coming," Baldr chuckled. "A half Sacred Beast now hunting them down, I wish I was there to see it in the flesh!"

"Which goes back to why I'm here, the Maku have reached my planet. They intend to either destroy it or bring it completely under their rule," said Josh.

"You must not allow that to happen!" said Fyra "The great Creator did not intend for planets to be slaves to rogue creations."

"So, I've been hearing a lot about Nephilim, who are they anyway? How come one of them defeated Kili?" asked Josh "And who is this great Creator?"

"When the Great Creator, the one commonly known as God by your people, created the universe, he made the Sacred Beasts, such as Fyra," said Baldr. "And he created the planets and the first mortal races. The Sacred Beasts were divine guides to the mortal races, they helped shape some of the planets, set their orbit just right for life, and aided the first once-mortal races in advancing to a higher state of virtue and a superior existence. Those who worked directly with the beasts and Creator attained this existence and were risen to a special class, which became known as Celestials. The Sacred Beasts passed some of that knowledge to the first Celestials, thus helping us create our technology in the early days as we were to assist and achieve great things for the good of the universe. But some believed themselves different from the Creator's intent. They believed they should have complete control over the mortal races that later came to be, so they attempted to enslave the other races and even battled other Celestials. In the end the Creator cast them away and stripped them of title and rank. But he could not take away their abilities as their technology is of this world and they had immense knowledge since they were among the first races. They procured their own means and wandered the world. Disturbing the mortal races and constantly causing random chaos. They are known as the Nephilim; they are sons of the Creator as are all of us but have lost their connection with the Creator completely. The Maku worship them as their deities since they are powerful and share some interests, but I never thought one would be as bold as to join them. This changes things drastically."

"So, the Maku are basically a band of fanatics who follow them?" asked Josh

"Imagine an entire planet of those fanatics serving an entity that only responds randomly when it desires," said Kili. "Our intel shows they have their leaders, and their own ranking structure but they are common mortals. A Nephilim joining them directly is unheard of before now. We believe the Maku's cause is only part of the goal of the Nephilim, so while the Maku worship them, the Nephilim seem to have other plans as well."

"Ok, so, back to the great Creator, he's God? So even in a world of Celestials and great beasts, there's a God?" asked Josh.

"Not a God, The God," said Kili. "He is the one who created everything and invented the original intelligent design. He willed the world into existence along with several other worlds. And has entrusted us with them."

"He created the Sacred Beasts and planted the seeds in the world that created us. With the help of the Sacred Beasts, some of our race and those of other races became Celestials. And he created the mortal races by intelligent design. Now many of us followed his guidance as we attained our Celestial status, but some took a different path at some point. The Nephilim are merely the Celestials who strayed from him when newer mortal races emerged, believing themselves superior. Then some mortal races followed. Creating the cult of the Maku," said Baldr.

"Which means they intend for your planet to join the Maku," said Fyra. "He intends to enslave every human in your planet to the Maku cause. But why the human race specifically?"

"They show great potential. In general, they are flawed, irrational, even self-destructive, but under the right conditions, their potential is nearly unlimited. The great Creator bestowed them with many gifts even if they were not present at the time the Celestial technology was made," said Baldr. "The Maku intend to make the planet their own and force that potential out of your species, they will kill millions, but will have new weapons and technology which will allow them to further achieve their goals. Of course, that's just speculation."

"That's enough speculation to raise an eyebrow," said Kili. "The reason so many of our races visited your planet in the past was for exactly that purpose. We saw the potential in your species that was bestowed by the Creator. We had to ensure we got to you and could protect your world before the Maku could completely dominate you."

"Well, then you must stop them," said Fyra "It is time, my daughter. You must go, please come back and see me. You'll always be welcome here."

"Thank you, mother. I shall return once I have completed my mission," said Kili warmly. The two embraced once more. A mother who had just met her child, and a child who had just met her mother, and yet their bond of affection was already undeniably strong.

Baldr shed a tear "I'm not crying, tis a beautiful moment and I have something in my eye." Josh chuckled slightly. The trio bade farewell to the Phoenix as she escorted them back to the edge of the bridge leading to her house. She returned to her beast form and flew high above them as they headed for the transportation chamber inside the city and left the planet.

CHAPTER 10

Round Two

Kili explained to the Celestials what had happened at the planet of the Olympians. This changed nothing of their mission but shed light on many questions the Celestials had regarding Kili and her origins. Finally, Pete returned with Cernunnos. He looked more confident in himself, and Cernunnos was a Celestial like none of the others. He was average height for a Celestial, just over seven feet tall and unlike his other counterparts he wore furs rather than armor. His body was a mixture of a tree-colored brown with a darker blue than the other entities. Runes shined in a lighter shade of blue across his body, but they looked more natural to him, like the roots of a tree. He wore no helmet but had two massive horns protruding from his head.

"I have trained the little mortal to the best of my ability," said Cernunnos. "He may now be of aid to your kind in your endeavors."

"And I wish he'd stop calling me that," said

Pete. "I stated many times to call me Pete."

"Apologies Pete, Cernunnos is rather stuck in his ways," said Kili.

"Very well then," said Odin. "We have been watching Earth, not very many significant changes have happened. Whatever the Maku had in mind, it has not yet come to pass. As I have witnessed with my own eye, this may well be a mission from which you may never return. Champions, feast tonight, fight tomorrow!"

The halls of Asgard had indeed a massive feast as Odin stated. Nobles and peasants alike from the kingdom came to feast with the odd trio. A half Sacred Beast Celestial, a human and they weren't sure what to call Pete. Dwarf? Half human? Half man? Either way, the festivity was incredible. Foods from all over the planet were served, beef from a bison equivalent on the planet, boar, even fish. The three were sent with a goodbye worthy of heroes as they prepared to leave the next day.

The trio landed with precision on the planet. Right on the rooftop of Alex's building. Josh had contacted Alex with his phone and set up the landing. The three traveled directly from Asgard thanks to using the Bifrost, all three of them landing simultaneously on the same rooftop.

"Dude, you have roof access?" asked Josh.

"Almost everyone in Boulder does, you have limited space here," said Alex.

"That's convenient," said Pete.

"You should see the bars man! It's wicked awesome! Of course, now they're all closed due to this pandemic but still!" said Alex. "So, got all your stuff figured out? Looks like you're back with a body."

"Yes, well… it's complicated," said Kili.

"Not as complicated as it will be to get to the big bunker. The facility is in alert level Delta thanks to the cyber security breach. It even made the news! They're blaming Russia as a cover-up until they figure out what the hell is going on. I got us all access to the facility, but it's severely limited. I told them I was waiting on a return call from your department, and I would bring in two guests who can shed some light on this, and well, here you are. I'm going Monday as an auditor and bringing you guys in. We should be good to go, but just out of curiosity, those aren't real CIA IDs, are they?" asked Alex.

"The nanodevice creates the IDs," said Josh.

"I can hack the database and temporarily assume the identity of three agents, or create three identities, but unfortunately they do get deleted a while later to avoid detection. Who do you need us to be?" asked Kili.

"I need three auditors, or basically just three official IDs for you guys that they can verify. If they ask, I am accompanying you as part of training for my potential next assignment, although I doubt I will go much higher considering the last incident. It wasn't my fault, they determined that, but neither am I out of the woods as the firewall did go down on my watch as well as the whole building getting wrecked by an alien," said Alex.

"I'll get working on that, we have two days, right?" asked Kili.

"More or less," said Alex.

"Better get busy then," said Kili as they headed for Alex's apartment.

The next two days Kili spent doing as she had stated, hacking the database of the government and creating the identities of the auditors and department guests that would appear. They were doing something highly illegal, but Kili's capabilities with technology were a century ahead of anyone in the planet, so getting caught was simply not a possibility, and their actions were in the end, for the good of the planet. Naturally, no one protested. Josh in the meantime tried to recreate his abilities from when he fought the Nephilim but to no avail. In the end his shield and sword had gotten stronger and lasted longer, but nothing compared to when he challenged the Nephilim in one-on-one combat. Josh, Pete and Alex caught each other up on all events. Everything that went on both on Earth with Alex, as well as everything that went on beyond in their journeys, from Pete's training in

Asgard, to the Phoenix being Kili's mother.

"It is your mastery of it," said Kili. "Think of it like developing a muscle; no matter how strong you become, you can always get stronger. It is limitless, but right now you are in the baby phases, which is why we rely so heavily on my powers."

"But how will I ever defend this planet alone if I'm always relying on you?" asked Josh.

"That is simple, is it not? You're not alone. And you're not supposed to rely solely on yourself. Every action I take, the Celestials watch over. If they deem their hand is needed, they will come. So far, the only reason the Asgardian army has not landed here yet is due to the statute of secrecy they are trying so hard to maintain. Your planet was not set to be revealed for at least another century. That is also likely why the Nephilim opted not to simply kill you or Pete next; it would have triggered a massive Asgardian intervention. The Maku are truly forcing our hand on secrecy with their invasion, but they are likewise somewhat fighting with a hand tied behind their backs," said Kili. "Either way, we will always be there for you when things are at their worst."

"Well, thank you. It's just I also want to pull my weight," said Josh.

"I didn't necessarily pull mine before I was trained. Much less before I mutated. A dwarf with a common shotgun, what good was I really?" asked

Pete.

"Now you can go beast mode and super kill things with your mutation," said Josh.

"And you have been touched by a Phoenix!" said Pete. "Although not inappropriately. Quite the shame, I hear she was hot!"

"Pete! That's my mother! Show some respect!" said Kili.

"Well, she is an older woman, although from what I hear so are you compared to us," said Pete.

"Pretty sure not the point," Alex chuckled, "but still funny."

This time instead of Josh's car, the four of them took a company vehicle. Alex had the vehicle signed out from his company the week prior. "For safety," he stated, "they sometimes point guns at unknown vehicles that simply appear at their facility."

The facility was indeed well protected, it was right next to an army base. Up a mountain through a winding road. At first, they had armed guards stopping them, some pointing weapons. Alex cleared the whole mess before Kili did anything drastic and they finally entered the facility. Inside the facility were massive server rooms. Space Command, as they called the main room, with many people working on computers and large world maps with trajectories.

"Wow!" said Pete. "This is literally the room

from where you can destroy the world if you want to."

The employee guiding the four through the facility nodded but eyed Pete carefully over this statement.

"I mean it always amazes me coming to places like this," said Pete to avoid more suspicion. "It's not every day you get to inspect the security of a nuclear site."

The entire site seemed in order; the cyber security environment seemed in good working condition. The facility's physical security seemed in order. Alex and the others grouped up in a conference room to discuss the results of the audit.

"It appears everything is in order. How come?" asked Pete.

"Maybe they haven't attacked yet. Maybe the defenses here were too good. We sure had a hard time getting in," said Josh.

"No, no, this is all wrong," said Kili. "The Maku don't give up on their prey due to an inconvenience. We would definitely see a sign though," said Kili.

"What kind of sign?" asked Alex as the entire room shook from a thunderous crash somewhere outside.

"That kind," said Kili as they ran to the main office, the area had several desks with computers and personnel on them. Some personnel dove for cover as the building shook with a second crash outside.

"What's going on?" asked Alex.

"We're being bombarded from the outside by something," said the manager at the facility. She walked over to a console with a screen and pushed a button. The camera feed outside showed large creatures emerging from each meteor that hit the ground. Each of the behemoths were roughly twelve feet in height, standing on two legs with leathery wings, in their hands what looked like rifles. The creatures fired towards the bunker as the soldiers guarding the area came to defend the facility with their weapons. The crossfire now becoming more intense between the two opposing forces.

"They're being engaged by… whatever those things are," said the manager.

"Draconians actually, regardless, we need to push them back," said Kili.

"You know what they are?" asked the manager.

"Yes, there's intel on them but it's need-to-know basis," said Kili. "I'll go outside and handle this issue."

"No, I'll go take care of it. You stay here in case any of them make it in," said Pete.

"You'll need back up!" said Kili. "We don't know how many of them are going to drop in."

"Uh… guys, I still have that figurine and smartwatch," said Alex. "I never used it."

"That's perfect! Alex, put the figurine on the ground and put the watch in front of it," said Kili as Alex did just that.

"Ok, now what?" asked Alex.

"Engage combat protocol Kenji," said Kili to the nanodevice. The device came to life and turned into a metallic liquid, which flowed right into the figurine. The small samurai quickly grew until it was taller than Kili. The small, detailed figurine was now about eight and a half feet tall, just as detailed, and moved independently.

"What is your order, master?" asked the giant android samurai Kili just created.

"Secure the perimeter, eliminate all threats," said Kili.

"Hai!" said the samurai as it bowed to Kili's command.

"Cool! A samurai robot?" said Alex.

"It was the easiest persona to load into the AI, and one of the most reliable," said Kili, "also the deadliest. I call him Kenji."

"Follow me, I'll have the bunker door open for a moment," said the manager, still astounded as she stared at the large samurai. She led Pete and Kenji to the bunker's upper door after several massive stairs and turns in the complex facility, finally leading them outside.

Inside the room, an alarm sounded off, the systems suddenly appeared to be going down. A warning came over the megaphone. "WARNING: FIREWALL DOWN, LAUNCH PROTOCOLS INITIATED!"

"Uh oh!" said Alex. "That's not good. That means nukes are about to launch." Alex tried to run to one of the computers only to find all the employees at the computers slowly standing up, they were still wearing work clothes, but their skins were green and scaly, their eyes yellow, they hissed as he approached. Alex ran back towards Josh and Kili.

"Umm… we have a problem," said Alex.

Josh approached them first. The reptilians attempted to attack by manifesting swords with their biochips, but Josh was ready. He clashed with the first one, blocked a blow from the second one as he sliced the head off his first opponent. The desks delayed the other four reptilians just long enough for Josh to defeat his second opponent and impale him with his sword. Three of the reptilians took on Josh, who had to retreat slightly as his sword and shield began to fade. One was foolish enough to take on Kili, who sliced him in two before coming to Josh's aid. Kili made quick work of the remaining two after Josh cut down one of his opponents. Her biochips manifested what looked like a steel wire, which she quickly wrapped around their heads and took them clean off. At the very edge of the room, stood the Nephilim that once defeated her.

"Well, I see you've made quick work of my men. I don't know how you survived our last skirmish, but shall we try again?" asked the Nephilim, smiling menacingly.

"Ok… you guys handle that, I will try to stop the launch," said Alex as the warning continued over the megaphone. Alex found a nearby desk with a working computer and began to work fast, reading and typing protocols as he tried to reactivate some security to prevent the launch of all the nukes.

"It would be unwise to try me, it shall not end like last time," said Kili to the Nephilim.

The Nephilim approached, pushing the last front two desks aside telekinetically. He had his tail out this time and was fully ready for combat. He drew two daggers infused with mistletoe, one in each hand. Kili fired up like a Phoenix as he moved in for the kill. He rushed her, daggers forward one swinging overhead and one thrusting forward. The daggers stopped just short of Kili, as if some invisible force was pushing them back making it impossible to stab her. The intense heat melted the daggers in his hands before even making contact with Kili's now glowing orange skin. Kili suddenly manifested wings on her back.

"What? No!" said the Nephilim as Kili drove a sword seemingly made of pure flames through him. "How dare you? I am a Nephilim… an ancient breed you insolent…"

"You are nothing but ancient history," said Kili as her other hand manifested a dagger made of flames and cut his head off, the sword on her hand went through his chest. As his body dropped lifelessly to the ground, it began to turn to ash.

One of the reptilians Josh impaled was still alive. He crawled to the nearest desk with a round blue sphere. The almost dead reptilian pushed the button in the center of the sphere, hissed as he smirked at Josh and Kili and dropped it on the ground. The sphere began to beep increasingly faster as it rolled towards the other desks.

"Kili, what is that?" asked Josh.

"A lightning grenade, now get down!" shouted Kili as the grenade went off, a sphere of pure lightning engulfing all the machines within a ten-foot radius. Kili and Josh dove just out of its range as it fried every machine in the room. Alex hit the ground as well as an electric current visibly traveled to every additional machine unlocking and opening every door controlled by an electrical circuit. The computer where Alex was working suddenly firing off sparks. Alex ducked just in time as his machine fried completely.

"Shit!" said Alex as they got up. "They fried every computer on this floor. We have no shot at cancelling the launch!"

"Did you see where the launch was aiming?" asked Josh. "What do they intend to fire and where?"

"Yeah! At us!" said Alex. "I stopped them from doing anything to the bigger nukes, but they still have that smart nuke I showed you armed and it's gonna hit the city!"

"Makes no sense. Why would they simply hit the city with a nuclear weapon?" said Kili.

"You all have no understanding of our great ways. An ancient weapon lies dormant in this city. You shall see…" said the Nephilim's disembodied head.

"Dude, how are you still alive?" asked Alex.

"He is dying, not fast enough," said Kili as she incinerated his head into a pile of ash, pure fire out of her palm like her nanodevice used to when it converted into a flamethrower.

"You know, he could have given us more information," said Josh.

"Nephilims only provide information when it is convenient for them. He would have stalled for time with falsehoods after this. We shall have to stop this last nuke manually I suppose. Alex, do you know the way out of the facility to where Pete and Kenji are fighting?"

"Yeah, more or less."

"Lead us outside. If the Nephilim was wrong, the nuke cannot detonate in the city. If he was right, it cannot hit the mark and power this ancient weapon he spoke of," said Kili.

Alex led the trio through the hallways, they bumped into the manager who had led Pete outside, and she led them to the closed bunker doors.

"We need this open," said Josh.

"Something's wrong with the console. It's dead!" said the manager.

"Step aside!" said Kili as she materialized the same flames from her hands she had before, shooting like an intense torch and melting her way through the door.

"Seriously, who are you guys?" asked the manager.

"We are the best your government can provide!" said Alex wittingly as Kili made a hole big enough for them to pass through.

Pete and Kenji had followed the manager running outside the door during Kili's melee with the Nephilim, Kenji's heavy armored feet making a loud metallic noise with each step he took. The manager opened the bunker door to reveal a firefight outside going on between soldiers and the giant dragon-like creatures.

"What was it Kili called these again?" asked Pete.

"The master called them Draconians," answered Kenji through his helmet, a somewhat electronic voice. The Draconians were firing blasts of energy out of their rifles while getting fired upon by the soldiers engaging them. "I will defeat as many as I can before I fall." Kenji drew his sword, it was a katana, only it was bigger than any katana a human could hold, appropriate for his size. Kenji held tightly to the katana and the blade began to glow like hot metal. Kenji charged fearlessly into battle, slicing an arm off the nearest enemy. The creature shrieked in agony before Kenji took his head off as he moved to challenge his next opponent.

"Well, handy lady. What's your name?" asked Pete to the facility manager.

"J… Ja… Jane!" said the manager, not believing her eyes on what she just saw. She fell to her knees as her legs were trembling terribly.

"Well J-Ja-Jane, my friends will need guidance on how to get here and we will surely need backup. Would you be so kind as to go get them for me and inform them we are at war out here?" asked Pete.

"Ye… yeah ok," said Jane.

"Thank you. Please get moving, this isn't my favorite part," said Pete as he took his shirt off and transformed into his werecat form. Pete had been given three weapons by Cernunnos, which he pulled out of his pocket now as he charged to assist Kenji. The small contents of his pocket became a spear, a shield and a short sword. He struck a nearby enemy who was firing mercilessly at Kenji.

His spear planted deep into the Draconian's chest while Kenji deflected every shot he could with his sword before Pete eliminated the large lizard. The Draconians began driving their fire away from the humans, who were taking heavy fire and assuming increasingly defensive positions as they suffered casualties and began to focus on Kenji and Pete. The duo was eliminating as many enemies as they could but had to fall back behind a concrete barrier. The soldiers assisting them at first pointed their weapons to fire at them but decided better against it as another blast from a Draconian rifle hit close to them.

"I will draw their fire. You hit them until you cannot fight anymore," said Kenji. Pete growled loudly and nodded. Kenji sliced the hands off the first enemy then impaled him, pushing him into a group and disrupting their formation as they again engaged him. Pete stepped out and threw his spear, hitting one of the enemies square in the chest at the center of their formation. The soldiers behind them pushed their firing line forward as Pete clicked a button on the last object in his pocket. The small orb quickly became a sword in Pete's hand, which he used to hack limbs off his next three enemies. To his side, Kenji was slicing through enemies but taking hits visibly. Blasts bouncing off his armor but tearing chunks of it. Pete caught a few close blasts with his shield but was slowly getting pushed back every time as Kenji was beginning to slow down. Pete caught two lucky blasts that threw him off balance and began to retreat again to the concrete barrier. Kenji tried to follow closely behind as he deflected some of the blasts but took more hits. The barrier stood near the bunker doors, which were sealed shut. Suddenly the door began to glow red, then melted a perfect round hole in which Kili and the others came out of.

"Where have you been?" asked Pete half reverted to his normal form. He was leaner but not as furry and had sharp teeth and amber eyes but a human head still, burn marks on his abdomen and shoulder.

"Busy. How you holding up?" asked Josh.

"How do you think?" asked Pete. Beside them, Kenji had just dropped with his back against the bunker wall, chunks of armor missing from him, sword no longer powered up in one hand and bits of circuitry showing, occasionally firing off a spark or two.

"I am sorry master," said the electronic voice behind the helmet, "I have done my best." Sparks coming from his chest, his pauldrons were gone showing circuitry. Kenji stood up and charged forward screaming "Banzai!" as he plunged his sword into one last enemy before being torn apart by blasts from the Draconian rifles.

"Banzai? Really?" asked Josh staring at Kili sarcastically.

"It seemed appropriate to add it to his programming, was I wrong?" asked Kili confused.

"He will be missed. He was a good robot," said Pete.

"Mourn him not, he cannot die if he was never alive," said Kili. "But unless we intend to join him, we need to do something. There's a nuclear warhead coming for our location. We need to redirect it."

"Well, you're the only one of us who can fly," said Josh. "We'll draw them out and take care of things here, you get the missile."

Kili nodded as she clicked her wrists and launched herself in the air. She materialized wings to stay aloft, only instead of the usual silver transparent wings made of light from her biochips, much larger fiery orange Phoenix wings materialized. They kept her aloft easier and seemed to really be able to fly as opposed to just glide. Her wings generated massive heat as they powerfully created lift. Kili could see the missile coming now. It was small for a nuke, but she knew it could still take out the whole city.

Kili materialized her two swords, she charged full speed towards the missile. She knew what she had to do, take out the propulsion system and guide the nuke out of the atmosphere. She was almost there, the nuke coming fast going directly above them. She intensified her blades as she approached it, ready to strike it just after the head of it when a blast from a Draconian rifle hit her square in the chest, knocking the air out of her. A second blast in the face and a third one in the shoulder. Kili barely scraped the back of the missile, causing it to spin slightly in the air as it still headed for its trajectory. Her armor generated by the biochips and her Phoenix powers kept her from severe injuries, but the blasts were still strong enough to knock her out of the air. Kili went down hitting the ground hard.

"NO!" shouted Josh as he and Pete began to push the line of enemies back harder until they finally reached the last Draconian. He was bigger than the rest, he was the one who fired the shots at Kili. Pete plunged his spear on his right shoulder as he charged through the last few of their kind who were again busy engaging the facility's soldiers. The Draconian seized Pete by the neck as he drew his sword and stabbed repeatedly at his arm. Josh placed his hands together and created a massive sword, which he struck against the Draconian's neck. The sword lodged itself against the creature's massive neck, dark red blood beginning to flow from the wound. Josh pushed the sword harder and concentrated, the sword finally slicing through the Draconian's neck. The large reptile released Pete to the ground as it fell lifeless. The five last members of the Draconians attempted to flee, but Pete's spear and Josh's swords found them faster than they could mount a retreat and so they too met the same fate as their leader.

Josh and Pete ran towards Kili, who had been on the ground, she was badly bruised and her shoulder burned, but otherwise ok as she got up.

"What in the Helheim man!" said Kili.

"We beat the Draconians. You ok?" said Josh.

"Yes, but the nuke hit the mark," said Kili as she got up and pointed at where the missile was landing. It hit square in the center of a park with massive red rock formations. The impact caused a mushroom cloud, but all the energy suddenly stopped in mid blast. You could see the bright light receding into the point of impact. Suddenly the rock formation at the park began to shift. The ground making massive fissures with the same light as the blast from the missile. Immediately after, they heard a loud roar. A massive creature raised its head. It was made of a mixture of the red rocks and what looked like scales. Its face resembled a dinosaur with a massive jaw and terrible jagged teeth. The creature began to stand revealing its massive body, armored by the rocks in some areas, it had a tail with a spike at the end, wings made of red stone mixed with grayish skin and arms long enough to walk in either two or four legs. The creature stood and roared loudly once more before taking a giant leap, landing square in the middle of the city. Panic spread immediately in the city as it now began to ravage the area. The local military and police response was likewise immediate, police initiating evacuation while some fired shots at the behemoth but to no use. It easily dwarfed the largest structure in the entire city. The military responded in a matter of minutes sending aircraft to fight the creature as all the city's emergency services either evacuated or tried to engage the behemoth somehow. Josh and the others stood on the mountaintop still watching from almost a mile away as the behemoth of a creature wreaked havoc.

"What now?" asked Pete. "This entire time we had Godzilla under the garden of the gods park!"

"Not funny Pete we are in deep shit!" said Josh.

"This is that so-called ancient weapon he spoke of. We call it a Leviathan. It is a destroyer of worlds. Made to conquer a planet and deliver it to its overlords," said Kili as she got up. She was still dazed from the hits and the hard fall she took, but otherwise ok. "Looks like the nuke was not enough to power any energy weapons it would have lying around but was enough to revive it. The Maku must have dropped this thing here over a millennium ago when we Asgardians first drove them off the planet."

"Sir, what do you suggest we do about this? Our weapons are useless!" said a nearby soldier. Josh had even forgotten they were there, their gun-

fire in the fight with the Draconians had distracted them and helped the trio win, but so far, their
weapons were truly as useless as the first time Josh
tried to shoot a normal gun at a Dragoon.

"Gather your wounded and secure them, Sergeant," said Josh. "See if you can get the bunker's
electronics up and running again. We are completely stranded until we can do that. Call for air
support, fighting that thing will take a lot of that
I assume." Josh was unsure the Sergeant who approached him would even listen to him but to his
surprise the Sergeant nodded and began moving.
Josh had never given a superior in his active-duty
days an order before, but now senior ranking personnel were following his orders to the letter. Josh
felt a surge of confidence in himself, pride even.

"I'll go with him, pretty sure I'm useless to you
guys on this one," said Alex as he followed the Sergeant back into the bunker.

"Kili, can you fly still?" asked Josh as they
watched the creature continue its rampage. Fighter
jets and helicopters had now mobilized in the air
and were actively shooting missiles and bombing
the Leviathan. Their weapons having little to no
effect against its hardened skin.

"I have to!" said Kili as she fired up. She quickly materialized Phoenix wings with an enormous
wingspan and thrust full speed off the ground at
the creature. Kili covered the distance between

them and the Leviathan in a matter of seconds and materialized larger blades than usual at her hands. Kili sliced at the creature's right arm mercilessly as she flew towards its head. She created a mini sun similar to the one her mother had made back in her planet when attacking Josh. You could see the helicopters nearby beginning to try to get away as they were getting pulled towards the gravity of her creation. It was about the size of a car now as she blasted the creature square in the face with it. The Leviathan staggered slightly as it took a step backwards, but then roared with raw fury as it swatted at Kili with remarkable speed for a creature that size. Kili dodged gracefully as the creature continued to swat at her like an annoying fly, only to be distracted again by the new blasts on its shoulder from another bomber run. Kili made her way back to the mountaintop quickly, landing near Josh and Pete.

"Can we blast it again with something bigger?" asked Pete.

"I just blasted it with a sun in the face and all that did was piss it off!" said Kili. "If you have a bigger blast handy, please by all means. Besides, that took its toll on me. Our technology is powerful and so are my mother's abilities, but our powers are not unlimited."

"We need to get closer. I do have a plan. Kili, can you set the nanodevice to send things anywhere? Like into a star?" asked Josh.

"Well yes, but it would be suicide!" said Kili. "Why would you want to send us there in a time like this, anyway?"

"I never said I wanted to send us. I meant him," said Josh as he pointed towards the Leviathan.

"You realize you need to get extremely close to him, right? And an object of that mass, it will take massive amounts of power. Another nuke maybe, and even that may not send all of him," said Kili.

"And just where the hell do you intend to find another nuke?" asked Pete. Josh pulled his cell phone out of his pocket. The battery Jura and Todd gave him was nuclear after all. He was about to ask about it when Kili met his gaze, she nodded at him.

"Well, we just need to send enough of him. What happens if it doesn't encapsulate all of him?" asked Josh.

"You'll see..." said Kili grinning as Josh handed her the nanodevice that was on his wrist and his cell phone. Kili created the holographic sphere and began working on the device. Pete approached Josh as Kili adjusted the nanodevice to full charge.

"You realize this will take more than Kili to do right?" asked Pete. "I myself am finding it hard to transform right now."

"Don't worry man, I got this," said Josh as he faced the large behemoth from the edge of the mountain. Josh materialized wings of fire, they extended out once before fading and were much smaller than Kili's which could seemingly sustain flight. "The Phoenix gave me one gift, it's time I use it."

"It is done," said Kili as she handed Josh the nanodevice again, this time it was bulkier and the screen was more elaborate. It looked much less like a smartwatch and more like some odd alien weapon now with what looked like claws for a wrist strap. The large battery added to its mass, and the screen displayed a red eyeball with a warning banner around it and several options. Josh held the device in his hand without attaching it to his wrist. "It will fry the device and it needs to make direct contact with the Leviathan, but it should send enough of him away to solve our problems."

"Sir!" said the Sergeant Josh originally had given orders to. "Communications have been established. We have Black Hawks coming in for our casualties and Apaches to provide further air support."

"Can you bring us closer to the beast, Sergeant?" asked Josh as he showed him the strange object in his hand. "We need to be on him to use this weapon, just get me close and I'll do the rest."

"Uh… yes sir!" said the Sergeant somewhat confused as to why Josh wanted to get close to the giant nightmarish creature, but relayed orders to his soldiers who set up three landing zones near-by. The helicopters landed, and the soldiers began loading their wounded. One of the helicopters remained empty as the other two took off fully loaded with the wounded from the battle.

"Sir! The last one said he will take you, but he is not coming in striking range of that thing!" shouted the Sergeant over the sound of the helicopter's rotors.

"That's fine! I just need to be close enough!" shouted Josh back.

"Roger! Get in!" said the Sergeant as he motioned for them to enter the aircraft. It had open windows and machineguns from the sides. Josh, Pete and Kili followed the Sergeant into the aircraft as it decollated from the mountain and towards the beast.

"Pete, can you transform one more time?" asked Josh while the aircraft flew towards the Leviathan.

"Yes, but probably only once more, and I don't know for how long!" said Pete.

"Morph and draw his attention with your spear. Sergeant, fire at him, aim for his eyeballs, when he attacks, get to safety. Kili...," said Josh.

"I will hit him with everything I got again! You just focus on getting to me in time to get away," said Kili as they reached the Leviathan. The door facing them opened, allowing Josh and Kili to jump out. Kili jumped first, manifesting her wings out of her back and flying towards the beast. Josh jumped soon after as Pete threw his spear, plunging right into the Leviathan's eye. The creature roared with rage as Kili sliced into its hard flesh tearing rocks and chunks of scale, creating a perfect gap as Josh materialized wings and glided down to the creature's body, the creature clawed at Kili and the helicopter as the Sergeant fired the machinegun mercilessly from one of the side doors. Pete was on the opposite side doing the same every time his side turned towards the giant beast. The helicopter finally retreated as Kili sliced at the Leviathan's arm, tearing rocky scaly flesh and finally drawing some blood. The creature winced from pain as it attempted to grasp Kili and was both cut by her sword and burned by her wings. Josh landed on the creature's back just below its neck where a few pieces of rock and armor were now missing and pushed the button as he planted the nanodevice in the Leviathan's enormous body as hard as he could. The device began flashing red and beeping increasingly faster.

"Now!" said Josh as he jumped from the large creature. He tried to form full wings again but couldn't. Kili grabbed his arm at the last moment and flew him away from the creature as he leapt from its back.

The radius of the sphere was larger than the

initial blast of the nuke that awakened the Leviathan. It did not, however, encapsulate the entire
beast. It cut off part of its wings, legs and fingertips. The sphere shot up into the sky at the speed
of light once it reached maximum size, severing the
body parts clean and leaving them to fall lifelessly
on the ground. Neon blue blood poured from the
severed parts pooling around the city. Kili landed
with Josh on a nearby hiking trail as she ran out of
power completely.

"We did it!" said Josh.

"Yes we did, but we are completely exhausted
in our abilities. We'll need to walk to Pete to re-
group," said Kili as the helicopter landed in a nearby open space. Pete came out of the helicopter,
morphing back to his normal form, followed by
the Sergeant to meet them at the trail.

"God damn you guys made a freaking mess,"
said the Sergeant. "Sir, who the hell are you guys
with, anyway?"

"Well, Sergeant, you see..." said Josh as Kili
stepped in front of him.

"That is classified, Sergeant," said Kili. "But if
I were to tell you anything, it would be that with
the technology you saw, there will be some vast
changes around here. Now if you would please
guide me back to the bunker we initially left. I have
some equipment to collect."

Without further question the Sergeant guided

them back to the helicopter. The pilot flew Kili and the others back to the facility they left. Kili approached the body of Kenji, the robot samurai laid in pieces on the ground. Kili touched several parts of the armor and the nanodevice assembled itself out of parts from the dead robot. It was larger than its original size, shaped more like a micro robot as it gathered parts off the fallen warrior. Still had the same screen for a face with the same eyeball awaiting attentively for its master's commands. Kili spoke to it as she always did.

"Memory wipe," said Kili to the device. The eyeball in the blue screen nodded and began shaping itself into a small missile. The little missile fired from the ground at the clouds hanging over the city, which quickly expanded over the entire area including their facility. Suddenly a drizzle began.

"Worry not, it shall not affect us. I had the nanodevice analyze the data and erase parts of critical data to maintain our secrecy. They'll know what happened and that the world was saved, but no one shall recall your involvement with the events of today," said Kili. "You can lead normal lives that way."

"Question is, will there be such a thing as normal?" asked Josh. "Didn't we majorly break that statute of secrecy?"

"Well, yes, but it won't be all thanks to you," said Kili.

"Guys!" said Alex as he ran towards them. "Dude, that was nuts! I got out here just in time to see you guys fight that thing!"

"Will Alex be affected?" asked Pete.

"He will know it was us. He had knowledge prior. That thing was coded specifically to erase us from memory of people who did not know us before today. Erasing memory is complicated on an intelligent species to say the least," said Kili as the drizzle began to fall on them.

As Josh and the others gathered to celebrate their victory for a moment, suddenly a light shined bright directly above all four of them. Before Josh knew it, his feet randomly left the ground at the speed of light…

CHAPTER 11

The Statute of Secrecy

Josh stood on a large round platform. It shined a bright white light. Beside him was Kili, Pete and Alex. At the edge of the room was a large desk with several greys standing before them. The table was tall and looked over the platform they stood on. At the edge of the table sat Jura, who waved and flashed a friendly smile the moment they arrived. One of the other greys looked at Jura disapprovingly. There were seven of them in total, wearing silver suits and varied in height from taller than Jura to shorter than Todd, who stood at the edge of the room.

"Well, this is not good," said Kili.

"What do you mean," asked Josh.

"The greys are here, and in a mothership. That means they're on a mission and in a larger quantity, and these guys are their council. Unlike us Asgardians and many other races, they aren't part of any human lore so much as judges on the safety of the universe, and enforcers."

"Is that good for us or bad for us?" asked Alex.

"Well, they are armed well enough to vaporize the entire planet if they see you humans as a threat to the rest of the universe… and considering an ancient behemoth just got awakened in your planet…"

"Bad for us," said Pete.

"Silence! We will now commence debriefing over recent events and determine the proper course of action over this planet!" said one of the greys who sat behind the tables. He was in one of the more centered positions and carried himself much more in charge than Jura or Todd, who sat quietly on the side tables. He looked furious. "You are the human the Asgardians bestowed the gift of integrated biotechnology?" asked the grey as he addressed Josh.

"Yes sir, that's correct. I am."

"Well, it's a fine mess that's made of your planet, your galaxy, and quite the disturbance for the rest of the universe. What benefit did this integration bring, if any at all, to the universal guardians?" asked the grey.

"Sir, if I may, the integration of our technology went extremely well for such a young species, and the benefits of bestowing this technology upon him far outweighed the risks," said Kili. "Josh has been instrumental in detecting the threat of the Maku in his planet and was the one who devised the plan to destroy the Leviathan once it was awakened."

"Silence Asgardian! Is the bipedal ape unable to form his own words so that you must speak for him?" asked the grey. Kili bowed her head with a look of discontent in her face. Josh had never seen her obey a command this reluctantly from another alien species before.

"The technology bestowed upon me allowed for me to deal the final blow to the behemoth sir. I was instrumental in saving my entire race and planet," said Josh.

"And the human you brought with you without abilities," said another one of the greys next to the angry grey who was asking questions originally, he had a calmer but still stern tone to him, "what is the purpose of him being here?"

"It's Alex, sir, and well, I have a top-secret clearance by my government. As far as they're concerned, I'm one of the most trusted individuals of my kind. I'm trusted with information that is not widely available to other members of my species. If we were to make contact with your kind, they would send someone like me."

"I see. You brought us not one diplomat but two," said another grey, this one sat in the very center of the room. "Well done, Asgardian. You are indeed a credit to your kind and may be the best to resolve this issue after all. Brief us on the events on earth and we shall decide the next course of action."

Kili began explaining everything to the greys, from her landing the first time on the planet based on the information she had been given, to the Nephilim involved with the Maku and finally the Leviathan that was released. The greys probed Kili, Josh and Alex with several more questions while Pete simply stood by with Todd, chatting about differences in their worlds.

"By the Lords! A Nephilim fully infiltrating an underdeveloped planet! And he easily infiltrated your most advanced infrastructures with ease! How corrupt can a race be to just allow for an infiltrator so easily? And a behemoth to be awakened in a world with the intent to merely hand it over to the Maku! This does prove quite the threat! What is the guarantee that their species will thrive, that the Maku won't succeed regardless due to this human greed and corruption or that there aren't any more awful ancient weapons dorment in this rock of a planet?" asked the grey who originally spoke angrily with them.

"Well, none, but..." said Kili as the alien interrupted her.

"I've heard enough! Perhaps wiping the planet may prove a better safety measure after all," said the grey as he pushed a button on his console. A light shined above them with a noise, similar to a turbine powering up. The platform in front of them lighting up brightly and intensifying.

"Whoa, whoa, whoa!" said Jura suddenly jumping out of his chair. "This is not what I signed up to the council for! You can't just wipe out planets on a whim!"

"You can't gauge the validity of the species based on the corruption of their governments! The Nephilim could have invaded any species! And Earth is a protected planet of prophecy to Asgard as well as many other races! You can't simply destroy a planet of prophecy!" said Kili.

"You're literally threatening to wipe billions of species off existence!" said Pete. "This planet is not just us, but billions of other species coexisting!"

"We've observed your planet, your dominant species, and your regard for or lack thereof for your own environment. Planet of prophecy or not, why should we take our chances on a species that gambles its very existence for its comfort and convenience?" asked the grey, the others merely observing his actions without intervention.

"Listen, we may be flawed as a species, many of us prone to greed, we may be destructive even to our surroundings, but that's not us entirely. That is not the human race as a whole! Yes, things may have been a bit out of hand, which created our circumstances, which created this invasion, but overall, people of our planet just wake up in the morning and try to do good things for the world around them!" said Josh.

"Do your own philosophers not say that the road to hell is paved with good intentions?" asked the grey.

"Yes, but people act upon their good intentions!" said Josh. "Think of all the sacrifices made by other races to ensure this one would continue, think of the millennia spent on us! You really intend to blast that away for the risk of the race turning to the Maku?"

"I died for them in combat once!" said Kili. "Literally took a dagger to the heart for them! Had I not been born the offspring of a Celestial and a Sacred Beast, that death would have been permanent! If it was all for nothing, we may as well all die right here right now!" said Kili. She also began to power up, her whole body turning a bright orange and her blades materialized to full power. For the first time the grey took a look of caution towards her. She did not show any intent to stand down and all in the room were sure she could obliterate the entire ship, killing them all faster than he could fire his weapon at the planet. Her body gave off intense waves of heat as she was beginning to float a foot off the ground, prepared to attack.

"Please, if you do this now, this is how the rest of the universe will see you. Will it truly make you better than the Maku? More virtuous? Will it make the rest of the universe feel safer or will the world just see another tyrant?" asked Alex.

The grey looked at him. Simple questions, but they seemed to impact him deeply. He looked from Alex to Kili, still armed and ready to pounce. The center most grey raised a hand to him in protest, indicating for him to power down his weapon. He nodded to the grey leader and with the push of a button the light receded. The machinery powered down, Kili likewise powered down, the air around them felt much less tense suddenly.

"You have been spared by our Magistrate, but your planet may not carry on as it was before. The statute of secrecy has been damaged beyond repair. So, in addition to the existing issues that have been caused, now there is that to take into consideration," said the grey.

"Thank you. It is quite nice to not have to murder one another in a diplomatic position. Would have made it complicated to explain to the All Father dropping your head at his feet," said Kili sarcastically.

"Insolent Asgardian!" said the grey. "I have been a member of this council before you even came to be of this world!"

"Then perhaps your brethren should have graced you with the temperament of someone fit to be in charge of making diplomatic decisions. Genocide isn't exactly diplomacy," said Kili.

"You little…" said the grey but again the centermost grey raised his hand to him in protest before he spoke again.

"Quiet yourself brother. The Asgardian does speak sensible words among us. To vaporize an entire planet over the possibility of an enemy conquering it is not the answer to the issue at hand. But to have the secrecy of the existence of all other species in the world end does pose a problem. Your species has dabbled in the question of being alone in the universe for centuries now, and today they have discovered the answer to that question. The issue is where to go from here," said the center grey.

"Well, you guys could continue to ignore us," said Alex. Josh and Pete looked at him in surprise for that remark. "I mean you've had minimal contact with us plenty of times, had contact with our higher-ranking personnel of our kind and even abducted some of us at times, so we kind of have known you exist for over half a century now, we just can't prove it."

"These encounters are never well-planned events so much as due to unforeseen circumstances, as well as some of our brethren having a certain curiosity about your kind," said the Magistrate as one of the greys surrounding him looked at Jura, who looked slightly embarrassed. "But this is a question of your species as a whole knowing completely about the existence of all other species. It's about all trade and business being now open to your planet as well as access to the technology of other planets and mastery of space travel. How can you be certain your species will handle that well and won't simply self-destruct once it has access to all that exists beyond their own planet?"

"We can't prove to you that we won't self-destruct. Just as your fellow councilman can't prove to you that we will. Those questions always land on a maybe, or a chance of either happening. But there must have been past planets that have been under the same circumstances, and they prospered in the end. Am I right? Earth can't be the first planet you make this decision upon," said Pete.

"The short human does state a good point. Many times we have made decisions upon planets and they proved to us more than worthy of universal knowledge and trade. Surely ignoring them as we have in the past and hiding our existence to them would be an option, but at this point it would not help in diplomatic affairs in the future. It would cause more harm than good. For the sake of peace and prosperity in the universe brother, I urge you to consider lifting the statute of secrecy," said another grey who sat close to the magistrate. Pete nodded his appreciation for the support but felt he could have left the 'short' remark out of it.

The Magistrate took a moment to consider,

he looked at Jura, who looked in agreement with the grey's words, looked at the humans and the Asgardian that accompanied him, and finally nodded at his fellow grey who had spoken.

"Very well. By executive order of the Intergalactic Republic of the Universe, we hereby lift the statute of secrecy allowing planet 303, also known as Earth, to enter intergalactic trade, communications and travel. Todd, take our guests to integrate with biotechnology as Earth is now authorized access to such. We will initiate communications with Earth's governments soon and establish the first peace treaty," said the center grey to Todd, who replied, "Yes, your Magistrate," before motioning for the others to follow.

"And you," said the alien who originally spoke as he pointed to Kili, "I am holding Asgard responsible to a degree for their actions. They will of course require guidance. Also, don't you ever power up against me again, Asgardian!"

"Yes, councilman, I will perform diplomatic functions and proper guidance as necessary," said Kili, "and well… my bad." Both Kili and the grey councilman smiled slightly at that remark.

Alex was the first one to have the biochips applied to him. The greys had a machine that consisted of a medical bed with two stations to rest your hands. Directly above the hand rests sat what looked like needles controlled by robot arms. The same crystals on both sides connected to the robot arms. According to Alex it "tickled, but also felt like getting a tattoo," as he now had the same biochips as Josh. Pete was next.

"Nifty tats!" said Alex "They're the ones that let you do all that crazy shit right?"

"Yes, but you have to train daily to be able to do stuff," said Josh. "Took me over a year to get decent at it with a lot of alien help and training."

"That's terribly impractical," said Pete.

"Relax bro!" said Todd. "It's like learning to ride a… what you call those things on your planet? The ones with the two wheels?"

"A bicycle," said Josh.

"Yeah, that thing! It's like riding one of those!" said Jura as he came into the room.

"Well, I'm sure this will make things more interesting," said Pete.

"Well, for the sake of a smooth integration, we do ask that you guys avoid publicly using the biochips in too flashy of a manner. At least until your species is more used to seeing them. It is like a lot of people here warned you Josh, everything will change," said Kili.

"Bro, I can't wait to be able to come down to earth and have a drink with some humans though!" said Todd. "It's gonna be awesome!"

"Well, first we have to address the whole issue of first contact and peace. Speaking of which,

Josh, you and the others don't really need to come back with me right?" asked Alex. "Do you guys wanna just go home?"

"Yeah, that would work," said Josh. "Wait, does that mean you're going home too, Kili?"

"Sadly, yes. My assignment is done with your planet for now. I have to report to the Celestials that Earth is now part of the Republic, and everything that happened."

"Will we see you again?" asked Pete.

"Well, Josh had a phone that could call me or these guys anytime, but that is gone unfortunately. We shall have Josh's phone replaced as well as provide you guys the same means to contact us. But meanwhile, look at the sky at night. You may not see us, but rest assured, we are watching you," said Kili. "Besides, you heard that pompous twit, Asgard, or rather, I as a representative of Asgard am to assist in guiding your world into prosperity. I am quite sure our paths are not done being crossed." She leaned in and unexpectedly hugged Josh. Josh hugged her back followed by Pete, whose arms at best reached her waist. Jura walked Josh and the others back to the platform they were beamed into the ship from. Kili reverted to her true form, crystalline with golden blonde hair and blueish skin, and waved goodbye as she was sent home. Alex was next, being sent to the exact spot he was picked up from, followed by Josh and Pete.

"Canyon City please, 6th Avenue," said Josh and Pete as Jura put in the coordinates.

"See you soon bro!" said Jura as Josh and Pete made their way finally back home.

Over the next months the grey alien species made first contact with the human world. The stage was set for mankind to realize they were truly not alone in the universe…

www.ingramcontent.com/pod-product-compliance
Lightning Source LLC
Chambersburg PA
CBHW060900190726
48286CB00002B/317